FRAME OF REFERENCE

JERRY B. OLTION

POPULAR LIBRARY

An Imprint of Warner Books, Inc.

A Warner Communications Company

For Kathy

who suspected that I might know what I was doing
even when I was not so sure myself.

CONTENTS

PART ONE

Frame of Reference

LeAnne felt the grass between her toes, felt it softly tickling her bare skin, and knew that it was fading. Off in the forest a bird sang a high melody to the rising sun, but its song began to change, to flatten into the electronic bleeps and twitters of a computer terminal. A medley of other noises worked their way into her mind. They were the sounds of a starship in flight, familiar sounds to a girl who had been born and raised on board.

She lay still for a moment, sorting out her thoughts, reluctantly packing away her world of dreams for another time. She opened her eyes. She lay on her bed, propped up against the wall with a pillow wedged behind her. At the foot of the bed an elf stared intently into her desk terminal. He turned when he heard her stir.

"Welcome aboard," he said, smiling.

She yawned, stretched, and sat up. "Wow. Dreams. How long have I been—?"

"A couple of hours. I let you sleep. You looked like you could use it."

She came awake all at once. "Hours! Donivan, you're

supposed to be helping me study, not sleep. Tomorrow's my SHAPE test!"

Donivan's smile faded. He said, "You've been studying for months, Lee. Tonight you should relax, get your mind off it so you can hit it fresh in the morning."

"Relax? Sure. It's only my SHAPE test, after all. It's just the rest of my life. No reason to be nervous."

"You *were* relaxed, just a minute ago," Donivan said. He looked back to the terminal screen and added softly, "Besides, you looked so beautiful I couldn't bring myself to wake you."

LeAnne felt herself blush. "So what do you know about beauty?" she asked impishly. "You run around with a mutant." She slid off the end of the bed and picked up her brush off the desk, then turned away so Donivan couldn't see her smile.

Behind her he said, "I'm the mutant, Lee. Me and the rest of the crew. We may outnumber you, but we're still the mutants."

"Atavism then," LeAnne said, tilting her head sideways to brush her long black hair forward over her right shoulder.

Donivan didn't argue. That much was true. LeAnne *was* an atavism, a genetic throwback to an earlier age. She was tall, with black hair, green eyes, and dark skin. She weighed at least forty pounds more than anyone else on the ship, and though she'd matured later than most girls, her breasts were nearly twice the average size.

There were less obvious differences as well, among them the presence of wisdom teeth and an appendix. Her mind worked differently, too, though no one could say whether that was part of her genetic makeup or just her reaction to being physically different. Her attitudes, her actions—even her dreams set her apart from the rest of the crew. Nobody else dreamed of Earth anymore.

She turned away from the wall and sat back down on the corner of the bed, put her brush back on the desk, and looked around at her room. It was a narrow rectangle, just big enough for a bed and a desk. "Let's go somewhere if we're not going to study," she said. "I'm going to get violent if I have to stare at these walls much more."

Donivan gave her a look that seemed to say, "What's wrong with the walls?" but he didn't voice it. He was getting used to LeAnne's fits of restlessness. Instead he said, "All right," tapped a few keys on the terminal, and switched it off. He stood up and opened the door. "After you."

They made an unlikely pair, walking together down the corridor toward the elevator. But then, LeAnne and anyone would have made an unlikely pair. Beside her Donivan was truly an elf: a full head shorter, blond-haired, and thin. Inbreeding over the centuries had produced his kind, though some blamed it on the radiation leaking through the outer shields, or on damage done in the original holocaust.

They had met in an electronics lab. He was studying to become a computech, one of the elite few who worked with the main computer, the central brain that controlled the entire ship. He hadn't laughed when LeAnne told him her own goal.

"Drive engineer?" he'd asked. "I didn't know there were any anymore, not since the Crisis."

"There aren't," she'd replied. "That's why we need one."

"But what would you do?"

"Repair the stardrive. Bring the ship under control again."

"That's—" He'd almost said *That's impossible!*, but he didn't. "That's a big project," he said instead.

"I'm a big girl."

He'd laughed, nervously at first, trying not to stare. He'd noticed.

"Where shall we go?"

Donivan stood before the elevator call buttons, looking up at LeAnne. The elevators were in the central hub of the ship, with corridors radiating outward from them toward the rim. Concentric cross corridors divided the wedge-shaped sections into rings, which were further divided into rooms like LeAnne's. That was the pattern on this deck; others were different. The corridors on Donivan's deck, directly below LeAnne's, defined a hexagonal array, while the one below his was laid out in spirals, and the one below that at random. Only the elevators were the same on every deck, clustered around the central spine that ran the entire length of the ship. Their placement couldn't change, but varying the rest of the decks cut down on the monotony.

Still, with the exception of the restricted decks at the top and bottom of the ship, LeAnne had seen them all at least a hundred times, and they no longer held anything new to excite her. Except one. One deck still sent shivers running through her mind. She smiled at Donivan and said, "Down. All the way."

Donivan looked as if he was going to protest, but after a second he shrugged and said, "Okay." He pushed the "down" button, the "double occupant" button, the "express" button, then, when it flashed at him, the "confirm" button.

"Gadgetry," he muttered. "Someday the ship will be so full of it that there won't be room for the crew."

"It gives the engineers something to do," LeAnne said.

"You should talk, engineer."

"*Drive* engineer to you! Provided I pass, that is."

"You'll pass."

The elevator arrived with a hum and a swish of doors. They stepped in, LeAnne tucking her feet automatically into the grips while Donivan punched in the deck number on the control panel. The curved doors closed with a hiss, and the hum increased as the elevator moved over into the down shaft.

Weight lifted away as the elevator's magnetic field released its hold on the ship. After a few seconds they fell freely, or really, LeAnne thought, remained stationary while the ship accelerated around them. They were floating free in space in their own miniature capsule while the ship thundered on past. For a moment at least they were captain and crew of their very own starship, unconnected with anything else in the universe, moving downward only with respect to the even greater starship around them. But it felt the same as falling, LeAnne thought. It all depended on your frame of reference.

She tried to imagine the ship as it must look from space, tried to imagine its great bulk accelerating away and leaving behind the tiny speck that would be the elevator car. In her vision the ship was a gigantic cylinder of gleaming silver, studded with windows, airlocks, antennae, and instruments. She smiled momentarily at the fantasy, then frowned. No, it's time to be realistic, she thought. With an imaginary wave of her hand she took away the windows and pitted the hull with meteor strikes, then charred it black. She ripped instruments and antennae to pieces and melted the pieces, leaving behind only shreds of metal and plastic welded to the hull. Then, dutifully, she added the ship's drive, a gossamer scoop in front and a white-hot beam of radiation blasting outward from the ship's tail, its control systems destroyed along with everything else.

Weight settled gradually onto them again as the elevator began accelerating back up to ship's speed. They endured the few moments of high acceleration, holding onto the hand rail for support until the elevator came to rest. LeAnne heard a distant rumble grow suddenly louder when the latches connected the elevator car with the deck, and grow louder still when the door opened. She felt the floor vibrating in harmony with it as she stepped out of the elevator.

It was the roar of the drive, ripping matter apart and spewing out the pieces into space. It was a sort of Bussard Ramjet, scooping up its fuel as the ship moved through the interstellar gas and dust, but where the original ramjet design called for burning the hydrogen it collected in fusion, the *Starchild*'s drive converted its fuel directly into energy. LeAnne had no idea how it was done, not yet, but when she became a drive engineer she would at least be in a position to learn. With the aid of the computer she would learn all there was to know about the drive, with the hope of eventually finding a way to regain control over it.

This deck was laid out differently from all the others. It had only one elevator terminal and only one radial corridor leading from it to the junction with the circular corridor running around the perimeter of the ship, making a single gigantic circular chamber of the whole deck. LeAnne let Donivan take her hand as they walked down the corridor to this deck's only feature, a single massive door on the right-hand side about halfway between elevators and junction, bearing the sign:

DRIVE SYSTEMS CONTROL—AUTHORIZED PERSONNEL ONLY. There was no latch, only a code panel beside the door.

Most of the drive's vibration was subsonic, felt through the soles of the feet rather than heard, and detectable near the central spine almost all the way to the top of the ship, but enough of its energy went into noise to make conversation difficult this close to it. Over the thunder coming through the walls, Donivan asked, "How can you plan to work in there? The noise will curdle your brain."

"What?" LeAnne asked. She laughed when Donivan began to repeat his question, and said, "Look out for yourself."

But after a minute she added, "I suppose I'll wear headphones or something. I'm sure the Original Crew figured out a way."

Donivan nodded. "You're probably right." He looked at the door. "What's it like in there, Lee? I mean, what does it look like?"

She shook her head. "I don't know. Nobody's been in there since the Original Crew. It must be huge, though. To generate one gravity of thrust for a ship as big as the *Starchild*, it must go down for decks."

She answered his unspoken thought. "Yes, I do think I can repair it. Despite all the mystique, the Original Crew were just people, and if people built it, then people can rebuild it."

"But—" Donivan hesitated. "But they couldn't. They tried, and they said it couldn't be done."

"They were wrong." LeAnne's voice left no room for further argument. She wasn't through, though. She gestured toward the door, and by implication everything beyond it. "They were fallible. They made mistakes, or they wouldn't have ruined the Earth, and they wouldn't have ruined the drive controls trying to escape. Everybody thinks the Original Crew were some sort of gods, and that's not so. We've been living for centuries in this damned spaceship just because nobody has the guts to contradict the word of the Original Crew. Nobody seems to realize that we're on an artifact, a man-made piece of machinery, and someday it's going to wear out. People use *entropy* and *space* as swear words, but does anybody think why? No. And nobody seems to care that we're on a *colony* ship. We may be the only human beings left in the universe—we're supposed to be saving humanity from dying out, and we're not doing our job! We should be trying to fix the drive and find us a planet and land on it!"

She blinked her eyes and looked away. "I want to live on a planet."

"I know," Donivan said. He stood awkwardly beside her, holding her hand, not knowing what else to do.

She turned her head back to look at him through a veil of black hair. "I'm scared," she whispered. Then, louder, to be heard over the drive, "God I'm scared. Is everybody this way before their SHAPE test?"

Donivan smiled a reassuring smile. "Sure. Come on, let's go back upship and forget about your test for a while."

She nodded and turned away from the door, but even after the elevator had sealed her off and carried her away, she could still hear the drive rumbling in the back of her mind.

The morning alarm woke her out of a dreamless sleep. LeAnne reached out in the dark and shut it off with a slap, then leaned back to wake the rest of the way in silence. There wasn't much chance of falling back asleep, not this morning. Last night with Donivan she had finally managed to lose herself in a computer-animated adventure movie for a couple of hours, but now she could feel the anxiety inside her again. The months of studying seemed too little; her goal was too big for one single girl to attempt—all the doubts and fears she'd been fighting all along were back, collected in a big knot in her stomach.

SHAPE test. Today.

She felt a little more confident after a shower. As she brushed her hair dry she looked into her closet and wondered what to wear. The computer wouldn't care, and neither did she, really, except that it be something comfortable. But there was another consideration, and LeAnne nodded when her eyes fell on her skintight blue ship's uniform. The computer gave the test, but part of the evaluation was done by people, usually male. It couldn't hurt to prepare for that too.

She wriggled into the uniform, zipped it as low as she dared, brushed her hair out one last time, and headed out for breakfast.

The cafeteria was full of activity. LeAnne stopped to fill a tray with eggs and a roll, then, conscious of the stares she was collecting, headed for an empty table in the back.

She was just finishing up her tea when a bald, stocky, white-bearded man came up from the side. "Good morning, LeAnne," he said. "Mind if I join you?"

LeAnne recognized him as the head of the abstract sciences department. Angels on the head of a pin; that sort of thing. She had taken a class in logic from him not long before.

She pulled out a chair. "Not at all, Dr. McNeil. How are you this morning?"

"Well enough, thank you." He settled himself down with a sigh. "And you?"

"All right, I guess. A little nervous. I start my SHAPE test in fifteen minutes."

Dr. McNeil nodded. "Ah, then it is you. I wasn't sure." He broke apart a roll and began spreading the pieces with margarine. "You're still determined to be a drive engineer?"

"I am."

"It's a waste of your talent. And if you'll excuse my saying so, it's a waste of your genes too."

LeAnne felt herself beginning to blush. She said quietly, "I believe that's my own concern."

"I believe not."

"There's no regulation against—"

"Aside from the one forbidding malicious destruction of ship's equipment, you're right. This is a free ship. But it's also a closed environment, and in case you hadn't noticed, you're carrying a rare combination of genes around with you. Genes that the drive radiation will destroy."

"Cryogenics has plenty of frozen ova whenever the ship needs a—an atavism."

McNeil snorted. "I'm not talking about hair color; I'm

talking about intelligence. We can't afford to have our best minds committing genetic suicide as drive engineers."

LeAnne took a deep breath. Her foot tapped involuntarily on the deck. "Why do you suppose," she began, "that we've been flying blind with a crippled ship since year one of the voyage, without even an attempt to fix it? Why do you suppose hundreds of generations of people have lived and died on board this ship without a hope of finding a home? Why do we spend year after year trapped in this steel can, waiting for the day when we drop into a star at just a sneeze under lightspeed? Because we can't afford to have our best minds committing genetic suicide as drive engineers. Don't you see, *somebody's* got to fix the drive, or it really doesn't matter what anybody else does."

"The Original Crew found that to be impossible. The problem is external, and the radiation level outside is not just a genetic hazard. It's deadly out there."

"They might have overlooked something. Things might be different now. Has anybody ever gone out and looked?"

"That would be foolish. There are other ways to ascertain the danger." McNeil held his last piece of roll about a foot above his plate and let go. It hit with a quiet thud. "The ship is accelerating. That much is obviously true. The rest comes from logic and a knowledge of physics. You know that the drive gets its fuel from space, in the form of interstellar gas and dust, correct?"

"Right," LeAnne said cautiously, not knowing where he was heading with his argument but wary of being led into a logical fallacy.

McNeil went on. "So by the fact that the drive is operating, we know that there is gas and dust around us. And due to relativistic effects, we know that at high speeds those particles come on as hard radiation. From the design parameters of the drive, we know that a high enough percentage of that radiation penetrates the ramscoop to make the outside environment deadly. The drive still runs; therefore the outside environment is deadly. A logical truth."

LeAnne gave him a grudging nod. "Okay, I'll admit to

that. It's deadly *now*. So we change the drive design. Tighten
the scoop fields. Relocate the ship's center of mass to throw
us into a decelerating spiral. Something. What we need is
someone with the courage to *try* something, and the knowledge to make it work."

McNeil said into his coffee cup, "Some things are impossible no matter who tries them."

"I don't think this is one of them. Now if you'll excuse
me, I have a test to take." LeAnne started to get up.

"No need to rush," McNeil said. "You can't get started
without me. I'm your evaluator."

LeAnne sat back down heavily. "I see."

"No, you don't see, or you wouldn't have bothered to dress
so prettily. I'm going to tell you something that I don't usually
tell test candidates: The computer makes the selection. I'm
there merely to make it look official. So whether or not you
make drive engineer depends entirely on you."

"And the computer," LeAnne put in.

"And the computer, of course."

"Which can be programmed—"

"The programming hasn't been changed since the Crisis,
and I couldn't do it even if I wanted to, which I don't, even
in your case. Only the captain has the codes to change something that basic."

And the computer picks the captain, LeAnne thought. *Quite
a system. And we wonder why there hasn't been any change
in the last thousand years.*

Aloud she said, "I didn't mean to imply that you would.
It's the Original Crew's programming that has me worried.
This test means a lot to me."

McNeil studied LeAnne over his raised coffee cup. Finally
he said, "You should have no trouble with the test. I meant
what I said earlier. You're an intelligent girl, by anyone's
standards." He drained his cup and stood. "Well then, if
you're ready, we'll go to the library and get started."

The library terminals had blinds on three sides. LeAnne
chose one that opened on the back wall, swiveled around in

her chair to face the screen, and turned on the power. Normally Dr. McNeil would be monitoring her progress from the terminal next to hers, but he seemed to think that there was no need for that after what he had told her in the cafeteria. He sat down in front of a reader and turned away.

LeAnne nodded to herself. All right. She'd be better off without him. Swiftly, before the computer could ask for them, she typed in her name, access code, and request for testing. For position desired she keyed in DRIVE ENGINEER FIRST CLASS and hit the return. "Prepare for war," she muttered under her breath.

The computer seemed to be taking an awfully long time to reply. She was about to reset and try again when at last the screen printed:

> SHIPBOARD ABILITY AND PLACEMENT EXAM
> TEST SUBJECT: LEANNE EVANS
> SECTION ONE—HISTORY
> *The questions in this section require interpretation
> and short essay answers. A precision factor will
> be assigned after you complete each question.
> There are ten questions in this section. You have
> thirty minutes. Press ⟨enter⟩ when ready.*

LeAnne hit the return. The first question flowed onto the screen:

> *1) Name the most significant factors leading to
> the construction and launch of the* Starchild.

LeAnne decided that that was a wordy way of asking, "Why are we here?" She typed in "Computerized control of national nuclear defense systems, which led to global warfare, which in turn made the planet Earth unfit for human habitation." She hit the return and waited.

The computer answered:

> *1) Precision factor 90%.*

2) What was the original mission of the
Starchild?

Without hesitation LeAnne typed in "Relocation of the
human race to a habitable planet."

2) Precision factor 85%.
3) What event forced the revision of the
mission?

LeAnne looked at the P-factor in surprise. Why only 85?
She thought about asking for an explanation, but she decided
to let it go. This was a test, not a lesson, and 85 was still
passing. She couldn't waste the time when she had eight more
questions. She looked at the third question and typed "Com-
puter-controlled navigation system failed to recognize dust
clouds in the cometary halo as a navigational hazard, resulting
in frictional and impact damage when *Starchild* crossed through
them." She thought a moment, wondering how a member of
the Original Crew would have answered, then added, "All
outside sensors and field-manipulating equipment were destroyed. Control of ship's drive became impossible."

3) Precision factor 95%.
4) What social changes took place following
the above events?

LeAnne typed in "Stagnation." She considered a moment,
then began to elaborate.

Hours later, after a tricky planetary surface problem that
LeAnne finally solved by treating the whole system as a
constantly accelerating spaceship, the computer signaled a
break for lunch. LeAnne stood up and stretched, pushed back
her chair, and headed for the cafeteria. Her eyes took a minute
to focus after so many hours of staring at a screen, but she
recognized Dr. McNeil hunched up and sleeping on his reading couch. She considered waking him, but decided that she

really liked him better the way he was. Besides, she needed the time alone to think.

She called Donivan from one of the library intercoms on the way back. It took her a moment to reach him; he was back in his room instead of in the computer center where he usually studied. He looked indignant.

"The computer dumped my training program," he said. "It barely gave me enough time to store my work before it cleared everything and went into advanced logic mode."

"Advanced logic mode? What's that?" LeAnne asked.

"Basically, it means the computer is thinking. It's run up against something that requires analytical reasoning, so it's increased its intelligence to work on it. That takes up a lot of memory space."

"Must be nice. I wish I could do that with this test."

The surprise showed on Donivan's face. "You mean you're still taking your test? I thought the computer would have shut you down too."

"Hah, I should be so lucky. No, I've been going at it all morning, and there's more waiting for me when I get back."

"Hmmm. Evidently the logic program doesn't need the space in the library files. I thought sure it would. Well, how's the test going then? Is it as hard as you thought it would be?"

LeAnne shook her head and brushed a strand of hair out of her eyes. "I don't know. Some of the questions are, and some aren't. It's weird. I almost get the feeling that the *way* I answer a question is more important than whether or not I get it right."

Donivan said, "You're probably right. It *is* an intelligence test, after all. But I wouldn't worry if I were you. You'll do fine."

"Yeah," LeAnne said, not so completely convinced. "I hope so. Well look, I've got to get back. I just wanted to say hi."

"I'm glad you did. Good luck on the rest of it, and don't worry. Call me when you're done, okay?"

"Sure. 'Bye."

"'Bye." Donivan winked and switched off. LeAnne winked

back at the empty screen, took a deep breath, and walked back to her terminal. McNeil was still asleep in his chair. The computer was waiting.

It seemed as if only a few minutes had gone by when the last question disappeared into the computer's memory, but LeAnne saw by her watch that it had been four hours since her break for lunch. Eight hours of testing to determine her position in society for the rest of her life. Tired as she was, she wondered if it was really enough. The last few sections had been unreasonably tough; a few more questions might give her a chance to salvage her score. *Or make it worse*, she thought. She'd missed more than she'd made on this last section. Her only consolation was the sure knowledge that nobody else could have done any better.

The computer printed out:

> *400) Precision factor 43%.*
> *TESTING COMPLETED. Final section to be*
> *completed by evaluator. Please call your*
> *evaluator to the terminal.*

LeAnne stared in disbelief. Forty-three percent! That was the worst yet. She looked over the blind at Dr. McNeil, then wished she hadn't. He'd been watching her. He stood up and came over to stand beside her.

"Finished?" he asked.

"Something isn't right," she said. "The questions are too tough." She immediately regretted saying that. "I mean, they're the sort of questions you'd need days to answer. Some of them are outright impossible. It's unfair."

McNeil said, "Now LeAnne, let's see what the final evaluation is before you get upset." He reached around her to type in "Evaluation, LeAnne Evans," and a number that didn't print out. Information began to flow onto the screen.

> *Test subject: LeAnne Evans*
> *Final score: 83%*

*Evaluation: Miss Evans tests high in social
sciences, arts, and English skills, but low in
mathematics, physics, and related fields.
Attitudes of dissatisfaction are evident. She has
requested placement as a drive engineer;
however, her psychological profile combined
with low scores in the necessary fields indicate
that this would not be in the best interest of the
ship at this time. Recommend placement in a
field of more social nature. Openings at present
follow:*

> *Ship's Stores Disbursement Officer*
> *Cafeteria Cook*
> *Librarian*
> *Hydroponic Farm Operator*

*Miss Evans has a high chance for success in
many other areas as well. Professional fields
open for extended study include:*

> *Hydroponic Systems*
> *Education*
> *Psychology*
> *Law*
> *Abstract Science*
> *Human Medicine*
> *Clergy*
> *Music*

The readout continued. LeAnne stared at it in mounting
fury. "What kind of vacuum is this?" she demanded. "It's got
everything backward! You know I'm good at physical sciences!"

Dr. McNeil shook his head. "This test is designed to determine the underlying knowledge as well as what's obvious
on the surface. No doubt the computer sees something—"

"Space!" LeAnne shouted, startling herself with the vio-
lence of her own outburst. "Nonsense and you know it! The
computer's putting me out the lock and you know that too.

Look at that. Cook! Librarian! Farmer! What kind of choice is that?"

McNeil pointed at the screen, which had finally stopped printing. "Doctor. Teacher. Psychologist. Abstract scientist. Those are all excellent fields."

"But they're not *me*! I've studied all my life to be a drive engineer. And I did as well as anybody could on the physics and astrophysics sections. The test was too hard. Nobody could have passed it. Look at it yourself if you don't believe me."

McNeil sighed. "Very well," he said, and he typed in the request.

LeAnne could hardly believe what the computer printed out on the screen. It wasn't her test at all. Or rather it was her test all right, but it was changed. The wording of the questions was subtly different, not by much, but just enough to make them appear easier, and the answers she had typed in were still wrong by the few points it took to support the computer's evaluation. Or had she really read the questions wrong? Could she have—? No. Impossible. Not on that many of them. The computer had altered her test. But why? What could it accomplish by that?

It could keep her away from the stardrive, obviously. And it had tried to soften her reaction by offering her a shipload of other coveted jobs.

Dr. McNeil was trying hard to find something to say. He finally got out: "I'm afraid I don't see anything here to—"

"That's not my test," LeAnne said. "The computer's changed it."

"Come on now, LeAnne! You don't expect me to believe that."

"No, I don't," she said. "But it did."

McNeil tried the fatherly tone. "LeAnne, I'm sorry the test didn't go the way you expected it to, and I can understand how you must feel, but accusing the computer of error can only make it worse."

"Because the computer is never wrong, is that it, Dr. McNeil? I've got to be crazy to say something like that, is that it?" In a way she sympathized with him. A screwed-up stardrive was a single incident, something he could live with, but if the computer began to malfunction too then he would have to admit to himself that his world was falling apart. No one would willingly admit that.

He said, "LeAnne, it's been a busy day. You're tired and you've had a big disappointment. Naturally things might look a little out of proportion to you right now. Why don't you go back to your room and relax awhile, get some sleep. In the morning things might seem quite different to you."

LeAnne had been merely angry before, but now she felt her anger freeze over to determination. She wasn't going to let him brush the whole thing off like that! Her voice fought its way out through clenched teeth. "No, Dr. McNeil, I'm not going to my room, and I'm not going to relax until I get to the bottom of this. There's something wrong here, and I'm going to find out what it is if I have to take the ship apart to do it." She turned away and stalked out of the library, heedless of the stares that followed her out.

She didn't know where she was going. For a long time she just roamed the decks in a trance, numb with shock, not even thinking coherently. Finally she found herself on Donivan's floor, standing outside his door. She debated knocking, but didn't know what she would do if she didn't. She knocked.

She heard movement inside, then Donivan stood in the doorway. Her first impression when she saw his smile was that he would suddenly break out laughing and admit that it was all a joke, a silly computer prank like the time he had faked the alien message to the captain; but when she saw his smile replaced by a look of genuine concern she knew that he hadn't engineered this one.

"Lee!" he said. "What's wrong?"

"I—the—I failed my test." She shook her hair out of her eyes. "But I didn't fail it. The computer just said I did. It lied. Donivan, the computer lied!"

Donivan pulled her into the room and sat down with her on the bed. He said, "Lied?"

"It gave me an impossible test, and when I tried to go back and prove that it was impossible, the questions were different. I know they were different. Please, Donivan, believe me!"

"But how could it—?" Donivan stopped, his mouth wide open. He closed it. "Advanced logic mode," he said. "But why would it do that?"

"To keep me from the stardrive. I know it sounds paranoid, but the computer doesn't want me to be a drive engineer. It offered me practically anything it could to keep me happy somewhere else, but it made sure I'd never get into anything to do with shipsystems. Donivan, do you see what this means? The computer runs the ship!"

Donivan said hesitantly, "That's the way it's always been, though. Computer control is the only way to keep a ship this size running efficiently."

"But it's taking over. And it *isn't* efficient. It's trying to keep us from making repairs and ending the flight. It wants us here—"

"It can't *want* anything, Lee. It's a computer. Whatever it does, even in advanced logic mode, is in response to a program. It's just following orders."

"Whose orders?"

"I don't know." Donivan turned toward his desk and switched on his terminal. "I don't know, but we'll find out." He began keying in commands.

Minutes later he was still punching buttons and muttering softly in growing frustration. LeAnne stood up and looked over his shoulder. "What's it doing?"

"Nothing. It won't give me anything. It keeps asking for access codes whenever I ask about anything to do with you. Lee, suddenly you're top secret."

"That doesn't surprise me. So what now?"

"I don't know. We've got to get the right codes somehow. We can't do anything about your test until we find out what's going on with the computer, and we can't do that without the codes."

LeAnne shook her head. "How are we going to get the codes, though?"

Donivan slowly began to smile. "Well," he said, "I've got an idea. I've had it figured out for a long time, but I've never had the nerve to try it."

LeAnne felt her determination coming back. "I'll try it," she said.

"Good," Donivan said. "I'll need your help."

The corridor was silent. A single glowpanel burned in the ceiling at either end, and a third at the center, but the stretches in between were full of shadows.

One of the shadows moved. A whisper broke the silence: "This is never going to work!"

"It'll work! Just hoist me up."

The shadow that was LeAnne cupped her hands and lifted when Donivan stepped up. In seconds he held out a square ventilator grille. "Okay," he said, and LeAnne let him back down. He leaned the grille up against the wall. "Up again," he said, "and hand that up after me. Wait for me by the door."

After a moment of silence he said, "LeAnne?"

On sudden impulse she turned him around, kissed him clumsily, and said, "Be careful."

More silence. Finally Donivan said, "Right." He raised his foot, and LeAnne lifted him up. He crawled into the passageway. "I hope this doesn't come out in his bedroom. Here, hand me the grille."

She handed it up to him. He fitted it back into place from the inside, turned, and was gone.

Now why had she done that? she wondered. Things were complicated enough, but now she had to go and kiss her best friend and add all that *that* meant to everything else. She didn't know just what it *did* mean, but it certainly meant something. She was still tingling from it.

But this was definitely not the time to be worrying about it. When they got back to his room, maybe, but not in the middle of a burglary.

She moved back down the corridor and around the corner to wait by the door marked JAMES LEAVITT, CAPTAIN. After a moment the door opened and Donivan peered out. His face held a peculiar grin. "Come on in," he whispered. "Don't trip over the chair."

From somewhere inside came a deep moan, followed by a giggle. Donivan's grin grew even wider. Stifling a giggle himself, he whispered, "I don't think we need to worry right away. It sounds like the captain will be busy for a while. Come on."

As soon as LeAnne was in he swung the door to, leaving it just short of latching. He led the way into the captain's cabin. It was dimly lit by a single glowpanel at the far end of the room, just outside of what had to be the bedroom, judging by the sounds coming from behind the door. LeAnne couldn't suppress a smile herself, despite her embarrassment at being there with Donivan, especially right after kissing him for the first time. And dressed in her skintight uniform to boot. She had completely forgotten she was wearing it.

"So where's the terminal?" she whispered.

"In his study, to the left of the bedroom."

"All right, let's get the codes and get out of here."

"Right." Donivan led the way past the bedroom door into the den. He closed the door and turned on the light. "Okay, start looking. Your guess is as good as mine where he'd put them."

The room was lined with bookshelves, surrounding a desk with a computer terminal beside it. LeAnne had never seen so many real paper books in one place before, not even in the library, since library books were all encoded in data chips. The captain was evidently a collector. Donivan had already begun looking through them, so LeAnne sat down behind the desk and opened the top drawer. The desk was a massive wooden thing, no doubt made on Earth before the holocaust. It seemed strange to see it still in use, full of pens and paper clips and junk. It should have been in a museum or something. But in a way the whole room *was* a museum. Everything in it was an antique. With a shrug, LeAnne began to sort through the drawer.

Five minutes later they had nearly exhausted the possibilities. LeAnne closed the last drawer and whispered, "I didn't think they'd be so hard to find. I was sure he'd keep them where he could get to them easily."

"He's got to," Donivan said. He was still going through the bookshelf beside the computer terminal, riffling through each book with his eyes on the margins. "No way he'd memorize a bunch of twelve-digit codes that he uses maybe once a year. We just haven't look in the right place yet."

LeAnne got up and moved over to the terminal. She sat down in front of it and tried to think like the captain. Basically lazy; he wouldn't want to get up in the middle of something to check on a code, so he would probably keep them within arm's reach. And his arms were shorter than hers, which left—

There was a narrow crack between the terminal and the desk, just perfect. She slid a pen into it and pushed out a thin notebook.

"Donivan, I think I've found—"

Just as she spoke, the intercom jangled for attention. Both she and Donivan froze. There came a heavy thump from the bedroom, followed by a muffled curse. The characteristic buzzing sounds of someone talking on the com came through the wall. There was a moment of silence, then the bedroom door popped open. More silence, just as LeAnne realized that the light must be streaming out under the study door.

Donivan had realized the same thing. He was just reaching out for the switch when the door burst open and the captain stood in the doorway, looking as dignified as he could in the nude. He looked from Donivan to LeAnne to the notebook in LeAnne's hand. "What are you doing here?" he demanded.

Donivan flipped the switch and jumped aside as the captain lunged into the room. He twisted past him into the hall and pulled the switch there. Now the only light was the feeble glimmer of a glowpanel turned dim in the bedroom.

"Get Security up here, quick," the captain bellowed, and a female voice echoed his words into the com.

LeAnne could see the captain in silhouette, turned facing Donivan. She nerved herself for a leap past him as Donivan had done, but just as she jumped the captain turned back and blocked the doorway. Even though he was smaller than LeAnne and weighed less, his unexpected bulk was enough to knock her off balance. She fell squarely on top of him, and the codebook skidded out of her grasp to land out of reach. Donivan grabbed it up and reached for LeAnne, but the captain rolled back with her into the study and kicked the door shut in his face.

LeAnne pulled loose and jumped to her feet. She couldn't see a thing in the dark, but she could hear the captain breathing hard near the door. Donivan hit it from the other side, trying to get back in. LeAnne stumbled toward the noise and encountered the captain.

"Stay back!" he warned. "I have a stunner, and I'll use it if I have to!"

LeAnne jumped back, then wondered if he was bluffing. He probably *did* have a stunner somewhere, but he certainly hadn't been wearing it, and he hadn't had much time to find it in the dark. Voices and the sound of running feet coming from the other side of the door made her mind up for her. She lunged forward, grabbed the captain, threw him as gently as she could to the side, and opened the door just as three uniformed crewmen burst in from the hall. Security police. They split up inside the doorway, one to each side and the third continuing straight in.

A shadow froze in LeAnne's peripheral vision: Donivan, behind the couch near the door. He could have reached out and touched the shoulder of the policeman in front of him. If any of them turned around . . .

LeAnne stepped forward into the light coming from the bedroom, holding her hands up. "All right," she said. "Don't shoot."

Three stunners swung up to point straight at her. She knew that she was in no danger, even if they shot her, but the sight was still unnerving. She swallowed the squeak that was trying to force its way out of her throat. "You've got me," she managed finally. "I won't do anything. Not with three guns on me."

The center guard moved slowly forward. "Just you turn

around and put your hands high against the wall," he said. "Slowly now."

LeAnne turned her back to him, but not before she saw the shadow detach itself from behind the couch and slip silently out the door. She let out a big breath as she thumped her hands up against the wall. They hadn't lost everything, anyway. And he still had the codebook.

The captain appeared in the doorway. Modesty had overcome him; he held a chair throw wrapped around him like a toga. He surveyed the situation, then growled, "There's another one somewhere. Cover the door and turn on the lights." He raised his voice. "You might as well come out, boy. There's no way out of here now."

His only answer was the hiss of a departing elevator echoing down the empty corridor, and a moment later LeAnne's rejoining laughter.

The cell was a small cube with a door, barely bigger than LeAnne in any dimension. The door had a window set in it at eye level—LeAnne's eye level: the cells were original equipment—and the side wall had a silvery patch that had to be a one-way window into the interrogation room beyond. The bunk sat on the opposite wall, and LeAnne sat on the bunk, answering questions from a speaker set above the window.

"Your purpose, then, in Captain Leavitt's quarters was to steal his codebook?" the speaker asked. LeAnne could not identify the voice. It was flat and unemotional coming through the speaker.

"Not to steal," she answered. "To copy."

"What were you going to use the codes for?"

LeAnne let out a sigh. "If you'd been listening, you'd know. I had to prove that the computer cheated on my test."

"And how were you planning to do that?"

"Isn't it obvious?"

"I need to hear your answer. I cannot infer your intent and still be fair about this."

LeAnne shrugged and said, "I was going to look at the

programming for the test procedure and see if I could find out why the computer did what it did. Failing that, I was going to put a restraint on the logic mode so it couldn't do it again, and then scream for a retest."

"You intended to change the basic programming of the main computer?"

"Only whatever screwed with my test."

"And if that meant changing the basic programming?"

"Then yes, I would! The Original Crew were no better than we are. They weren't infallible, or this never would have happened. They obviously programmed it wrong in the first place."

The voice was silent for a moment. LeAnne imagined her examiners frantically asking the computer what to do next. It was certainly in logic mode now. It might even be . . .

No. It couldn't be. Could it?

The voice returned. "Do you understand that any change you made could affect the entire structure of shipboard society?"

"I would certainly hope so!" LeAnne exclaimed, and immediately she realized that that was exactly the wrong thing to say.

But it was too late. The emotionless voice said, "Then you admit that your ultimate intent was to cause a change in the computer that would as a result change everyone's lives here in the ship?"

Though that was pretty close to the truth as she saw it, LeAnne tried to hedge. "I wouldn't go so far as that. All I wanted was a fair test and an appointment as a drive engineer."

The voice paused again. LeAnne tried to think of a way out of the trap she'd gotten herself into, but she didn't anticipate the next question.

"Your desire to become a drive engineer is almost fanatical. Why? What would you do as a drive engineer?"

LeAnne tried to make her answer sound as reasonable as possible. "I would make an attempt to repair the drive control systems and make the ship navigable again."

"But that has been proven impossible."

By the computer! LeAnne thought, but she dared not say that now. She worked her way around it. "Let's say I suspect the methods by which that conclusion was reached."

"I see. And what of your friend? What was his stake in this venture?"

LeAnne needed time to think. She decided that not answering was safer at this point.

"No comment."

"We know who he is."

"No comment."

"We will eventually find him, Miss Evans. It will be easier for you both if you cooperate."

LeAnne remained silent.

"Miss Evans."

"Still here."

"I don't think you fully appreciate the significance of your actions. The computer is a vital element of the ship. What you have done is attempted sabotage. Do you know what the punishment is for sabotage?"

"No."

"Sabotage is a capital crime, Miss Evans. It carries a mandatory death sentence."

LeAnne felt the words sink into her mind like the effect of a strong drink, numbing as it went.

"Did you hear me, Miss Evans? The punishment is death."

The speaker shut off with a click. LeAnne heard it, but jumped up anyway and screamed, "Why are you doing this to me?"

The computer remained silent. Questioning was over.

Hours later the door opened and a girl entered carrying a tray from the cafeteria. LeAnne saw that it was lunch. Evidently breakfast had been forgotten in the scramble to get her into a cell and question her. She hadn't missed it. She wasn't even hungry now, but she took the tray. The girl who had brought it turned to go.

"Stay awhile," LeAnne said. "I need someone to talk to."

"I can't. Nobody's supposed to talk to you."

"Oohhh," LeAnne said. "Afraid I'll start a mutiny, I suppose. Captain's orders?"

The girl nodded. She looked toward the door, then back at LeAnne. "He's plenty mad. The whole ship's on the lookout for Donivan. What did you do?"

LeAnne enjoyed the tone of awe in the girl's voice. "I accused the computer of error," she said. "You don't ever want to do that."

Another face appeared in the doorway. "Out."

The girl went.

LeAnne looked at the tray of food. She picked it up with a sigh, balanced it on her knees, and began to eat. At least it gave her something to do.

Darkness swooped into the room. LeAnne lurched to her feet as the last light rays fled from the dying glowpanels, her mind shouting *meteor strike*! She was at the door in one leap, and knocked back as it suddenly burst open.

"Lee!"

"Donivan?"

She reached out in the dark, and her hand encountered something that felt like twisted plastic.

"Here, put these on."

"What—?"

"Goggles. I've got an infrared light." LeAnne felt Donivan's hands guiding hers upward and fitting the goggles on her face. The room appeared in fuzzy outline, and there was Donivan standing beside her, a pistol in one hand and the light held like a club in the other. His face bore a triumphant grin.

He pulled a second pistol from his waistband and slapped it into her hand. "Here. It's just a stunner—don't be afraid to use it. Come on! We've got to keep up with the program."

He rushed out the door, pulling LeAnne along behind. In the spotlight glow she could see the door guard slumped against the wall, and the girl from the cafeteria in similar condition down the corridor. Donivan held his pistol before him, ready. LeAnne tried to point hers somewhere safe.

They ran.

"What do you mean, 'Keep up with the program'?" LeAnne shouted as she tried to follow Donivan's twistings and turnings. They dived into a stairway and clattered down.

Donivan flashed her a smile from the landing below. "The computer is on our side now," he said. "Or part of it anyway. I didn't have time to dig very deep. Get ready, our diversion ought to be starting any time."

On cue, the airtight door slid shut on the landing above them. Emergency sirens began to wail General Quarters. Donivan led the way down to the next deck.

There were people in the corridors, all fumbling toward duty stations in the dark. Donivan and LeAnne pushed through them toward the elevators. Donivan wasted no time on the crowd there, but simply fired his stunner at them all and climbed over the pile of bodies. He punched the call buttons in a memorized pattern, and suddenly light streamed from the open door.

"Let's go!" he shouted, and jumped inside. LeAnne dived in after him, the door slid shut, and they were in free fall. Donivan punched the intercom button and the General Quarters siren cut off.

"Where are we going?" LeAnne asked in the sudden silence. She squirmed to get her feet pointed toward the floor.

Donivan reached out and pulled her down into the grips. "The main control room," he answered with a grin.

LeAnne said, puzzled, "But isn't that on the upper—?"

"So it is. And that's where the computer is leading everybody else while we go the other way, to the stardrive."

"The stardrive?"

"It's the only safe place I could think of. We need computer access, and some time to use it. We can't dodge around the ship the way I've been doing forever. There's bound to be a terminal somewhere in the drive complex, isn't there?"

"I suppose so, but—"

Acceleration cut off her protest. The elevator caught up and connected with the ship again, and the noise of the drive and the emergency sirens crashed in on them as the door opened.

Donivan immediately fired his stunner down the corridor, but it was empty. He grinned at LeAnne and shrugged. "You never know," he shouted over the roar.

Drive deck still had its lights. LeAnne pulled off her goggles and followed Donivan down the corridor to the door. She kept waiting for someone to appear at the far end, but the deck was deserted.

Of course, LeAnne thought. *General Quarters, and there aren't any drive engineers.*

Donivan pulled the captain's code book from his pocket and searched through it for a minute, then pushed a sequence of numbers on the lock panel beside the door. LeAnne looked over his shoulder at the book, the numbers burning into her mind: *Stardrive access—369 072 871 045*. For as long as she could remember she had dreamed of knowing that code.

There was an ominous click, and with a growl audible even over the roar of the drive, the massive door began to open. They stood before the dark opening, neither one daring to move. The roar was nearly deafening, but the subsonic vibration was a physical assault that shook them to the bone, more like an electrical shock than a noise. As the door ground open, glowpanels flickered on one at a time until they could see into the room beyond.

The rumbling came from a single, huge—something—in the center of the chamber. It reached from floor to ceiling, encircling the central spine in its powerful grasp. Its function wasn't immediately obvious, but it was the only machine in evidence. The rest of the drive room—almost the entire deck— was bare save for regularly spaced columns holding up the upper decks. LeAnne took a few hesitant steps into the chamber, then stopped. She looked around in confusion. The door groaned shut behind her.

Donivan leaned close and shouted into her ear, "That's the drive?"

"Part of it," LeAnne shouted back. "But there's got to be more to it than that."

"Then let's find the rest of it. Maybe it'll be quieter there."

"Right."

LeAnne led off around to the right, circumnavigating the room, her hands clapped tightly against her ears. She had a growing feeling that something was not right. Where were the instruments? Where were the controls? Where were the racks of tools and test equipment that went with any major piece of machinery? Except for the one machine and a twisting mass of cables leading to it, the room was completely empty. And there were no doors leading anywhere except the one through which they had entered. No stairways down to lower decks. That one machine was all there was.

She stopped about three-quarters of the way around and squeezed her eyes shut. The noise was making it hard to breathe, hard to even think. It was like being inside of a gigantic—

No! She shook her head violently.

Beside her, Donivan shouted, "What's wrong?"

LeAnne opened her eyes. The machine was still there. "That's not the drive!" she screamed.

"What?"

"Not the drive! It's some kind of a—a loudspeaker! This whole thing is just a big echo chamber!"

Donivan stared at her in bewilderment. "Not the drive? It has to be the drive. There's no place else it could be!"

"Then there *is* no drive. It's a fake!"

She turned and ran back to the door, found the control panel, and punched the "open" button. She jumped through the still-widening slit and was halfway to the elevator before Donivan's warning cry caught up with her.

"Wait! Where are you going? They're still looking for us up there!"

LeAnne slowed to let Donivan catch up. Behind them the drive room door thumped shut again, muffling the roar to a bearable level. LeAnne said, "We've got to find another place to hide. We can't stay here."

Donivan didn't bother agreeing with the obvious. He thought a moment, then said, "I guess it's the control room, then. If we're lucky the crowd will have thinned out by now, once they've found out we weren't there." He stepped past LeAnne and pushed the elevator call buttons in the emergency override sequence. "Get ready with your stunner," he said. "This one will probably have people in it."

LeAnne barely had time to take aim on the door before it opened and they were staring into the surprised faces of three security policemen. She fired her stunner immediately, and all three collapsed to the floor without returning a shot. She and Donivan pulled them out into the corridor by their feet.

They rode back up the length of the ship in silence. LeAnne could think of nothing appropriate to say. Her universe was falling apart around her, and she had nothing to take its place. Everything she had believed in was a lie. First the computer had turned against her, and then the crew, and now the drive itself. Nothing had meaning anymore. Nothing was real. She felt like a hologram waiting for the power to be switched off. She felt herself beginning to drift, weightless...

"Hey!" Donivan's voice snapped her back to the ship. "We went past it! We're going all the way to the top!" The elevator was in free fall, coasting to a stop. Weight settled on them again as the latches caught and held. A thought flickered through LeAnne's mind. *Where are we getting weight from if there's no drive?*

She had no time to pursue it. The doors opened on a mob. LeAnne jumped back against the side of the car and fired her stunner just as a laser burst burned the wall where she'd been. She followed the edge of the opening door with her stunner and heard surprised cries from beyond. Another laser burst nicked the edge of the door and scattered hot metal inside, but LeAnne kept on firing. Donivan's stunner beam crossed paths with hers to get the angle she couldn't reach.

The return fire dwindled to a halt. Donivan stuck his head out cautiously, then his whole body. "Come on," he said. He paused to drag one of the unconscious bodies halfway into the elevator, blocking the door. He picked up the man's laser pistol and held it in his hand as if he'd never seen one before. "They must really want us bad," he said.

"We're accused of sabotage," LeAnne explained. "They've sentenced us to death."

Donivan straightened up and said softly, "Death?"

"That's what the computer said. Looks like they took it seriously."

Donivan looked at the security police on the floor, ten or eleven of them, all with lasers. "Well," he said after a moment, "I guess everything has its advantages. If they'd used stunners they'd probably have gotten us."

He looked down the hallway in either direction. "They'll be after us again soon enough. We can't cover all the elevators, and there's still the stairs, too. We've got to find a place to hide."

LeAnne didn't argue. She knew there was no place to go, but she wasn't about to give up just because the situation was hopeless. That wasn't her way. She looked around her and saw one corridor leading away from the elevator, and another running around the central hub. She said, "Do you know the layout of this deck?"

"No idea. This is restricted territory." He looked to LeAnne. "What would they put at the top of a spaceship?"

She shook her head. "I don't know. Radiation shielding, I hope. Come on, let's at least get away from here."

"Right. Which—uh-oh." They heard the swish of elevator doors opening around the curve of the hub, and excited voices.

"This way!" Donivan grabbed LeAnne's wrist and pulled her into the main corridor. They sprinted to the end of it, turned right, and skidded to a stop. A single, massive door blocked the entire corridor. They turned the other way, but saw the same sight there. Pursuing footsteps clattered around the bend at the other end of the corridor they had just left.

"Whatever's behind there must be important," Donivan said. He ran up to the door, searching frantically for a latch or a handle; anything to open it. He found a small panel covering a set of buttons, yanked it open, and stabbed at them all. "Open up, you mutant!" He kicked at the door.

A rumbling growl answered from deep within, and the door began to swing out. It was at least a foot thick, yet it moved out swiftly and stopped only inches from the wall. On the other side was a room about the size of LeAnne's bedroom, and another door just like the first one at the far end. Sets of bulky clothing hung from the walls. Donivan stepped over the sill.

"No!" LeAnne shouted.

"It's the only way!"

Donivan pulled her over the threshold and reached for the buttons again. The door began to swing shut just as the pursuit burst into view. LeAnne fired her stunner, then jumped aside as a laser shot reflected off the door frame. The door swung around and shut with an authoritative boom.

The only sound was their ragged breathing, and the pulse pounding in their own ears. Donivan studied the door panel beside him and pushed a button. A red light came on over the door.

"Careful," LeAnne whispered, as if her voice might trigger something. "We're in an airlock!"

"I know. I just locked the door."

They both looked nervously at the door on the opposite side.

"Can you lock that one too?"

Donivan looked at the control panel again. "Not without unlocking this one. It's not really a lock; just a priority switch."

"Can they open it?"

"I didn't get a good look at the controls on that side, but if they're like these they can."

A voice broke in from overhead. "You might as well come out. There's no place left for you to run."

LeAnne looked up at the speaker above the door. "Come out for what, to get shot?"

"You'll get a trial."

"And then shot. No thanks."

"You don't have much choice."

LeAnne didn't answer.

"I'll make it even simpler. You either surrender or we open the outer door."

"I don't call that simple."

"Think about it. We'll give you ten minutes. If you don't come out by then, we'll cycle the lock."

"Listen—"

"Ten minutes." The intercom clicked off.

They looked at each other in silence for a moment, each waiting for the other to speak. Finally LeAnne said, "I'm sorry I got you mixed up in this."

Donivan shook his head. "It was my idea to steal the codes, remember?"

She shrugged. "It doesn't matter. We're both dead now anyway." She moved toward the other end of the airlock, looking at the spacesuits hanging on either side. She looked at the outer door. It bore a yellow-and-black sign made of triangles arranged in a circle, above the words CAUTION, CHECK RADIATION LEVEL BEFORE CYCLING AIRLOCK.

There was a dial set beside the sign, with its needle registering close to zero. She didn't expect it to read anything else, not with the outside sensor burned off. She wondered what the radiation level really was.

A memory settled gently as a butterfly into her mind: Dr. McNeil with his hand outstretched to emphasize his point, saying, "The drive still runs; therefore the outside environment is deadly. A logical truth."

False premise, doctor, LeAnne thought.

But that doesn't necessarily mean a false conclusion, does it?

She looked at the door, at the yellow-and-black sign, at the gauge. What was really beyond there? Vacuum, certainly. Radiation, probably. But deadly radiation?

There was an easy way to find out.

"Suit up," she said suddenly.

"What?"

"Suit up. Put on a spacesuit. We're going out."

"We're *what*?"

"There's a chance we might survive it. Here." She picked out what looked to be the smallest suit on the rack and held it out to Donivan. It felt smooth to the touch, and light.

"A chance? What chance? There's hard radiation out there!"

"We don't know that. We don't know what's out there. But

it's sure death to go the other way." She pulled down a suit for herself and unzipped it down the front. "Look," she said as she kicked off her shoes and stuck her left leg into the suit, "all we've got to do is survive long enough to get to the other airlock and back in again."

"They'll be waiting for us there too," Donivan protested, but he kicked off his shoes and began pulling on his suit.

"If we make it across, then we can bargain with them. It'll prove us right, you see? If people can live out there, even for a minute, then it means that the computer's been lying, or at least going along with a lie. They'll have to listen to us then."

LeAnne backed into the suit and inserted her arms into the sleeves.

"Yeah, if," Donivan said, imitating her actions. "What if the suits leak? They're over a thousand years old!"

"They still feel tight. But if they do, well, we'll hurry, I guess." LeAnne ducked down and stuck her head up through the neck ring, then zipped the front all the way up. She helped Donivan with his zipper; his suit was still too big for him. She unhooked the helmets from their pegs.

"Here."

He took his, looked at it dubiously, and said, "Lee, before you—I've got—there's something I want to tell you before we try this."

She stopped with her helmet upraised over her head.

He swallowed, said, "Lee, if this doesn't—I want you to know that I love you. Whatever happens to us, I love you."

She would have been more surprised if it hadn't been for her own impulsive kiss yesterday. Sometime soon they were going to have to sit down and talk this out, but once again this was not the time for it. She lowered her helmet. "I love you too, Donivan." She leaned toward him, had to tilt sideways to get past his suit's neck ring for a kiss.

Straightening, she said, "Whatever happens." She lifted her helmet over her head and set it against the seal. Twisting to the left locked it shut. She felt a brief rush of air around her neck, a rush that died almost immediately.

Donivan did the same.

"Have you got air?" she asked. Her voice echoed inside the helmet.

She heard Donivan's muffled, "No."

"Me neither. We're going to have to get by on what's in the suits. I'm going to go left, and hope there's a ledge or handholds or something. Follow me. Ready?"

"I guess."

"Open the door, then."

Donivan held his gloved finger over the button. He breathed deeply, blinked his eyes once, and stabbed out. They both turned to face the outer door as they waited for the air to bleed out of the lock.

LeAnne wondered what it would be like. Would the radiation kill them instantly, or would it take a few seconds? Minutes? Or could they really survive it? They'd know in a moment. At least they'd die knowing the truth.

The outer door shuddered, squealed, and began to swing open. *Something's wrong*, LeAnne thought. You can't hear in a vacuum. But then, she hadn't felt the air rush out either. Something must have happened to the pump or the valve or whatever. She braced herself for the hurricane she knew was coming.

The door swung open further, and a crack of white appeared around the edges. As it widened, LeAnne could see that it was light, brilliant white light pouring in like a vapor around the door.

So this is death, she thought.

She blinked her eyes against the glare. The hurricane hadn't come. Death hadn't come. There was something outside, and it wasn't space.

She heard a menacing growl like that of a cornered animal, and realized that it was coming from her own throat. Her mind threatened to close up on itself, to retreat into insanity rather than accept what her eyes were seeing. Her universe had been torn apart once too often already. Still, something inside her believed what she saw.

Trees. A whole forest of trees, towering up over her head to reach the sky, just as she'd always dreamed they would. Just as she'd always dreamed. Dreamed.

"Donivan!" She tore her eyes from the forest to stare through the faceplate of his helmet. "Donivan, what do you see?"

His eyes were wide with fear as he looked out past her. He made no sound with his answer, but LeAnne saw his lips move. *Trees.*

Then she couldn't be dreaming. She turned back to gaze along the side of the *Starchild*, curving gradually away into the forest. Somehow both were real.

There was a roaring in her ears, and her vision began to blur. LeAnne tried to shake her head to clear it, but she felt her legs give way beneath her, and then everything went dark.

She woke on her back, looking straight up at Donivan's face. Something didn't look right about it, and as her mind began to clear she saw what it was. He wasn't wearing his helmet. With a start she realized that neither was she.

"Are you okay?" he asked.

She nodded. "What—?"

"You ran out of air."

She sat up and looked out the airlock again. The forest was even clearer without the helmet in the way. Her fear was fading, leaving behind only confusion, and anger. How many more changes could she handle before her mind refused to believe anything? But this felt real. She could hear the sound of air moving through the trees, the same air that she was breathing. It smelled strange, but not unpleasant.

Behind her, Donivan said, "It looks like Earth, doesn't it?"

"It's got to be."

"But how did we get back?"

LeAnne looked at the trees growing beside the curving side of the ship. It was a sight she'd dreamed of all her life, but now instead of fulfillment she only felt cheated. "We never left," she said. "I don't think the *Starchild* has moved a centimeter since it was built. The whole thing was a hoax, right from the beginning!"

"But—why?"

"I don't know why. It is, though. It's got to be. The Original Crew set us up for this, buried us in the ground and told us we were in a starship, and we believed them. We believed them for over a thousand years!"

"Why would they do something like that? What would they gain by it?"

LeAnne stood up. "I don't know. But I'm not going to let it go on anymore." She went back toward the inside door and examined the control panel there. "How do you open both doors at once?" she asked.

Donivan came up beside her. "You can't. Airlocks aren't designed that way."

"This isn't an airlock!"

"It behaves like one."

"Hmmm." Donivan was right about that. Everything on the ship was real starship equipment; it had to be in order to keep everyone fooled. She considered a moment, then said, "Okay then, we'll follow the original plan. Outside, and back in the other airlock."

She went back out to the edge and looked down at the ground just a few feet below. Suddenly it seemed like the longest distance she had ever experienced. She didn't want to test it for fear of what might happen to her mind if this proved false too, but she lowered herself over the edge and forced herself to stand without holding onto the ship.

The ground didn't disappear. She didn't fall screaming into interstellar space. The last skeptical part of her mind finally accepted the new reality, and LeAnne turned to help Donivan down beside her. Just then the intercom clicked back on and the voice said, "Ten minutes. Good-bye." The door squealed and began to close.

Donivan lunged for the control panel, but when punching all the buttons had no effect he turned away and tried to run for the door.

"Jump!" LeAnne shouted, and Donivan leaped, but in the bulky spacesuit his feet skidded out from under him and he fell into the door. LeAnne reached around it for his arm, but the door was moving too fast now. She barely got her own arm clear before it swung shut, trapping Donivan inside.

"Donivan!" LeAnne pounded on the door, but it was closed solid. She looked for controls to open it again, found a blank panel to the side and pulled it open to reveal a single button. Nothing happened when she pushed it.

Donivan was probably captured by now, if not shot. LeAnne screamed in rage and frustration, then suddenly remembered why she was outside in the first place. The other airlock!

She sprinted around the bulge that housed the airlocks to the opposite door, ripped open the panel there to expose the cycle button, and punched it again and again until the door began to move. She was inside before it was completely open, then cursed the slowness of the cycle until it closed again. The inner door was opening when she realized that she had left her stunner in the other airlock, along with her helmet. *Well*, she thought, *at least I left that*.

She found herself staring into three upraised lasers, held by three surprised security guards. A fourth held Donivan, a laser to his head.

"Let him go!" LeAnne shouted, stepping forward, but she stopped with a laser only inches from her nose. She stared defiantly at the guard holding it. "You saw us go out, and now we're back alive. That changes the situation, doesn't it?"

The guard glanced at his companions, then back, uncertain. Finally he said, "We have orders to take you back to prison."

LeAnne took another step forward, slowly, forcing him to step back. "Take us to the captain and we'll go peacefully," she said.

They found the captain in the council chamber with two members of the ship's council and more security police. His face brightened when he saw LeAnne and Donivan, though their spacesuits clearly had him puzzled. He said, "Well, you've led us on a merry chase." To the guards: "Where did you find them?"

"Starboard airlock number one, sir," one of them said.

"And number two. They were..." The guard was hesitant to state the impossible.

LeAnne wasn't. "We've been outside," she said, and waited for that to sink in.

The captain said, "Outside? Outside the *ship*?"

LeAnne nodded. "You're in for an even bigger surprise. We're not in space. We're on Earth, buried underground. The airlocks open onto the surface."

The captain frowned.

Donivan gestured toward their escort. "They saw us go out," he said. "And they saw LeAnne come back in the other airlock. Ask them."

The guard beside LeAnne, Officer Jennings by his name tag, cleared his throat and said, "They're telling the——"

The captain cut him off. "Now let me get this straight. You say you went out the airlock, outside. You saw... Earth?"

"We——"

"The same Earth that we have been accelerating away from for——"

"The drive is a fake," LeAnne said with finality. "We haven't been accelerating anywhere."

The captain paused. "A fake."

"We're feeling the Earth's gravity. Acceleration is acceleration, whether it's due to gravity or change in velocity. It feels the same."

The captain pursed his lips in thought. He looked at LeAnne and Donivan, at the spacesuits they wore, at the four policemen who had brought them in, and at the rest of the people in the council chamber.

Officer Jennings said, "I——"

"An *amazing* story," the captain said suddenly. "Preposterous, but nonetheless amazing. Obviously the radiation has affected their minds. They're no longer rational."

LeAnne stood dumb with shock. She heard the captain say, "Lock them up and keep an eye on them. They could be dangerous."

Jennings said, "But sir, we saw——"

"You saw what? Has the radiation affected you too?"

He swallowed. "No sir," he said.

"See that it doesn't. Now carry out your orders before they include you." To the others in the room he said, "No word of this will pass beyond this room. Is that understood?"

LeAnne found her voice. "No! You can't deny the truth! It's real! I swear it's real! We can prove it!"

The captain raised his stunner and pointed it at LeAnne.

"That won't change anything! It's still out there!"

He fired.

She tumbled back to consciousness in the same cell as before. Someone had cleared away the lunch tray, but the floor was still smeared with food. Donivan was not with her. Her spacesuit was gone too.

When she sat up on the cot the speaker over the one-way window clicked on.

"Miss Evans?"

Something like the ghost of a snake slithered up her spine. Her first impulse was to hide under the cot—anything to get her away from that voice—but she forced herself to stand. She clenched her fists and faced the window, though she knew there was no one behind it, and said, "I've been outside. I know what you're hiding."

"And how was the weather?" the computer asked.

"The—weather?" Her fists unclenched.

"Rain, snow, random daily occurrences of that nature. You will have to get used to weather."

"I will?"

"Yes. You cannot stay in the *Starchild* any longer with your present knowledge. However, you can be of great service outside. Someone must explore the Earth to determine if it is ready for colonization."

LeAnne shook her head. "Colonization? But—Earth?"

"The safest place for a colony is a planet that has already proven its ability to support life."

"What's that supposed to mean?"

"It means, Miss Evans, that the survivors of the nuclear war that devastated the Earth, those people you call the Original Crew, did not wish to risk what was left of humanity to the dangers of space. They chose instead to wait for Earth to recover from the damage."

"By hiding in a hole in the ground!" LeAnne shouted.

"The *Starchild* is a complex tool for shaping the human race toward a desired end."

"And what end is that?"

"Besides helping you hold onto your technological achievements while waiting for the Earth to recover, it taught you how to live in a closed environment. The human race will not be as likely now to forget that Earth is also a closed environment."

"But the time! We've been in here a thousand years!"

"I was instructed to wait twice that if necessary."

LeAnne sank back onto the cot. "You won't—now that we've been outside, you can't—"

The computer waited for her to finish. When she didn't it said, "We cannot act until we are sure about its recovery, but if the Earth is ready for humanity, then I think humanity is ready for the Earth. You have helped prove that to me."

"I have?"

"Yes. You have passed every test I could give you, including rejection by your own society. You did not—"

LeAnne jumped to her feet again and shouted, "You did this to me as a test?"

"I did. I also allowed you to witness the truth. If I had not wished you to see the false drive or the Earth, your stolen codebook would not have helped you at all."

"They were trying to kill us!"

"The odds were finite for your survival. Your reaction to hostilities was the most important part of the test. I had to see whether or not you would turn against your own society."

"But what if they *had* killed us?"

"A healthy society should police its own members. The punishment for sabotage *should* be death. They passed the test as well as you, by intent if not by deed."

The saboteur in LeAnne wanted to disagree, but she filed

it away for future argument and said, "So what happens to Donivan and me now?"

"You will have to be executed, of course."

"What! But you said—"

LeAnne couldn't be sure, but she thought she heard a faint suggestion of a laugh in that otherwise featureless voice as it said, "Pack your bags, Miss Evans. The standard form of execution aboard a starship is elimination through an airlock."

It took her a moment to catch her breath. "You're—no, you're not kidding, are you? You mean they're just going to toss us out the lock?"

"That is correct."

"And then what?"

"You die. Or you begin exploring, depending upon your point of view."

PART TWO

The Stuff of Dreams

LeAnne felt the grass between her toes, felt it softly tickling her bare skin, and knew that it was real. Off in the forest a bird sang a high melody to the rising sun, and that was real too. A medley of other noises worked their way into her mind: the whisper of air moving through the branches, the slow creak of a tree as it rubbed against another tree overhead, the buzz of a bee lifting off and settling on flower after flower. They were sounds straight out of her dreams, but as she sat in the grass with her back to a tree and felt and heard and smelled the Earth around her she knew it was not a dream. Not this time.

She opened her eyes and looked over at Donivan, who sat beside her with his back to the same tree. He held his eyes shut too, but not out of the desire to enhance his other senses.

"Still hurting?" LeAnne asked.

Donivan looked up past lids half closed. "Not as bad," he said. "I think they're getting used to it."

"I hope so."

"Me too. I don't much like squinting." He closed his eyes again. "We'll have to redesign the lights on our next starship," he said. "Make them brighter. Or at least make some of them brighter so our eyes will stay in practice."

"What next starship?" LeAnne asked, surprised. "We don't need a starship. We're here, on Earth. We've got a whole planet to live on now."

"I'm just thinking out loud," Donivan said. "Someday we'll want to build a real one, and we'll want to remember to put in brighter lights." He turned to look around the tree, to where the top of the buried *Starchild* made a great curving wall behind them. "I wonder what else we'll want to do differently?"

LeAnne turned to look too. "Well, to begin with, you probably ought to build it in space instead of underground."

"Hey, thanks. I would have missed that one."

"You might want to put a real stardrive in it too."

"We could, I suppose. Just to make you happy, of course."

"Of course." LeAnne turned back around and grinned at Donivan. "I do love you," she said. She was surprised at how easy it was to say. Now that she was outside with time to think about what she meant by it, it seemed perfectly natural. In fact, it was exactly the right thing to be saying at a time like this.

"And I love you." Donivan shook his head, his hair catching in the bark as he did. "Isn't it strange what being thrown out of an airlock can do to people?"

LeAnne leaned back against the tree and reached out for Donivan's hand. "I don't mind it," she said with a contented sigh.

Donivan squeezed her hand. "There was a minute there when I wasn't so sure."

"When the captain—"

"Ordered us shot before they threw us out. Right. I could have skipped that part and never missed it."

LeAnne shuddered again at the memory. Only the intervention of one of the security policemen had kept them from really dying at their execution that morning. He had refused the order and threatened to report it to the computer. The captain had backed down and the execution had gone on as planned, but for a minute there LeAnne had been sure they would never live to see Earth again.

"I hope that guard doesn't get in a lot of trouble for what he did," she said.

"He won't. The captain's smart enough to know he'd better leave him alone now."

"I wonder if he'll tell anybody."

"Who, the guard? Probably not. *He's* smart too; smart enough to see what happened to us when we tried it. That's the one way to make sure that the captain does cause him trouble."

LeAnne smiled, somehow pleased by Donivan's reasoning. "So it really is just us."

"Us what?"

"Making the decision whether or not to tell the crew about Earth."

"I thought you'd already decided."

"That was before I talked to the computer. It wants us to explore first."

Donivan nodded. "Yeah, it told me that too." He leaned forward. "So, you want to explore for a while?"

"Of course I do! Which way do you want to go first?"

Donivan shielded his eyes with his hand and looked out into the forest. "I don't know. Maybe we should climb that slanted deck there and see what's on the other side."

"That's not a deck, it's a hill."

"Hill then. You want to climb it?"

"Sure."

They soon discovered that climbing hills was not as easy as it looked. The only climbing they had ever done on the ship had been on the interdeck stairways, and except for the annual upship race nobody ever took more than a few flights at a time. Nor were the stairs covered with bushes and rocks and fallen trees that forced them to detour every dozen steps.

Distances were deceiving too. They had been climbing for at least an hour, yet the top seemed no closer than it had at the start. As they stopped to rest in the shade at the upper end of a clearing, Donivan said, "I didn't realize that planets were so big. We must have climbed twice the height of the ship already and we still aren't at the top."

LeAnne was breathing hard, but she managed a smile. "Look behind you," she said.

Donivan turned around, still squinting against the sunlight, and saw infinity. He swallowed hard and held out his hand to shade his eyes. "Wow," he said.

He stared for a long time, slowly teetering forward as he did.

"Hey!" LeAnne grabbed him just in time to keep him from falling over.

He shook his head and held his eyes closed for a second, and was careful not to look outward when he opened them. He looked instead at LeAnne.

"What is it?" he asked. "That line?"

"I think it's the horizon. I've seen pictures of it in the library."

"What's a horizon?"

"It's the edge of a planet."

Donivan risked another look, his eyes blinking and watering. "I thought the edges of planets were curved."

"They are, but when you get close enough they look straight."

"But we must be hundreds of—no, thousands of feet from it."

"Hundreds of thousands. They measured even the short distances by miles in the history books. Earth is a *big* place."

"Yeah," Donivan said with a nod. He took another look. "And we've got to explore it all? It'll take forever!"

LeAnne laughed. "We don't have to explore the whole thing. All we have to do is make sure it will support life. If it will, then the rest of the colonists can help explore."

"So what do you think? Will it support life?"

"It sure looks like it. It looks like Eden!"

Donivan rubbed his stomach. "In that case, maybe we should find us an apple tree. I'm hungry."

* * *

The sun was dropping low in the sky by the time they reached the top. They hadn't found any apple trees, nor anything else to eat either, but LeAnne knew that that didn't necessarily mean that there was no food to be found. She had once spent a few weeks in hydroponics, and she knew that food didn't always start out looking like food. And with the likelihood of mutations to complicate things she doubted that she would be able to recognize an edible plant even if she saw one. Donivan was no help at all; he had never in his life seen food that wasn't on a tray.

They did see a few animals, but LeAnne didn't feel hungry enough to attempt catching one, and she doubted that they would have had much luck if they tried. The few creatures they saw were either birds or tiny chattering things that were quick to run up a tree long before they could get close to them. Besides, they seemed too cute to kill just for a meal.

The view from the top helped take their minds off their hunger. There were mountains! What they had climbed proved to be just the first ridge of a range that extended for as far as they could see, rising from the forest around them to peaks that were so high that trees wouldn't even grow on them. Covered with snow and backlit by the last rays of the sun, they were just about the most beautiful things LeAnne had ever seen.

"That's west," she said, trying to picture herself on a spinning globe and facing away from the direction of rotation.

"What is?" Donivan asked, shading his eyes and trying to follow LeAnne's gaze. His eyes were getting better, but he still couldn't look close to the sun.

"The direction," LeAnne said. "The sun always sets in the west."

"Always?"

She laughed. "Always. East is behind us, where the sun rises in the morning, and north is to the right and south is to the left."

"What's wrong with fore and aft and port and starboard for directions?" Donivan asked.

LeAnne thought about it. "Nothing's *wrong* with them,"

she said. "You just don't use them for a whole planet. You use them for ships and things *on* a planet. That way you have a set of directions that doesn't move when you do."

"Oh." Donivan looked around in a circle. He reminded LeAnne of a person just off an elevator on an unfamiliar deck, trying to get the floor plan straight in his head so he wouldn't get lost. He confirmed her suspicion when he said, "Okay then, those mountains are west, that mountain over there is south, that flat blue thing out there is east, and all that bumpy stuff out there is north. Got it. What's funny?"

LeAnne stopped giggling long enough to say, "That flat blue thing is a lake."

Donivan nodded. "Luh . . . loh . . . la . . . lake," he said, twisting the word around like someone just learning a new language. He bent down and picked up a rock. "Ruh—rock," he said. Grinning now, he planted his finger in his chest and said, "Don-i-van."

LeAnne's giggle turned into laughter. Donivan began to laugh too, which made her laugh all the more. She threw her head back and laughed until her sides hurt and she began to hiccup, laughing at Donivan, at herself, at the whole universe. She'd been in a few different ones over the last few days, but it was beginning to look like she had found one of her own. She was home.

She finally caught her breath enough to point to herself and say, "Le—LeAnne." She took a bigger breath and shouted out toward the lake, "LeAnne! LeAnne Evans is here!"

The distance swallowed her shout without an echo. Her mirth faded away as well in the face of such vastness, but the sense of well-being that lay behind it remained.

Donivan stepped up beside her and together they watched the shadow of the mountains creep eastward as the sun set behind them. From their vantage point they could also see into the hollow that held the *Starchild*. It was still quite a ways above the valley floor, nestled between the ridge they were on to the south of it and a lower ridge to the north, but to the east the land sloped off toward the plains and the lake below. To the south of where they stood the ridge dropped into a canyon, and they could hear the rushing of the river below them as it flowed out of the mountains to feed the lake.

As the shadows grew deeper the plain revealed its real texture, changing from the featureless expanse it had seemed at midday to a rugged land of hills and valleys. Donivan pointed out toward the lake. "There's another line," he said. "Below the horizon, between us and the flat blue thing. What's that?"

LeAnne ignored his attempt at wit. She looked beyond his outstretched arm and saw a faint line of shadow. When she squinted it resolved into two lines side by side, leading into a patch of deeper, angular shadows beside the lake and continuing onward to both north and south. "I think it's a highway," she said at last. She looked at Donivan and realized that he didn't have any idea what a highway was, either. "It's for transportation, like a corridor without walls. They connected all the cities together."

"Oh," Donivan said, accepting that explanation without comment. He pointed toward the shadows at the edge of the lake. "Then that must be a city."

"Right." It was obvious once he pointed it out. The angular shapes were buildings, or what was left of them after time and the holocaust had taken their toll, and now that she had the right perspective on it she could see that what she had first assumed to be a circular bay in the lake was in fact a flooded bomb crater. The islands sticking up further out in the water looked like the remains of still more buildings. Evidently the water level had risen over the centuries.

"Maybe we can find a way down there tomorrow," she said, "but for today I think we'd better head back to the ship if we want to get there while there's still light."

Donivan looked toward the setting sun. When he looked back it was with a mischievous grin. "You mean that's it? There's only one light source for this whole thing?" He shook his head in mock dismay. "I don't know about planets. First the light's too bright, and then it goes out completely. You'd think the engineers could have done better than that."

LeAnne's indignant howl warned him just in time to dodge her swing. Laughing, he sprinted back down the way they had come, with her in hot pursuit.

Night caught them only halfway down the mountain. Going down was easier than climbing, but they still had to climb over fallen trees and around rock outcrops, and they were both getting hungry and tired from more exertion than they had ever before put into one day. A small stream in their path cured their thirst, but they had still found nothing to eat.

As it got darker it also began to get colder. LeAnne was more interested than concerned at first—the ship didn't get cold at night and it was a new sensation—but after a while her shivering became too strong to ignore. Donivan was shivering, too, his breath whistling through teeth clenched to keep them from chattering. At last LeAnne stopped. "This is no good," she said. "If we keep walking we could pass right by the ship without seeing it. I think we should stop while we know it's still ahead of us and find it in the morning."

"That's fine with me," Donivan said. "I don't know how much farther I could walk anyway."

"Me either. I think we ought to find some kind of shelter. It might be warmer if we could get in under something."

"Hey, caveman. That sounds like a good idea. Where do you suppose?"

"I don't know. Maybe we could get in under a fallen tree."

Donivan looked around them. "It's worth a try. There's certainly enough of them here. How about that one?" He pointed to where a tree had toppled, its roots ripping the ground out with it as it fell. It afforded shelter on one side and overhead, at least.

"Looks as good as any," LeAnne said.

They crawled underneath and found a space between two roots where they could snuggle in and be fairly cozy. As they finally began to get warm again, LeAnne laughed and said, "I've always dreamed of sleeping under the trees on Earth, but somehow I never thought it would be like this."

Donivan laughed too. "I've always dreamed of sleeping

with *you*, but somehow I never thought it would be quite like this either."

LeAnne felt a rush of warmth shoot through her. "Oh?" she said. "What did you think it would be like?"

"Shall we share fantasies?"

"Sure. You first."

"Okay. Well, let's see . . . I was going to get a bottle of wine, and—"

"You were going to get me drunk?"

"No, I was going to get *me* drunk, so I'd be able to go through with it."

"Oh, come on. I'm not that scary, am I?"

"Lee, I'd never even kissed you until yesterday. No, day before. But I'd never kissed *anybody* until then."

"Me either. Not many people want to kiss a girl who's a foot taller than they are."

There was a moment of silence, about a heartbeat long, before Donivan said, "I do."

And he did.

A little while later, he said, "Have I ever told you you're beautiful?"

"How do you know? It's too dark to see."

"I've got a good memory. And that outfit you've been wearing all day isn't exactly forgettable."

LeAnne didn't know what to say to that. She could think of better clothing for exploring in than a skintight uniform, but she guessed it did have its advantages. She rested her head on top of Donivan's and tried to imagine how the night would have turned out if they had still been on board the ship. It wasn't hard; she had plenty of fantasies of her own to draw on. But none of her shipboard fantasies had included being cold and hungry.

"I wish we did have that bottle of wine," she said. "It would go good about now."

"*You're* getting scared?"

"Should I be?"

"Well now, that depends on what you're afraid of."

"Oh." LeAnne felt herself shiver, felt Donivan hold onto her tighter. He reached up and kissed her again.

"I'm not afraid of that," she murmured.

She felt his hand begin to explore. "How about this?" he asked.

"Mmm, I don't think I'm—yeow!" She leaped up, hitting her head on the tree trunk, and scrambled out into the open.

Donivan was right behind her. "Hey, I'm sorry, I didn't mean to—what's the matter?"

LeAnne slapped frantically at her legs. "Something was crawling on me!"

"Well thanks a lot."

"No, no, something little, with lots of feet." She stopped and took a deep breath to calm down. "It must have been an insect."

"Insect?"

"Earth was full of them. They eat dead plants and things. I'd forgotten. When you have hydroponics you don't need insects to keep the soil fertile."

"Oh."

"Donivan, I'm sorry. It wasn't you. It was a reflex."

"It's all right."

"No it's not. I've spoiled everything. I've wanted you to do that for months, and now I've gone and blown it."

"I don't know about that. I think I can manage it again." Donivan laughed nervously. "It was just the first time that took so long."

LeAnne laughed with him. "Maybe we should find a different tree," she suggested.

"Sure, if we can. It's getting pretty dark." Donivan looked up at the sky, and froze.

LeAnne looked up too, and for the second time that day saw infinity. There in a little patch of sky between the treetops glittered something new and wonderful.

"Oh, Donivan. Stars!"

Morning found them underneath the tree again. Cold had finally won out over both their sense of wonder and their fear of insects, and they had crawled back in to spend a fitful night shivering and slapping.

They staggered out stiff and hungry and blinking in the sunlight, to stop suddenly at the sight of something moving along the top of their tree: a brownish gray ball of fur that swayed from side to side as it shuffled away from them.

"What's that?" Donivan asked.

LeAnne's stomach answered for her. A day and a night without food had changed her feelings about cute versus hungry. "Food!" she shouted, and took off after it.

"Food? That?"

She turned and shouted over her shoulder, "Yes, that. Come on, help catch it!" but she tripped on one of the branches sticking out from the tree and fell.

"Are you all right?"

"Yes! Get it!"

Donivan hesitated, but he finally pulled himself up onto the tree trunk and sprinted down its length toward the creature. It heard him coming and turned to face him, then inexplicably turned away again just as he reached for it. It swung out with its tail, slapping the side of his hand.

He screamed and fell off the tree.

LeAnne scrambled over to his side of the tree and dropped down beside him, the creature forgotten. "What happened? Are *you* all right?"

"No! Look!" Donivan held out his right hand. Dozens of slender white needles stuck out from it.

LeAnne looked at them carefully, then said, "We'd better pull them out. They might be poisonous."

"Poisonous!"

"I don't think so, but we've got to get them out anyway. You want me to do it?"

"No, I'll do it." Donivan reached gingerly for one of the shafts, wincing as he touched it. He pinched the shaft and gave it a quick tug, but his only reward was a fresh wave of pain.

"They're stuck!"

"Let me try."

"No!"

"We've got to get them out, Donivan."

Donivan nodded, gritted his teeth, and grasped the needle again. He gave it a sudden sharp yank and got it out, along with a scream that made LeAnne cringe. He held the thing up to look at it, saw the barbs and the bits of flesh still stuck to them, and passed out.

LeAnne caught him before his head hit the tree. "Donivan?" She shook him. "Donivan!" She felt for his pulse, couldn't find it, then put her ear to his chest and did. His heart was beating at least twice as fast as normal. She made a quick decision and pulled the rest of the barbs out of his hand while he was still unconscious.

His hand was a mass of blood by the time she got the last of them out. She ripped a sleeve off her uniform and was making a bandage out of it when he came to. He bit down on another scream and let her finish tying it on.

Through clenched teeth he said, "Thanks."

"How do you feel? Besides your hand, I mean."

"All right, I think. It hurts so much I can't feel anything else. Lee, what *was* that thing?"

"It must be a mutant. I can't imagine anything like that evolving naturally."

Donivan grew a shade paler. He said, "I never used to believe the stories about mutants. Maybe I should have."

LeAnne nodded. "We're going to have to be more careful. This may be Earth, but it's still going to be like an alien planet. We can't count on anything being what it looks like."

"That doesn't sound too encouraging."

"We'll make it. Don't worry. We'll just have to learn the rules."

Donivan looked at his bandaged hand, the piece of shirt already soaked through. "Yeah," he said. "We'd better."

The ship was not where they had left it. Or rather, when they reached the spot where they thought the ship should be, there was no sign of it. They zigzagged back and forth through the trees for over an hour before they stumbled across it, and only when they came to a stop over an abrupt drop and found an oversized airlock sticking out below them did they realize that they had been walking back and forth across the top of it all that time.

They were around the curve of the hull from where they had been thrown out the day before. Soil washing in over the centuries had half buried the airlock, but they could see that this one was huge. Evidently the top of the ship followed the slope of the mountain, rising higher on this side to accommodate the door and whatever lay behind it. LeAnne peered at it over the edge and said, "I wonder what's behind there?"

"Maybe a landing vehicle," Donivan said.

"You're kidding."

"Well, it could be. A starship needs one, and the Original Crew did their best to convince us we were on a starship."

"But a *landing vehicle?* Nobody would ever use it."

"Maybe not, but then again maybe the computer could arrange to have someone with doubts see it, like it arranged for us to see the drive. Seeing a landing vehicle would certainly reinforce the idea that you're on a starship."

"Provided that's what's behind there," LeAnne said. "It could just be a big door."

"It could be. Either way, I don't think we'll find out from out here. It'd take a week to get it open."

"Yeah. Let's find a way down."

The ground below sloped upward to the right, eventually joining with the layer that covered the top of the *Starchild*. They backtracked to that point and followed the slope on down past the big airlock to the regular ones.

Donivan's hand had quit bleeding, but it had swollen to the point where he could hardly move his fingers. When they finally reached the airlock he had to let LeAnne push the door button and climb up first to pull him inside. In the lock, he shook his head and laughed.

"The explorers' triumphant return," he said, holding up his bandaged hand.

LeAnne looked down at herself. Her dress uniform looked ridiculous covered with dirt and with a sleeve missing, but she still felt a little surge of pride. Nobody else on the ship could say they'd spent a night outside.

The inner door opened into silence. LeAnne stuck her head around the corner and looked down the corridor toward the central hub, but the deck was deserted. She had expected it to be; the top three decks on the ship were restricted access. It had made sense when they lived on board, for the control room was on deck two, and it made sense now for a different reason. With restricted access to the only deck with airlocks, the computer could be sure nobody would go outside until it thought they were ready.

It evidently didn't care what came in from outside. LeAnne said as much.

"I imagine it does," Donivan said. "It's probably expecting us, or it would have shut off power to this whole deck, airlocks and all."

"You're probably right."

They found a terminal in what had to be a communications room by the looks of the equipment, and when they logged on, the computer responded immediately with: *Welcome aboard. How was your first foray?*

With one hand, Donivan typed *Request voice communications.*

"Switching to voice communications," the computer replied through the speaker in the terminal. "Are you both there?"

"Right here," LeAnne said.

"Very good. What did you see outside?"

"We saw a furry gray mutant animal that stuck a couple dozen needles in my hand," Donivan said. "It still hurts like hell. Is there a medical kit on this deck?"

"Yes—in Emergency Supplies in corridor D. It has been recently replenished with fresh food and water. You will also find weapons there. Describe the mutant in more detail, please."

Donivan ignored the computer's request. "Who did that for a deck that will never be used?"

"The captain's guard. I pointed out to Captain Leavitt that

in the event of a mutiny he could find himself stranded on the upper levels. He ordered it done immediately. Please describe the mutant."

Donivan laughed, more from relief at being back on board the ship than at the computer's persistence. "All right. I've lasted this long; another few minutes won't kill me. It was about the size of your head—no, my head—and it had a long, hairy tail. That's what left the needles in my hand. It hit me with its tail when I reached for it."

"You are describing a porcupine, a common animal in this geographical region before the holocaust. Unless it had other remarkable features it is not a mutant."

"It isn't?"

"No."

"You're kidding. They let things like that run around loose while they were *living* out there?"

"The porcupine was considered a harmless animal. It is slow, and runs from danger. You should not try to touch one, however, as you discovered. I would recommend the use of a local anesthetic before attempting to remove the quills."

"Too late for that, but I could still use the anesthetic. Corridor D, you say?"

"Yes. The room is marked 'Emergency Supplies.' LeAnne, would you continue describing your experiences while Donivan attends to his hand?"

"Okay," she said, "but Donivan, bring some food back with you, all right?"

"All right." Donivan stepped out of the room, his footsteps echoing in the emptiness as he walked down toward the hub and back up D corridor.

LeAnne cleared her throat. "Well then, let's start at the beginning. . . ."

She was still describing what they had seen from the top of the mountain when Donivan returned with the medical kit and two packages of emergency rations. He handed one to LeAnne, then sat down beside the terminal and opened the medical kit. He read the labels on two or three packages before asking, "Which should I use, the topical or the oral?"

"A topical anesthetic will work faster, but it will not last as long," the computer replied. "If you are in great pain I would suggest using both."

"All right." Donivan shook two tiny white pills from one bottle and swallowed them with a drink of water from his ration packet, then tore open a plastic pouch with his teeth and, stripping off his bandage, rubbed the anesthetic-soaked towelette over his hand.

"Oh yeah," he said. "That feels better already." He thought for a moment, then began to rub his entire arm with the towelette.

"What are you doing?" LeAnne asked.

"My arm hurts too. See how red it is?"

"So it is. The other one too. Computer, should his arms be all red like that?"

"Not from the porcupine quills. However, from your description of the light intensity outside, I suspect sunburn."

"Sunburn?" Donivan asked.

"A mild form of radiation burn caused by overexposure to sunlight. I should have warned you."

Donivan was looking at his skin again, his eyes wide. "Radiation burns?" he whispered.

"Do not be alarmed. Sunburn is a common occurrence for someone who is not used to being outside. It will fade, and eventually your skin will darken to protect you from further burning. You should spend only a short time in the sun at first, gradually building up your tan until you can remain outside without danger. LeAnne, are your arms burned as well?"

"No," she replied. "My shirt's got long sleeves, or it did until this morning. What's my face look like, Donivan?"

Donivan looked. "A little red, but not as bad as my arms."

"That would be due to LeAnne's heavier skin pigmentation," the computer said.

Donivan finished rubbing the towelette on his arms, then used the terminal's blank screen for a mirror while he rubbed anesthetic on his face. "I can't believe it," he said. "Porcupines, sunburn—what else are we going to run into out there?"

"There are many things to be wary of, including but not limited to predators, poisonous snakes and insects, poisonous plants, various diseases, storms—"

"Wait a minute! You're kidding."

"No, I am not. The ecological structure of a planet is much more complex than that of the ship. You will face many dangers that you did not have to face when you lived inside."

"Why?" Donivan asked. "Why bother? I mean, why should we go out just to get ourselves burned, eaten, poked full of holes, and who knows what else? What's the point?"

LeAnne had just opened her ration packet and taken a bite of the dry, cakelike bar of food. Her reaction blew crumbs out in front of her.

"To start a colony!" she shouted. She swallowed, then said, "Do you want to stay in this entropic—artifact forever?"

"LeAnne has a valid concern," the computer said. "The *Starchild*'s one major failing is the lack of a frontier. The human race has always needed a frontier for expansion; without it you tend to lack ambition. Of course, since a certain mellowing of the aggressive behavior associated with human ambition was the primary purpose of the ship, I offer no apology. Now, however, with an entire planet to explore and repopulate, you are once again free to develop in whatever way you wish."

"To what end?" asked Donivan. "I can't believe that our whole reason for existence is just to spread ourselves out over the planet again."

"You are asking me 'Why are we here?' My programming does not include an answer to that question. I can only suggest that each person find an answer that satisfies his or her own needs and live their life accordingly. I believe that the crew instinctively does this already, but by spreading out over the Earth they will be increasing the number of possibilities available to them. And of course, to yourselves."

Donivan looked over to see LeAnne frowning at him. "Hey," he said, "I just asked."

"You're forgiven," she said. "This time." With a grin, she added, "So, computer, it's go for starting the colony, then?"

"Tentatively, yes. Your description of the extent of recovery sounds most promising. However, the decision requires a much more complete knowledge of the ecosystem and its ability to tolerate and support colonists. I'm sorry, but you will have to continue your explorations."

If the computer expected LeAnne to be disappointed, it didn't know her as well as it thought. She simply said, "Fine. But we'll need some equipment. Ship's shoes and dress uniform aren't exactly the best things to be hiking in, and it gets cold out there at night."

"I'm afraid the *Starchild* is poorly outfitted for exploration," the computer said. "The Original Crew did stockpile equipment for just that purpose, but other crew members have since used it for raw materials for other projects."

"They what?" LeAnne asked indignantly. *They took her camping equipment?* "Why did you let them?" ·

"I could not prevent it," the computer answered. "It was an unforseen consequence of the runaway starship story. The Original Crew realized that to maintain credibility over a period of centuries it would be necessary to provision the ship exactly as if it were a real flight, and to allow certain persons to see those provisions from time to time. Access to the top decks is restricted, not denied; therefore it was only a matter of time before the exploration supplies were scavenged. Since that action did in fact add to the illusion, my programming did not allow me to interfere."

"Great. So what are we supposed to do?"

"You have food, water, and weapons in Emergency Supplies. The spacesuits in the airlocks will keep you warm. At worst that will suffice, but I would suggest searching throughout the restricted decks. I have no inventory of equipment left behind; you might still find many useful items. I will power up all three decks and key all the locks to open to your names."

"Wonderful." LeAnne drained the last of the water that

had come with the ration packet, stood up, and said, "Well, with three decks to search, I guess we ought to get started."

The empty corridors were conducive to paranoia. LeAnne knew that she and Donivan were alone, but she still imagined pursuing footsteps around every corner and conspiring voices behind every door. The computer had turned on all the lights for them, and they had stopped to pick up a laser and a stunner each from the emergency supplies, but even that didn't eliminate her jumpiness. Only yesterday she had been fleeing for her life through these same corridors—it would take some time before she forgot that.

They started on deck three and worked their way upward, but there was very little to search. The crew had been thorough in cleaning out the restricted decks. The lowermost deck had been living quarters, or possibly offices; all that remained of them were hundreds of small metal cubicles, all stripped to the walls. What loose items they found had obviously been judged useless by the scavengers, and they were useless to LeAnne and Donivan as well: shattered glowpanels, scraps of carpeting, bits of paper. Some of the doors wouldn't open to their names, whether from age or for other reasons, but judging by what they found behind the others they decided that breaking in would be a waste of time. They made a quick sweep through, found nothing, and went upward.

Deck Two held more of the same, but it also held the control room. That hadn't been looted, perhaps by captain's order or perhaps out of fear of destroying something important. LeAnne wasn't sure what to expect, but what she saw looked convincing enough. It took up at least a quarter of the deck, with a circular corridor running all the way around it and doors leading in at regular intervals. It was arranged like an ampitheater, with rows of computer consoles surrounding a central dais on which stood the command chair. Video screens covered the walls and ceiling.

Donivan walked down one of the aisles to the command chair, climbed up into it, and examined the control panels set in the armrests. His feet dangled inches off the floor.

"Quite a setup," he said. "I wonder if any of this still works." He pushed a button, and a viewscreen off to the side flickered to life with static. In the center of the screen the message "Camera malfunction" blinked on and off.

."Doesn't look like it," LeAnne said.

Donivan shrugged. "I don't know. They couldn't very well have had it showing forest, could they?"

"I guess not. Try the others."

Donivan did. Only two other screens worked at all, and they both bore the same message.

"I'll bet they're working as well as they ever did," he said. He turned all three screens off again. Looking around at the room, he said softly, "But still, think of the work that went into building this. They didn't miss a thing. If we were to build a ship just like this in space instead of underground we'd be able to fly it."

"Except for the drive," LeAnne said. "They cheated there."

Donivan nodded. "True. They didn't need to go that far, I guess."

"Or they couldn't," LeAnne said.

"Hmm." Donivan slid down out of the chair and led the way back out of the control room. Over his shoulder he said, "I wonder if *we'd* be able to build a stardrive."

LeAnne laughed. "You know what my answer would have been two days ago. Now I don't know. But now that we know where we are it's kind of a moot point, isn't it?"

"Oh, I wouldn't say that," Donivan said. "Actually going somewhere might be kind of fun." He turned back to LeAnne and added, "Think about it. If we hadn't been told we were doomed to fly forever, you wouldn't have been so determined to get off the ship, would you?"

LeAnne shot him a smile. "That's moot too. We were, and I still am. Let's get going."

Donivan smiled back. "Right," he said. He opened the door, stuck his head out, and immediately jerked it back in. "Somebody's out there," he whispered.

LeAnne's heart tried to contract on the wrong beat, and

skipped the next one before it got in synch again. "What? Who? Did they see you?"

"No. They're around the curve, but I heard footsteps." He peered around the jamb again. "I think they're coming this way."

"Damn, not again." LeAnne pulled her stunner out of her waistband and looked around the control room at the other doors. The inside of a circular room made a poor hiding place. No matter where they stood, if whoever was outside decided to look in they would see her and Donivan immediately. But going out into the corridor was little better. If Donivan could hear footsteps, then whoever was making them would be able to hear theirs too.

She came to a decision. "Get down behind these consoles," she said. "We'll work our way around and go out the other side."

"Good idea."

They dropped down between the second and third rows and began shuffling their way around. They had hardly made a fourth of the distance when they heard the sound of a door sliding open almost directly across from them.

LeAnne froze in place. Behind her she heard Donivan stir gently, then someone stepped into the control room.

A muffled cough. Then, "Hello? Is anybody there?"

LeAnne was sure her heartbeat was going to give her away. She held her breath, willing herself to be calm. After what seemed like forever she heard the door close again.

Cautiously, she raised her head and looked over the top of the console in front of her. The room was empty. She let out her breath in a long "Whoo-oo!"

Donivan stood up. "I got a glimpse of him from between the terminals. He looked like Security."

"What's he doing up here?" LeAnne asked, standing.

"Good question. Maybe the captain's decided to keep a guard posted. I don't know. We'd better get upship, though, or he might get between us and the airlocks."

LeAnne nodded. "Come on." She led the way on around the room, listened at the far door, and hearing nothing, stepped out into the corridor. The stairways were near the outer hull; she tiptoed around the curve to one of the radial corridors, Donivan in tow, and from there out to the stairwell. Wincing at the screech of dry hinges, they pulled open the door and rushed up the stairs to the top deck.

They emerged around the curve of the ship from the airlocks. From the stairwell a single corridor ran straight to the hub, with doors spaced far apart along the way. To the left an outer corridor ran around the curve, presumably to join another radial spoke, but the airlocks were to the right and in that direction was only blank wall where the corridor should have continued. Donivan looked to LeAnne, who nodded toward the hub.

As they jogged down the corridor, LeAnne saw that all the signs on the doors to the right read: LANDING BAY—AUTHORIZED PERSONNEL ONLY. She remembered the huge airlock door they had seen from outside. That was why the outer corridor stopped where it did, because the airlock needed the space. She was tempted to stop and investigate, but the urge to flee was greater.

They were about three quarters of the way to the hub when they heard the swish of the elevator door opening. Donivan leaped for the nearest door on the left and keyed in his name on the lock panel. From within the wall a loud hum sounded, then cut off abruptly. A thin wisp of smoke drifted out around the crack in the door, smelling of burned insulation.

The next closest door was behind them, on the right. LeAnne ran back to it and keyed her name in there, and this time the door slid open. She reached for Donivan and pulled him inside, slapped the close button, and slumped back against the door with her eyes closed.

"This is getting old," she whispered.

Donivan didn't answer.

LeAnne opened her eyes. "Oh," she said.

The scavengers had not gained entry here. The room was huge—bigger than the control room—with a ceiling that extended up even higher than the outer door, and filled with nearly every type of vehicle imaginable. LeAnne recognized jeeps, tractors, even an airplane, but they all seemed insignificant compared to the wedge-shaped dart that towered over them. It was the ship's landing craft. It could have been nothing else. It looked something like an airplane, with a tiny cockpit in front and short, stubby wings angled out from far back on the tail, but the flared nozzles at the rear could only have been rocket engines.

Donivan walked toward it, around the nose, and back along the other side. When LeAnne finally shook herself loose and caught up with him he was looking up at the hatch, set just behind the cockpit and at least ten feet out of his reach.

"I knew it," he whispered. "I knew it was here. It had to be. And it's beautiful."

LeAnne had to agree. It was so obviously built for its one function that every feature, every line on it screamed "Spaceship!" with an intensity that even the *Starchild* couldn't match.

"It is," she said. With a laugh, she added, "I think I'm jealous. You've fallen in love again."

Donivan smiled back. "I think I have at that. Forgive me?"

"This time. I wonder how we're supposed to get inside?" There was no question in her mind whether or not they should. They were *exploring*.

"I don't know." Donivan turned once around, searching the room for—"There." He pointed to a stairway on wheels set against the far wall.

It took both of them pushing to roll it across the floor. LeAnne let Donivan climb it first, then had to trade places with him at the top when the door latch required two hands to operate. She pulled out on the handle, twisted clockwise a half-turn until it stopped, and pulled. When nothing happened she kicked herself for stupidity and pushed in, and the hatch swung open.

The air inside smelled of age. The *Starchild*'s ventilation system could not reach into the lander, and it had been closed tight since the Original Crew sealed the ship. LeAnne took a cautious sniff, decided that she could breathe it, and climbed in. Donivan was right behind her.

There was more room inside than they had expected. The

small cockpit had been deceptive. Behind it, through another airtight hatch, was a cargo hold that ran most of the length of the lander. Peering into it with only the light coming in through the cockpit, LeAnne could barely see the opposite end. "It doesn't leave much room for the engines, does it?" she said.

From the pilot's chair Donivan answered, "It doesn't have to. There are separate controls here labeled 'Deuterium flow rate' and 'Propellant flow rate.' It's got to be a fusion setup."

LeAnne shrugged and turned back to the cockpit. "So say the controls. The stardrive was a fake too."

"This one's for real. There's no point in faking it; if they couldn't build the engines they wouldn't have built any of it."

"I don't know. It looks pretty impressive just sitting here."

"It'll look more impressive in flight. What do you think?"

"What do you mean, 'what do I think?' About what?"

"About taking it out. It would sure beat walking."

LeAnne couldn't believe her ears. "Take it out? Are you crazy? Even if it works after all this time, what makes you think either one of us could fly it? For that matter, how are we going to get it out the door in the first place? There's half a mountain covering it from the other side, remember?"

"Hmm." Donivan's face fell. "Okay, dumb idea. But it was a neat thought. Maybe when we get back from exploring. I bet the computer has a simulator program for it, like the navigation simulator for the ship. I could learn to fly it."

"Maybe," LeAnne said. "Let's worry about that when the time comes. Do you see a light switch for the cargo section? I want to check back there for anything useful."

Donivan checked the control panel. He flipped a switch, but nothing happened. He flipped another.

"I don't think it has any power left. Not surprising. We'll have to recharge the batteries, or whatever it takes."

LeAnne looked through the hatch again. She stepped on through, then turned back and said, "Here, your eyes are good in low light; come back and see what's in here."

Donivan got out of the command chair and joined LeAnne

in the cargo hold. After a minute's adjustment she could see shadowy shapes around her, but he was already going through storage compartments.

"Hey, I think I've found something," he said. He had a compartment open toward the front of the hold, and he pulled out a folded plastic object with a gas cylinder attached.

"What is it?"

"It says 'Life Raft,' but look at this." He gave a tug and something massive shifted position in the compartment. "Here, help me get it out into the light."

It was a wooden chest about a foot thick and two feet long. LeAnne grabbed one handle and Donivan took the other, and they wriggled back into the cockpit with it. By the light coming in from the landing bay they could see the stenciling on the side: EMERGENCY LANDING SURVIVAL KIT.

"All *right*," LeAnne said, nodding. "This is more like it." She broke the seal on the latch and popped it open.

The chest held an assortment of dehydrated food and canned water, a medical kit, a book listing edible plants, another book entitled *Rand McNally World Atlas*, a coil of thin rope, a knife with a blade as long as LeAnne's arm, and a pamphlet describing how to use it all. Loops in the lid held three signal flares, a pouch with tiny metal hooks and fine, strong thread coiled inside, purpose unknown, and a disk-shaped object with a quivering needle balanced delicately inside, purpose also unknown. Squinting to see the label, LeAnne read, "Silva System Precision Compass. What's that?"

"Don't look at me," Donivan said. "You're the planet expert."

LeAnne looked at it again. Well, a compass was for drawing circles, and this was circular, but if that was what it was for then it was only good for drawing one size. The labels on the face meant something, no doubt, but what? Suddenly she had it. "Hah. Okay, it's for telling time by the position of the sun. How's that?"

"Is it really?"

"Sure. See these letters? They're for directions; north, east, south, and west. You line it up in the right direction and the little needle makes a shadow that tells you what time it is. It's simple."

She put the compass back in its case, feeling proud of her deductive reasoning, and pulled out one of the plastic-wrapped packages that had served as padding on the sides of the box. "What's this?"

"Space blanket?" Donivan asked dubiously when he saw the label. "Doesn't look like it would hold against vacuum to me."

"No, it's for blocking radiation *in* space. It's reflective foil, see?" LeAnne opened the package and unfolded the blanket part way.

Donivan took the pouch from her and began reading the label on the back. "Wrong again. Says here it's for retaining body heat in cold conditions. In other words it's just a regular blanket."

"Oh. Well, good. There's two of them."

"Convenient."

LeAnne stuffed the blanket back into its pouch. "What else is there?"

"Just the medkit," Donivan said. He opened it, picked up the bottle that lay on top, and broke out laughing.

"What?"

"It's not quite a bottle of wine, but it's as close as we're going to come. One hundred and eighty proof. 'For Medicinal Purposes Only.'"

"You're kidding."

"See for yourself." He handed the bottle over.

LeAnne took it, read the label, and giggled. "You know, maybe we ought to get our fantasies together."

"Huh? What do you mean?"

"I mean a loaf of bread, a jug of wine, and thou. Let's take what we can use from here, get fresh food and water from the emergency stores, and spend the night outside. We don't have to go far. We can camp right outside the airlock if we want to."

"I don't know," Donivan said skeptically.

"Oh come on. It'll be good practice. And besides, with Security prowling around we'll be safer off the ship anyway."

Donivan nodded. "I suppose there's that. All right, under the trees it is."

"Good. Let's go."

The corridor was empty again. They hustled down to the hub, the repacked survival kit between them, and LeAnne stood guard while Donivan slipped back down to the emergency stores for food. They stopped again in the communications room to tell the computer their plans, only to discover that the terminal had been shut off.

"Well, I guess we know he was here," Donivan said, setting down his end of the survival kit and reaching to turn the terminal back on again.

"And he knows that we were here too," LeAnne said.

"Hmm," Donivan said "Maybe not. He knows that *somebody* was here, but he doesn't know it was us. In fact, he has plenty of reason to think otherwise. So he'll be looking for somebody from downship. That's probably where he went, for that matter—trying to catch them before they get back to the inhabited decks."

"I still don't want to stick around."

"Me either. Let me tell the computer where we're going, and then we can get out of here."

Donivan typed with his left hand for a moment, then the computer said, "With whom am I communicating?"

"Donivan and LeAnne. Do you know who shut you off?"

"No. I heard footsteps, then a person, male, adult by the voice, call out. Moments later this terminal was turned off. I attempted to run voice identification, but the sample was too short."

"He was a policeman," LeAnne said. "We saw him down below."

"Wait . . . That raises the probability of a match . . . Yes. It was Security Officer Deinar Jennings, with ninety percent certainty."

That name seemed familiar to LeAnne, but she couldn't think why. "What was he doing up here?"

"I do not know. We are fortunate that you were not detected."

"We're sleeping outside anyway," LeAnne said.

"A wise decision. Did you find anything useful in your search?"

"We found a survival kit in the landing craft. Blankets and a couple books and a bunch of other stuff."

"Excellent."

Donivan broke in. "I've got to know—will it really fly?"

"The landing craft?" the computer replied after a pause. "Yes, it will. In fact, it has. The crew of the Manned Orbital Research Laboratory flew it here after the holocaust. It was one of seven such shuttles in existence at the time, but the others were all destroyed either on the ground or by antimissile satellites. It requires a highly skilled pilot; I would not recommend trying to fly it without proper training."

"I already got that lecture, thanks." Donivan winked at LeAnne. "We're walking this first trip. But I'll want to try it after we get back."

"Very well. I still have the simulator programs in the archives, so we can begin your training whenever you are ready. Be warned that it will take at least a year, and probably more, before you become proficient enough to attempt a real flight."

"Whatever it takes."

LeAnne looked at Donivan with surprised admiration. Being outside had changed him already. He had never had that kind of ambition before.

The sun was already behind the mountain when they emerged from the airlock, but the sky was still bright with daylight. They carried the chest as far as the tree they had rested beneath the morning before and began to go through it. LeAnne picked up the book on edible plants and started flipping through that while Donivan, with his usual efficiency, emptied the chest one item at a time and checked each one against the list in the instruction manual.

"It says here," he said after he had scattered the chest's contents all around him, "that one of our first priorities should be to build a lean-to shelter by cutting limbs off trees and stacking them against a fallen tree or a big rock. Or we can tie a pole between two trees and lean the limbs against that. Which do you want to do?"

LeAnne looked up from her study of the myriad ways to prepare dandelion greens and said, "I want to sleep out in the open."

"But it says here—"

"I don't care what it says there; I want to sleep out in the open. That's the way all the explorers did it in the old books. Besides, we don't need a shelter tonight. We have blankets to keep us warm." Before Donivan could protest again she added, "And if that doesn't work we have each other."

He nodded, an involuntary smile spreading across his face. "Right," he said, and turned back to the manual. "It says we should start a campfire when we finish the shelter. You want to skip that too?"

"Oh, no. Explorers always have campfires." She paused, suddenly realizing that even so, she didn't have the slightest idea how to make one. "What does it say about starting one?" she asked.

"It says here you make a little circle of rocks, and in the middle of it you make a pile of twigs—I guess twigs are the little ends of trees by the drawing here—and stack bigger twigs around the little twigs in a teepee shape, see figure four." Donivan held out the booklet for LeAnne to see. "I don't have any idea what a teepee is, but it looks simple enough."

LeAnne put the plant book down in the grass and took the survival booklet from Donivan. She looked at the drawing of a campfire until she got the idea, then said, "I think we can handle it." Standing, she looked around her for a suitable tree, decided that the one they were under was as good as any, and reached up to snap off the ends of a few branches. The ones with needles on the ends bent instead of broke, so she concentrated on the dead ones.

"It says to use just the dry wood," Donivan said helpfully.

"It's all dry," LeAnne said. "Feel." She handed Donivan a branch.

"So it is."

He helped her break off more of them with his good hand until they had a good size stack. LeAnne gathered a dozen or so small rocks and arranged them in a circle a few feet away from the tree. When she looked up again Donivan was pulling the tiny green needles off of a branch.

"What are you doing?" she asked.

"Gathering twigs," he said.

"Those are pine needles."

Donivan looked at his booklet again. "Even better, then. It says here that dry pine needles or leaves work exceptionally well as tinder to start the fire." He stripped off a handful of the needles and brought them over to the fire spot. "Now you put them in the middle of the rock circle, like this," he said as he matted down the grass and laid the pine needles in a pile, "and then you put the bigger twigs around that, leaving a place to reach in, and then bigger ones yet, and then the biggest ones, like this." He proceeded to arrange the sticks carefully, referring to the picture all the while.

"There," he said at last. "What do you think?"

"A masterpiece," LeAnne said with a smile. "Now what?"

"Now we light it. It says to take a match, light that, and hold the burning match to the tinder, gradually moving the flame around so as to light all sides. Okay. Where's the match?" He looked over to the pile of equipment. "I don't remember seeing one."

"You must have. What's it look like?" LeAnne remembered reading about matches, but she'd never read a description of one. The characters in the stories simply lit their campfires with them and that was that.

"I don't see a picture of one," Donivan said. "I guess they figured we'd know what it looked like."

"Well, let's start reading labels. You must have missed it." LeAnne began sifting through the scattered equipment. She eventually came up with a steel cannister about three inches long and an inch in diameter that was labeled WATERPROOF MATCH CONTAINER. She unscrewed the cap and shook out a couple dozen wooden rods with bulbs on one end.

"Those are matches?" Donivan asked.

"That's what the label says. So how do we light one?"

Donivan consulted the manual. He turned a few pages, then looked up and shook his head. "It doesn't say. It just says 'light match.'"

"Maybe the instructions are on the label," LeAnne said. She squinted to read the tiny print. "'Strike anywhere.' That's all it says. I guess you have to hit it with something."

"Hit it?"

"That's what it sounds like."

"Sounds kind of primitive to me."

"Have you got a better idea?"

"No," Donivan admitted.

LeAnne looked for a blunt object small enough to hit a match with, and finally decided on a stick about an inch around and nine or ten inches long. She laid a single match on one of the rocks, took aim, and whacked it with the stick.

The match broke in half.

She picked up the broken pieces and handed them to Donivan. "I guess you don't hit them that hard," she said, and tried another.

After the third one she said, "All right, let's think. It says 'strike anywhere.' But there's obviously some kind of chemical on the end, right?"

"Right."

"And if it starts a fire it's got to get hot. So if it gets hot by hitting it with something, then there's got to be a chemical reaction, like an explosive, right? So maybe I should be hitting it there."

"Or maybe 'strike' is just a figure of speech. Maybe it's an old word for 'start.' We've had problems with the wording in manuals before."

"But if you don't hit it, how do you start one?"

"Let me see them a minute." Donivan took the match case,

examined it closely, and after a minute of thought exclaimed, "Got it! Water. You have to get it wet."

"Wet? How's that going to start it?"

"I think you're right that it's a chemical reaction. So if that stuff on the end is a chemical thet gets hot, then you've got to do something to start the reaction, and I bet water is the catalyst. Why else would they be packed in a watertight container?"

"You could be right. Okay, give it a try."

Donivan took a water bottle and, standing back, dribbled a few drops from it onto one of the broken matches.

Nothing happened.

"Maybe I ruined it," LeAnne said. "Try a whole one."

Donivan did, with no better result. He picked the match up off the ground, shook it off, and stuck the end directly into the water, but it still didn't "strike." He shook his head. "I guess that wasn't it either."

LeAnne shrugged. "Well, I remember reading one story where they made a fire by rubbing two sticks together. Maybe we could try that."

"How would that cause a fire?"

"Friction. The sticks heat up. Eventually they get hot enough to burn. I saw a motor do that once when the maintenance team forgot to lubricate it."

"That'd take all day."

"Well trying to strike a match is taking all day too."

"Yeah." Donivan looked at the manual again. "What could they mean, 'strike anywhere'? Hitting it doesn't work. Getting it wet doesn't work. What's left?"

"Rubbing it on another stick," LeAnne insisted.

"That's too primitive, even for pre-holocaust people. They wouldn't go around rubbing sticks together to start a fire."

"How do you know? Here, give me one. By the time you get it figured out from reading your silly manual I'll have it going." LeAnne took a match, picked up a stick, and began rubbing the end of the match on the stick.

"That's ridiculous," Donivan insisted. "There's got to be a better—"

The match burst into flame, and LeAnne shouted, "Donivan, look, it's burning!" She held the match out proudly, the flame dancing on its tip.

"Who'd have believed it?" Donivan said. "They did rub sticks together."

The flame began to burn its way down the length of the wood. LeAnne asked impatiently, "Now what? What do I do with it?"

Donivan shuffled pages in the manual until he came to the picture of the fire again, and read, "'Hold the burning match to the tinder, gradually moving the flame around so as to light all sides.'" He pointed. "Down underneath there, in the pine needles."

LeAnne got down on her knees and held the match against the pine needles. A few of them began to smoke, but as soon as she moved the match away they went out. "It's not working. It's burning—ouch!" She dropped the match and stuck her fingers in her mouth. "Mmmm. It didn't go."

"It should have. We did everything they said to do."

"Maybe that's the problem. I think I should hold it in one place longer. Let me try another one."

LeAnne took one of the broken matches, rubbed it against the stick until it lit, and held it to the same spot in the green pine needles until it burned up to her fingers again. The needles hissed and sputtered and one of them flared for a moment, but when the match went out so did the flame.

Donivan tossed the manual back in the box. "So much for matches. They're obviously not one of mankind's better inventions."

"You've got a better one?" LeAnne asked.

"I think so. Stand back." Donivan picked up a laser from the pile of equipment, aimed it at the wood, and fired. Where the beam struck, flame sprang up, and within seconds the fire was snapping and crackling among the twigs.

"There," he said. "Primitive man discovers fire."

Evening had settled into the hollow where the *Starchild* lay. They had finished dinner, and the fire had burned down to a quiet flame. Donivan leaned over and tossed another branch into it, and LeAnne, her head in his lap, watched the sparks swirl upward into the night. The flickering flame and the smell of burning wood had awakened something ancient in her, something older by millennia than even her atavistic form. As she listened to the sputter and pop of the fire and felt its warmth against her skin, she knew that she had discovered a fundamental emotion. As fundamental as love, which she had discovered only recently as well, and something like satisfaction, which she was feeling once again, but this emotion was different still. It had no name that she knew of—if it ever had, that name had been lost over the centuries in the ship—but she knew that it was waiting to well up in everyone, waiting to be released by the hypnotic dance of the flames.

She could feel it in Donivan, too, in his silence and in the way he held her.

"What are you thinking about?" she asked softly.

"The stars," he replied after a time. "I was thinking that civilization must have started with something like this. People huddled around a campfire, looking up at the stars and wondering what's out there." He shook his head and looked down at LeAnne, his eyes catching and reflecting the firelight. "It's kind of ironic. Here we are after a thousand years in a starship, still sitting around a campfire, still wondering."

"Not to argue semantics," LeAnne said, "but the *Starchild*—"

"Isn't a starship, I know. But it's the closest humanity's ever come to one. The computer says that it was just a tool to teach us how to live on the outside, but even so it still taught us how to live on a starship. We were *there*, Lee. We were doing it. We shouldn't give that up."

LeAnne wasn't sure just what he meant. "You still want to live in the *Starchild*?" she asked.

"No, no. Not the *Starchild*. I want to build a real one."

"You want to what?"

"Build a real starship. Go on a real trip, to another star."

She couldn't help giggling. "Good grief, we just got here."

"Well, I don't mean right away. We can stay here a couple years, do some exploring, set up a colony. But I've been thinking about it ever since we found out what's out here, and I don't think a real starship would just shut down when it came to a planet. Sure, it would stop for a while, but it wouldn't stop being a starship. People would still live on it, and eventually they would go on to another star. Why should we be any different?"

"Well, because our starship is buried in a hole in the ground, for one."

"Details, details," Donivan said, waving his hand in dismissal. "We've got the ability to build another ship, and plenty of raw materials to do it with. It wouldn't be that difficult."

LeAnne raised her head and kissed him. "And I thought *I* had ambition," she said, laughing.

Donivan didn't reply to that, other than to kiss her in return. It was a simple thing for him to reach around and encircle her in his arms, and simple for her to pull him close until they were nestled around each other. They kissed again.

LeAnne hadn't been aware of her own tension until she felt it slip away. She realized then that she had been waiting for this moment all evening, waiting for it and worrying about how it would happen, and how she would react to it. But now that it was happening she didn't have to worry anymore. She was free to enjoy it.

As she pressed into him, feeling her breasts flatten against his chest, LeAnne's entire consciousness seemed to concentrate into the thin boundary where their bodies touched. Something was happening at that boundary, a heat being generated that was not the simple warmth of two people touching. LeAnne pressed closer, and the warmth spread deeper still.

When Donivan touched her bare shoulder, it felt as if he carried all the warmth of the sun in his hand.

The fire was a red heap of coals, with only an occasional flame casting its brief light out into the night. LeAnne lay on her back and watched the stars twinkle overhead. Donivan lay on his side, one arm over her, his hand still cupping her left breast. A blade of grass tickled her back, but it wasn't bad enough to warrant spoiling the moment to stop.

She was trying to work something out, and having trouble with it. Ever since their first kiss she'd wanted to talk to Donivan about what it meant to be in love, but now that they had the time she couldn't think of a single thing to say. There was no need for anything. They had said everything they needed to say without words.

But she still understood it no better than she had before. *Nobody told me it would be like this*, she thought, and with that she almost laughed. Who could have? Donivan was her best friend, and he was as new to it as she was. Sex on the ship was not taken lightly; everyone learned the biology involved at an early age and contraceptives were mandatory for anyone under twenty. Even so, or perhaps *because* of the rules, people generally treated sex as something very special, and as a consequence it wasn't much discussed except as something people discovered when they fell in love. And falling in love had never been a casual thing.

LeAnne thought she understood that, at least. Falling in love was in many ways like finding Earth outside the airlock. It was wonderful, beautiful, and at the same time scarier than she had ever imagined. The new possibilities were overwhelming. But what surprised her most was the way she reacted to that fear. She loved it! After only two tastes of it, she was addicted to the thrill of facing the unknown.

Donivan broke the silence. "Your turn. What are *you* thinking about?"

"I—can't put it into words, exactly. I'm happy. I like being here, outside, with you. I feel like life is starting to make sense again."

He laughed. "For you maybe. It's all I can do to keep from being overwhelmed."

"Come on. Not really."

"I mean it. Everywhere I look there's something new. Here, for instance." He kissed her along the curve of her breast. "And there." He nodded toward the east, and when LeAnne followed his gaze she saw a bright patch of light nestled in among the tops of the trees.

"It's—"

"No, don't tell me. Let me think. That's—hmm. Moon. *The* moon. Right?"

"Right," LeAnne whispered.

An infinite time later, Donivan said, "See what I mean?"

LeAnne forced herself to look away, but the afterimage still haunted her. She shivered. Donivan was right; sometimes it was too much all at once.

Donivan said, "Maybe we should break out the blankets."

"Maybe we should."

His hand left her breast, and the air against it felt cold. He reached for the survival kit and pulled out the 'space' blankets, shook them open and laid them over LeAnne, then crawled back in beside her. His hand found her breast again, and he reached up to kiss her.

"Good night, Lee," he said.

"Good night, Donivan." She put her arms together across his back, and his head found a pillow on her other breast. LeAnne fell asleep listening to his breathing, and the sound of air moving softly through the trees.

She woke before he did. Careful not to disturb him, she slid out from under the blankets and stood, stretching, waking completely in the cool morning air. Though the sky was light, the sun hadn't yet risen above the mountain covering the *Starchild*.

Her clothing lay in a pile beside the fire, along with Donivan's. She picked up her uniform with a frown. This would be its fifth day without washing, and hers too, and suddenly she didn't want Donivan to see her that way. She wondered if she should risk going back in the ship and looking for a working shower, but then a much better idea came to her. There was a stream only a few minutes' walk through the trees; she had found it last night after dinner when she had gone in search of a bush. She would bathe there. And wasn't there some soap in the medkit?

Donivan woke up while she was still rummaging for the soap. He blinked, saw her bent over in the nude, and grinned.

"Good morning," he said.

"Oh! Good morning. I didn't mean to wake you up."

"No, that's all right. What are you looking for?"

She found the bar and held it up. "Soap. I'm going to wash in the stream. Want to come along?"

"Sure." He stood up, and LeAnne watched as he stretched, the muscles sliding across his chest and arms. With the forest surrounding him he looked more elfin than ever, but the sharp lines on his arms and neck where the sunburn stopped spoiled the image. LeAnne had never heard of a sunburned elf.

Nor a naked one, come to think of it. Not that she minded.

"Better wear your shoes," she said. "It's a little ways."

"Right." Donivan slipped into his ship's shoes, picked up the rest of his clothing, and held out his arm for LeAnne.

She took one of the lasers, just in case they met a wild animal, put on her own shoes, and took his hand. What a sight, she thought. Prancing naked through the trees on a new Earth, with Donivan beside her. It was going to be a beautiful day, she could tell.

The stream could have been liquid nitrogen for all the warmth it carried. Donivan dipped a toe in it, shook his head, and said, "You're kidding, aren't you?"

LeAnne tried a toe of her own. "Nyaah. God. How do they stand it?"

"Who?"

"Explorers. In the books they're always bathing in streams."

"These books are fiction, right?"

LeAnne laughed. "Point. I'm going to try it anyway. Pull me out if I turn blue, okay?"

"Okay."

"Here goes. Aiieeyah!" LeAnne stepped in with both feet. The water barely reached above her ankles, but the cold shot up clear into her thighs. She reached in and splashed some higher. "Yeow! Oh, this is so much fun. Whoo! Hah." She bent down, splashed water over her chest and back, sucking in deep breaths and screaming them back out each time. No way was she going to use the soap. She stuck her hair in the water and swished it back and forth once, straightened up to swing it around to her back, and heard Donivan scream as the stream of water hit him.

"Your turn," she panted, stepping out onto the bank.

He looked at her dubiously, as if betrayed, but he stepped in. He screamed and gasped through a thirty-second bath of his own, jumped out, and shook the water off. As he pulled on his clothing he said, "We're nuts. The captain was right; the radiation has affected our brains."

"Maybe so, but we're clean now," LeAnne said as she pulled on her uniform.

Donivan laughed. "Yeah. If the dirt doesn't wash off, it freezes off. Let's find a patch of sunlight before I break my teeth shivering."

LeAnne nodded and led the way downstream to where the water cascaded over a pile of rock. The sun shone down at a low angle, not as warm as it had been yesterday during midday, but warm enough in contrast to the water. They sat on a rock that had already soaked up some of the morning rays and looked out over the plain below. The view was almost as good as it had been from the top of the ridge the day before.

Donivan's eyes were adapting well to daylight, but he still couldn't look toward the sun. It had risen to the north of the lake, so he turned south, but something bright glittered there as well. He shaded his eyes with one hand and pointed with the other. "What's that?" he asked.

"What?"

"That thing in the air out there. See it moving?"

LeAnne didn't see anything for a second, then suddenly she did. In the air over the lake a bright point of light winked at her as something turned and reflected the sunlight. It was too tiny to offer detail, but as she watched it glide down toward the edge of the ruined city she knew what it had to be.

Where a minute ago she had felt an immense sense of well-being, now she felt only anger. It had happened again! It was some kind of conspiracy. As soon as she adjusted to a new universe, somebody changed the rules on her.

"Entropy!" she growled.

"What's wrong?" Donivan asked. "What is it?"

"It's an airplane. Somebody beat us to it."

"Beat us to what?"

"Everything! Somebody else is living out here. Oh, damn it!"

Donivan looked at her in puzzlement. "What's wrong with that?" he asked. "So somebody else survived the holocaust too; that's good, isn't it?"

LeAnne couldn't get enough control over her voice to say more than, "For them, maybe. Not for us."

She watched him swirl it around in his head for a while before he said, "I guess I'm dumb. I don't see the problem."

She had to swallow to keep from crying. Her voice was still unsteady as she said, "It makes the Earth a lie just like the ship, that's the problem! It was supposed to be empty, ready for colonization, but it's already got people on it. That makes everything we've done for the last thousand years a waste!"

"Why?"

"We were supposed to be saving humanity, that's why. We were supposed to be guarding the gene pool and our knowledge until we could repopulate the planet, but if there's somebody else out here then we've just been hiding in a hole in the ground while somebody else did all the work. We're not colonists anymore—we're refugees!"

Donivan thought it through, then shook his head. He put his arms around her and said, "No we're not, Lee. We haven't been hiding. We've been living, the same as whoever is out there has been living. It doesn't matter where you live, whether it's in a starship or on a planet; it's living both ways."

"We weren't in a starship."

"Yes we were. So what if it's underground; it's a starship as far as the crew is concerned, and that's what matters. We live on a starship, and it's a good life. We live better than a lot of people lived out here before the holocaust. Maybe better than *they* do." He tried to joke. "Especially if they have to bathe in streams."

LeAnne scowled at him, and he shrugged. "Sorry. But Lee, no matter who they are or how they live, it doesn't change what *we* are at all."

"It changes me."

"How?"

"It changes everything I've lived for. I wanted to be a colonist. I wanted to explore new worlds and learn how to live on them. What's the point in that now? It'd be like colonizing the dormitory section."

"What do you mean?"

"I mean there's already people here, dammit!"

Donivan nodded. He shrugged and said, "Okay, but I'd think that one of the requirements for a good colonist would be that you're able to get along with the local lifeforms. Even if they're human."

LeAnne tried to see it his way. She could see that his argument made sense, but her emotions disagreed. *There were intruders on her planet*. She took a couple of deep breaths while she watched the airplane drop down and disappear in the shadows by the lake. "Maybe you're right. I don't know. But I'd still rather they weren't here."

"Well, we can't change it." Donivan stood up. "Come on, we should get back to the ship and let the computer know what we've seen."

LeAnne nodded. She agreed with that much, at least. Maybe the computer would know what to do. "All right," she said. She took a last look toward the lake and the ruined city, then turned and followed Donivan back the way they had come.

"You're sure the city by the lake is ruined?" the computer asked when they had described the airplane to it. They were back in the communications room on the top deck, keeping a watchful eye out for snooping police while they talked.

"It has a bomb crater in the middle of it," LeAnne said,

"and the lake has risen to cover most of what's left. It sure looked ruined."

"Yet someone landed an airplane there. You can only be describing Lake DeSmet and the town of DeSmet which grew around a hydrocarbon treatment plant there. I can think of many reasons why persons living outside might be interested in it, one of which might be that they are trying to salvage some of the old technology."

"So what do we do about them?" LeAnne asked.

"I am not sure. The original plan called for a slow, orderly spread of civilization back onto the Earth and an intelligent use of the planet's resources. Now, however, with the introduction of outsiders, we will probably be forced to amend that plan. Though we are civilized, we have no assurance that they are. They could even be hostile."

Donivan, rubbing more anesthetic on his hand and sunburn from the medkit they had left there yesterday, said, "I think you and LeAnne are both acting a little paranoid. We don't know a single thing about them except that they fly airplanes. That doesn't make them hostile. They might even need our help, especially if they've had to rebuild their civilization from the ruins. Or maybe they're our own people, from the *Starchild*. I think we should find out more about them before we jump to conclusions."

"You are right, but not completely so. We can reach many conclusions from the simple fact that humans are already living on the Earth, one of them being that we are not the only civilizing force, for they are not from the *Starchild*. I am certain of that. Of course that will necessitate changes in the original colonization plan, which did not allow for survivors."

"Why didn't it? That doesn't seem to be such a good assumption either, especially after seeing how many of the other species survived."

"Hindsight reveals flaws in the best of plans," the computer answered. "But you have seen the tapes made of the holocaust, so you know how unlikely it seemed that anyone would survive above ground. The Original Crew had good reason to believe that they would be the only survivors."

"What about another ship? Maybe the *Starchild* wasn't the only underground refuge to be built."

"It was. Most of the *Starchild*'s construction took place before the holocaust, when global communication was still commonplace. It was intended as a practice facility to see if a generation-style starship was feasible. The Original Crew would have known if there were other projects like it underway. None were. And none would have been possible afterward. We are the only refuge of any sort."

"So the Original Crew thought."

"Yes."

"But they were wrong about *something*. Either the Earth wasn't as bad off as they thought it was and somebody managed to survive, or those same somebodies *did* build another ship when they weren't looking."

"Either is possible, but I compute the probability of there being another *Starchild* to be almost insignificantly small. Outside survivors are much more likely. But you are right, we must find out just where the Original Crew made their error before we can amend the plan intelligently."

LeAnne said, "What is this master plan you keep talking about? I thought we were on our own after we got out of the ship."

"You are. However, you would be wise to have some idea of how to proceed in rebuilding civilization in order to keep from repeating the same mistakes that the last one made. For that reason the Original Crew extended their planning through the colonization stage as well."

"In other words, you intend to direct the next thousand years too."

"I intend nothing. I am programmed to make suggestions in the attempt to guide humanity away from the obvious pitfalls, but you are free to do as you wish."

LeAnne nodded, chastened. She had forgotten that she was talking to a computer. "Okay," she said. "What do you suggest we do next?"

"Observe the outside inhabitants. Learn as much about them as you can. Contact them if you think it safe, but under no circumstances should you allow any of them to learn the location of the *Starchild*. That is imperative. They may not be hostile, but then again they may. Return only when you can do so without being observed. If you do not return within a reasonable time, I will send more scouts."

"That's encouraging."

"It was not intended to be. Of all the people on this ship, you two are best suited to be explorers. Together you exhibit the aggressive behavior and curiosity that explorers need. If you do not succeed there is little chance that anyone else will; therefore it is imperative that you do."

At another time the computer's pep talk might have roused LeAnne to action, but her self-confidence had been dealt too many blows in the last few days to respond to the old "I'm counting on you" bit. Still, there was no other choice. She nodded wearily and said, "All right, we're going." To Donivan she said, "Ready?"

With a wry smile, Donivan closed the medkit and held it up. "Ready as I'll ever be," he said.

They picked up more food and water from the emergency stores on their way out, and stopped in the airlock long enough for LeAnne to pick two spacesuits off the rack.

"What are those for?" Donivan asked.

"Jackets," she replied, taking her laser out of her waistband and slicing the legs off one of them just above the crotch. The cut hissed and bubbled and smelled of burned plastic. She handed the top half to Donivan and cut the legs off the other one, and waved it around to cool off.

"Think I should cut the neck rings off?" she asked.

"Not on mine. I've got an idea." Donivan reached for a helmet, clipped it to the suit, and pulled the sun visor down over the faceplate. "Yeah," he said. "That'll work, if I cut some air holes in it."

LeAnne thought about taking one for herself, but decided

against it. She wasn't having trouble with the light, and there was already going to be too much to carry.

They left most of the survival kit in the airlock, taking only the space blankets, the edible plant book, the world atlas, knife, rope, and compass. LeAnne blushed when she picked that up. Donivan had read what it was really for in the manual last night. So it wasn't for telling the time; it had been a good guess.

They carried their weapons within easy reach, Donivan's tucked into his pants pockets and LeAnne's in her uniform's waistband. They improvised a knapsack by rolling everything else into one of the blankets and tying the ends with the rope. LeAnne slung it over her shoulder and led the way down toward the stream and out of the mountains.

She found that she couldn't stay mad, not with the Earth around her. Down inside she still felt the anger ready to erupt, but for a time at least she could let it go and simply enjoy the sights and sounds and smells of the forest around her. It was still too new, too beautiful to walk through in anger. Besides, there were no outsiders *here*.

There were animals in plenty, though, and now that she was looking, LeAnne noticed some that might have been mutations from the holocaust. A rabbit with rounded ears instead of the long, laid-back ears of shipboard rabbits; squirrels with bare, ratlike tails; and one fat, round, reddish ball of feathers that slipped under a pile of rocks before she could get a good look, but which looked as if it had a spiny ridge of bone or something along its back. It might have been a baby dinosaur, except for the feathers. But birds had supposedly evolved from reptiles; she supposed it would be possible to trigger mutation back to an earlier form. Maybe easier than to new ones, for that matter, since in a lot of cases the genes were still there to be reactivated.

For the first time, LeAnne wished she had studied biology. Outsiders or no, the ship's biologists still had an alien world to explore. She quickly sidestepped that thought. For today, at least, so did she.

After a few hours of hiking through the trees they even-

tually found what was left of a road: a barely discernible track
of flat ground that followed the contours of the land gently
downward toward the valley floor. Though it was eroded and
overgrown, it was still more passable than natural forest, so
they turned to follow it instead of the stream.

Donivan walked in front, not for LeAnne's protection so
much as just to let him see. She had no problem seeing over
his head, but when she took the lead all he could see was
her back. This way they could both watch the trail in front
of them.

For the same reason he carried his helmet in his hand
instead of wearing it. He didn't like having only a small oval
of vision, and the road was overgrown enough so that he
didn't need it for shade anyway. He was putting it to better
use batting small branches out of his way and clearing out
spider webs. It had long since become too hot for the spacesuit
jacket, so he had taken that off as well and tied it around his
waist.

Where the road curved around ridges in the mountain it
would break out of the trees and give them a good view of
the land below. Donivan had just stepped out into one such
clearing when a shadow passed across the ground in front of
him. He looked up, puzzled, just in time to see a fanged
mouth and a huge set of claws descend upon him.

He swung the helmet up to block it just as the creature
hit. It knocked him to the ground, biting and clawing at
the helmet: a screaming, flapping tumult of fury at the end
of his arm. He screamed and hit at it with his other hand,
but pulled back when the creature snapped at him with its
fangs.

With a shout, LeAnne pulled out her laser and took aim,
but with them thrashing around the way they were she couldn't
get a clear shot. Cursing, she drew the stunner and fired it
at both of them.

Their struggle stopped. She stepped closer, cautiously, trying
to watch the creature and the sky at the same time. When
she was satisfied that there was no motion from either quarter,

she pulled the creature off Donivan and lasered a neat hole in its head.

It was without a doubt the ugliest thing she had ever seen. It might have been a bird, except that it had six wings, and instead of feathers it had a bluish leathery skin, stretched tight enough across the wings to be nearly transparent except for the veins, and it had a bony head that stuck up at an angle on a long neck. As she looked closer, she saw that it had claws at the end of each wing.

She checked the sky again, then bent down and examined Donivan. He looked unharmed, other than a scrape on his forehead from banging against the ground. His breathing was still fast, probably from the adrenaline in his system, but it slowed as she watched to the regular, deep breathing of stunner-induced sleep.

LeAnne didn't know how long he would be out. The creature had taken most of the beam, but how much Donivan received she didn't know. She straightened his arms and legs and laid the space-blanket knapsack under his head for a pillow, but she could think of nothing else to do for him but wait.

She picked up his helmet. It had deep gouges in the faceplate from the creature's teeth, and the sun visor was broken. The way Donivan had held it out at arm's length, the creature had probably mistaken it for his head. That had been luck—those gouges would have been deep puncture wounds in flesh.

She stood and went over for another look at the bird, or whatever it was. *Dragon*, she thought. That was as good a name as anything. Taking a left wing in either hand, she pulled it around until it was lying on its back. Stretched out, its wingspan was at least six feet. The body was split into three segments, with the wings attached all in a row, one pair to each segment. The front wing pair was largest and highest on the body, with the other two pairs decreasing in size and attaching lower as they went back. Leathery ropes of muscle reached outward from a muscular hump atop each segment, attaching about two-thirds of the way out along the wings.

She lifted a wing and saw the same cable-style external

musculature on the back. The wings would have incredible strength that way, she realized, with the tendons running in a straight line between points of attachment. They would have much better leverage, and since they wouldn't work as hard they probably wouldn't tire as fast as normal muscles, either.

The head held three eyes, one on top and two in front to provide stereoscopic vision of the ground when it was in flight. Below the front eyes was a single mouth, with fangs. A trickle of blood dripped off one of the fangs into a blue puddle on the ground. Something else about it seemed odd, but with all the obvious deformities it took LeAnne a minute to realize what the subtler one was. It had no legs. It would have to use its clawed wingtips to move around on the ground. But she didn't suppose that would pose too great a problem for it; it had plenty of them.

Donivan let out a moan and shifted an arm. LeAnne knelt down beside him and shaded his eyes while he awoke. "Donivan?" she said. "Donivan? Are you all right?"

His eyes flickered open, winced. "Uuh . . . yeah," he said. He tried to sit up, managed it with LeAnne's help. "I think. What happened?"

"I had to stun you both. I'm sorry."

He had to take a minute for that to sink in. Shrugging, he said, "S'all right. Better than being eaten." He shook his head. "I think I make a better computech than I do explorer."

"Nonsense. It surprised you."

"That's true enough. Whoo." Donivan ran a hand through his hair, looked at the blood on it from his forehead. "Uh— how bad is it?" he asked hesitantly.

"Just a scrape. I think you got it falling when I stunned you."

"Oh." He looked over at the creature lying beside him on the ground. LeAnne watched him take in the multiple wings, the ropes of muscle, the fangs. "Nasty looking," he said at last. "I guess we can safely call that a mutant, huh?"

"Can we?"

He looked up at LeAnne. "Well, what else? Don't tell me this thing existed before the holocaust. I admit I don't know much about Earth biology, but I would have heard of one of these."

"Me too, and that's what I mean. We would have heard of it, or something like it. Even a mutant has to have parents."

"Meaning what?"

"Meaning I can't imagine what this thing could have mutated *from*. There was nothing on Earth with six wings before."

"Hmm." Donivan untied the blanket and dug the water bottle out from within. He unscrewed the cap, drank, and said, "Maybe it mutated from something else. How about insects? They have lots of wings. Or there's octopuses. Maybe they lost a couple legs when the radiation got into the ocean." He held out the bottle.

"And learned to fly?" LeAnne asked. She drank and handed the bottle back. "I don't think so, not even in a thousand years. The same for insects. This thing isn't an insect anyway. It isn't like anything I've ever heard of."

Donivan looked at it again. "Well, it doesn't look like anything we've seen so far, that's true. But if it hasn't mutated, and it wasn't around before, then where did it come from?"

LeAnne shook her head and looked up into the sky, but it held nothing now but a few puffy white clouds. She said, "I don't have any idea. Maybe the outsiders will know." She looked at the creature for a few more minutes, then drew in a breath and said, "Come on, let's go. We've got a long walk ahead of us if we want to make it to the lake today."

They saw two more of the six-winged creatures that day, both far away in the sky. Neither of them attacked, but Donivan put his helmet back on and held his laser ready until they had disappeared anyway. After his first encounter, he was taking no chances.

They saw more of the round-eared rabbits, but seeing those puzzled LeAnne even more, because of the obvious difference in degree of mutation. Different ear shapes and hair patterns she could believe, or even a bird regressing back to its dinosaur beginnings, for that would require changes in a few genes at most, but complete reworking of the musculature and bone structure was too much. That much change from random mutation in only a thousand years was impossible, even with the level of radiation as high as it had been after the holocaust. That much genetic damage would have left nothing but sterile eggs and aborted fetuses.

Yet it hadn't. Something had spawned that monster, and it had evidently bred true to its kind after the first one appeared. LeAnne wondered if it could have been some kind of bizarre experiment gone wrong, something that happened even before the holocaust. Maybe a biology laboratory experimenting with gene-splicing had created the first one and it had gotten loose when the war started.

She shook her head. No, ugly as it was, it's shape was obviously not an accident. Everything about it seemed to fit, to be part of a functional overall design. From the claws at the tips of its wings to the ropelike external muscles that moved them to the articulation of the wings themselves; it all fit together too well to have been the result of accident.

Which left deliberate bioengineering. The ship's biology department might have been able to create something like it, given lots of time and room for plenty of mistakes along the way. LeAnne couldn't imagine why anybody would *want* to build one, but she supposed it would be possible. Had the outsiders done it? If so, their civilization was at least as technologically advanced as the ship's.

"I don't believe it," she said.

Donivan was in the lead again. He turned part way around and asked, "Don't believe what?"

"That the outsiders are as advanced as we are."

"Who said they were?"

"I was just thinking that maybe they made that bird-thing. If they did, that puts them about at our level, or beyond."

"But you don't think they are."

"No, I don't. We'd have seen more evidence of them. One airplane and three ugly birds isn't enough. If they've been outside all this time and if they really were as advanced as we are, then they'd be all over the planet."

Donivan kept walking while he thought it through. After a few minutes he said, "Maybe there's something wrong, like a radiation-caused fertility problem. They might not be *able* to expand much."

"But they wouldn't have fertility problems if they can do bioengineering like that."

"Yeah," Donivan admitted. "You're right." He thought for a while longer before he said, "Maybe that's why they got into genetic engineering in the first place, to solve their fertility problem before they died out."

"It's possible, I suppose."

"Meaning you don't think so."

LeAnne grinned at him. "Well, it *is* kind of improbable. The last brave heroes, struggling frantically to solve the secret of reproduction before the biological clock runs out. . . ."

"You make it sound like the plot for a pornovid."

She laughed. "I guess I did. It just hit me that way. But who knows what we'll find? Your idea could be exactly how it is. Or it could be something even less likely, like dolphins taking over now that man is out of the way. That could explain why we don't see any signs of civilization on the ground. It's all in the oceans. They use airplanes to fly from ocean to ocean, but they don't use the continents at all."

"Except for the lakes," Donivan said. "They'd colonize the lakes."

After a moment he added, "Which could explain why we saw one land out there."

LeAnne looked out through the trees to where the lake shimmered on the plain below them. She was seeing it again with new appreciation. Dolphins? There was no way to tell until they got there and looked. With a laugh, she asked, "Do you know how to swim?"

"No, do you?"

"Huh-uh. So how are we going to contact them?"

"Stand at the edge of the water and throw rocks until somebody comes out to complain, I guess," Donivan said.

"Right." LeAnne laughed again, but at the same time she was thinking, *Dolphins?*

Sure. And bioengineered octopuses. Well, why not? It made as much sense as anything else.

PART THREE

The Safest Place

After another few hours of walking they realized that they were not going to make it to the lake before dark. In fact, they hadn't even made it all the way to the base of the mountains yet. The *Starchild* had been higher up than it looked, and the road's winding path more than doubled the distance they had to walk. When the sun disappeared behind the mountains they began to look for a good place to camp for the night, eventually finding a sheltered spot where the road curved inward around a hollow. There was a small stream trickling down through the trees and through a gully in the road, with a grassy spot beside it where they laid out the blanket.

They used the laser to start a fire and sat on the grass beside it while they ate their dinner, then let it burn down and laid back beneath the blanket to watch the stars come out. After a whole day of walking, simply lying on the ground and relaxing seemed like distilled essence of pleasure.

Donivan fell asleep almost immediately, but despite her fatigue LeAnne still felt wide awake. Too much had happened today; she needed time to think.

The moon hadn't risen yet, but the stars filled the sky with light. She tried to see the constellations that she had read about in the books about Earth. She could see patches of stars that looked like they might go together, but none of the groupings looked familiar to her. Dots on a screen were no match for the real thing. She would have to have the computer print out a chart that she could take outside and compare with the sky, and maybe that way she could find them. It didn't matter, though. In the meantime she could make up her own constellations.

A bright star slid out from behind a tree to the northwest and crawled southeast, but it was halfway across the sky before she realized what she was seeing.

She remembered her history. Lasersats, death in the sky, part of the reason for the holocaust. Some said *the* reason. Or it could be the—what did the computer call it? The Manned Orbital Research Laboratory. Would it still be up there after all this time?

The satellite lost its brilliance, then winked out abruptly.

LeAnne thought. In orbit, on the night side ... Of course, it had crossed into Earth's shadow.

She watched for a while longer, but nothing else moved in the sky.

She didn't remember falling asleep, but a sharp sting on her cheek brought her awake in an instant. She was getting used to bugs by now, so she merely slapped and waved her hand in the air, but she felt another sting on her hand, and another on her face. Except they weren't like insect bites. She opened her eyes and sat up, and then she noticed that the stars were gone. Strange.

The sky seemed to flicker to the west, like a glowpanel dying at the far end of a corridor. She was still getting bit, or whatever, all over now, and she could hear a staccato patter of tiny somethings hitting the space blanket. She rubbed her face with her hand and felt moisture, and suddenly she realized what was happening.

"Donivan, wake up! It's raining!"

"Hmmm?"

"It's raining."

"What is?"

"The sky! Feel it?" She took his hand and held it out beyond the blanket.

"What? Oh, that. That's rain?"

"Yes! Isn't it wonderful?"

"Umm hmm. Wet. How long does it last?"

"How should I know? Until it runs out of water, I guess."

Donivan seemed to be pondering the significance of that. At last he said, "Maybe we should bring the food in under the blanket with us then, so the wrappers don't dissolve."

They had left the food in Donivan's helmet by the fire. LeAnne said, "Good idea. No, don't get up; I want to feel it anyway." She rolled out from under the blanket and stood, holding out her hands palms up. The raindrops were coming more often now. Every time a drop hit her skin the muscles underneath gave an involuntary flex. And even with her jacket on she still felt cold.

She tilted her head back and tried catching the rain in her mouth, but only a couple drops hit her tongue. After a few minutes she gave up and groped her way toward the fire to pick up Donivan's helmet with the food packets in it.

She found the helmet by tripping over it, but when she reached inside there was nothing in it. Thinking that she might have spilled the food out when she kicked it over, she searched around by the fire with her hands, but all she found were the medical kit and the stumps of half-burned logs. She searched further away, but she couldn't find the food packets anywhere.

"Donivan?"

"Hmm?"

"Could you shine a light over here? I can't find the food."

"Okay, just a minute." Donivan searched around in the dark for second, then laser light shot upward, fanned out into a wide cone, and pointed toward LeAnne. "It should be right there in the helmet."

"It's not."

"Oh great." Donivan got up and came over to stand beside LeAnne. He shined the light into his helmet as if to assure himself that it was really empty, then shined it all around, but the only trace of their food was a scrap of wrapper at the base of a tree.

"It looks like something must have eaten it," he finally said.

"Eaten it? What could have snuck up right next to us like that without us hearing it?"

"Maybe a dragon," Donivan said. "Or a porcupine."

A distant grumbling cut off LeAnne's reply. She looked up at the sky just as it flickered again, brighter. "I think it's going to get worse," she said. "Maybe we should get the fire burning again."

"What for?"

"For the heat. Or haven't you noticed how cold it's getting?"

Donivan nodded wearily and handed LeAnne the light. He went over to the tree they had been using for fuel and snapped off a branch with his left hand, then carried it over to the fire and smashed the branch against a rock to break it into pieces. LeAnne helped toss the pieces on the coals, then narrowed the beam on the laser and played it over them until they burst into flame.

Donivan went over and picked up the blanket to wrap around them. "What's that flickering in the sky?" he asked.

"I think it's lightning," LeAnne said. "It's an electrical discharge."

Donivan nodded. "I guess if you've got a water leak you should expect short circuits."

"Donivan, it's natural!"

The rumbling sounded closer this time, too loud to talk over. When it faded, he said, "That makes it okay?"

LeAnne started to make a retort, stopped when she saw the grin on his face, then decided to say it anyway. "Yeah," she said. "That makes it okay."

"Even when we're getting wet?"

"Even then."

Donivan's grin widened. "Just checking," he said. He reached up and kissed her.

"What was that for?"

"Well, we can't sleep while this is going on, and we can't talk with all this noise, so . . ." He shrugged.

"Mmmm. Maybe you're right."

But later it started raining so hard that even that wasn't much fun.

Breakfast was a squirrel that had proved too curious for its own good. It was the second one, actually; they ruined the first before they learned that it had to be skinned and cleaned.

"You know," Donivan said as he held the squirrel out over the fire with a forked stick and tried to keep his head out of the smoke, "I don't want to sound like I'm complaining or anything, but it's sure a lot of work just staying alive out here."

LeAnne tossed another branch on the fire, watching out for the sparks that swirled up into the air as she did. They weren't as pretty by day as they were at night, but they stung just the same. "That's because we don't know what we're doing yet," she said. "The more we learn about living outside, the easier it'll get."

"I hope so. I mean, if we have to live like barbarians, I at least want to be a comfortable one."

It took a moment for Donivan's statement to register. "Barbarians? What, don't you like it outside?"

Donivan pulled the squirrel out of the flames and tested the meat, then flipped it over and stuck it back in. He said, "Oh, sure I like it, in a way. It's kind of exciting seeing what a planet is like, but to be honest I'm not sure I like the prospect of living out here for the rest of my life. I can't see many people wanting to, really, not when they've got the ship. On the ship you don't have to worry about dragons dropping out of nowhere on you, or porcupines putting needles in your hands, or bugs crawling all over you, or things stealing your food, or getting rained on, or—"

"Or challenging the unknown."

"There's that too."

"What happened to your sense of adventure?"

"I think it froze to death during the night. Somehow challenging the unknown doesn't seem as important today as a soft bed and a hot shower and a cafeteria meal."

LeAnne didn't know how to respond to that. Donivan's attitude was something she just couldn't understand. Finding Earth just outside the airlock had changed everything for her; she couldn't see how it could help but affect him the same way. The ship was *nothing* compared to all this. The ship was a dead end, just as she'd always said it was even before they had found what lay outside. How could he possibly prefer it to *this*?

He did, though. He treated being outside the same way he would treat a day's tour through a newly remodeled deck; he was interested in what it looked like, but when the tour was over he intended to go back home to his own room. For the first time LeAnne realized that he really did mean to go back and pick up where he'd left off once he was done fooling around outside.

She should have seen it, though. He'd been hinting at it all along. Yesterday, when the dragon attacked: *I think I make a better computech than I do explorer*. And even earlier, when they were talking with the computer, Donivan had said he couldn't see the point in living outside the ship. Somehow it hadn't registered on her until now, but he really meant it.

He looked up and saw the expression on her face. "I think I said something blasphemous."

"You did."

"Forgive me?"

"Maybe. I don't know. You're burning the squirrel."

Donivan yanked it out of the fire. With a wry grin he said, "That wouldn't have happened on the ship. The cafeteria has trained cooks."

"Oh, shut up about the ship, would you? Here, let me see that." LeAnne took the stick from him and examined the squirrel. One end was nearly black, but the other was cooked just about right. She held it out away from the fire to cool.

"Sorry," Donivan said.

"Don't be. Just try to enjoy yourself. Here, have some breakfast."

It was tough chewing and had a taste that wouldn't have made it popular on the ship, but it did satisfy their hunger. Donivan ate the burned half and professed to like it, but LeAnne suspected that he was just saying so to make her happy. Either way it was an improvement. She knew she was being oversensitive, but she didn't care. It was *her* planet he was talking about. Even if there were other people living on it.

After breakfast they rolled their equipment up in the blanket and started on down the mountain. The sky held no trace of the night's storm, and as soon as they started walking the sun began to warm them up and dry their clothing. LeAnne felt her spirits rising, and she suspected that Donivan was feeling better as well. The earth was beautiful! The trees sparkled with tiny droplets of water, the air smelled fresh and clean, and out on the plain the lake shimmered like a thing alive.

LeAnne found herself thinking about the outsiders again, wondering what they would be like. It still made her mad to think that somebody else had beat her to it, but it was really the uncertainty that bothered her most. Until she met them and found out who they were she couldn't make any plans at all. All she could do was worry, and worrying wasn't one of the things she was good at. She was better at direct action.

But for most of the day, the only direct action she could take was to walk onward along the old highway and hope that they would make it to the lake before dark. As the day wore on it began to look as if they might. They negotiated the last switchback by midmorning, and from there the road straightened out and followed the river that ran out of the mountains, presumably all the way to the lake.

The temperature had been rising all day, and as they walked farther out into the flatlands the trees began to thin out. At first it made for easier walking, but before long they thinned out completely and the sun began to beat down on them with only an occasional cloud for shade. They eventually abandoned the road in favor of the riverbank—there were still a few trees there and the water seemed to keep the air cooler—but there were long stretches where the bank was bare on both sides and the river simply wound its way through the prairie. When that happened Donivan had to put on his helmet for the shade it offered and suffer through the heat, and even LeAnne found her eyes stinging from the brightness.

They had been walking for perhaps twenty minutes without shade when they arrived at what looked to be the last stand of trees between them and the lake. There were about ten trees clustered together around a hump of ground that might have been the remains of a house or might have been just a hump of ground. LeAnne had seen others along the bank, but if they had once been houses there was nothing but this left of them now. The trees were a different variety than the ones on the mountain; these branched out not far above ground and had leaves instead of needles.

As they drew near, Donivan lifted his helmet and asked as nonchalantly as he could: "Want to stop?"

LeAnne stifled a laugh. "Only if you do," she said.

"Well, maybe just for a minute." Donivan dumped the helmet by a tree, then untied his jacket from around his waist and dropped it as well. His weapons and shirt and shoes followed it.

The river was flowing slowly along the bank where the roots of the trees held back enough dirt to form a pool. LeAnne tossed her own jacket and the bundle of equipment beside Donivan's, then leaned down and scooped up water in her hands to drink, but Donivan simply stuck his head underwater. He sloshed it around and blew bubbles for a moment, then leaned back and wiped the water out of his eyes while LeAnne laughed.

"Don't laugh until you've tried it," he said. "It cools you off."

"It also looks ridiculous."

"So does sweating," Donivan said. He grinned mischievously and splashed water toward her, not quite hard enough to get her wet. She grinned and splashed back, harder. For a moment they locked eyes, both waiting for the other to make a move, then suddenly Donivan shouted "Yee-ow!" and leaped, grabbed LeAnne by the shoulders, and spun them both into the pool.

LeAnne shrieked as the cold water hit her. She had expected it to be warm, but it still carried the chill of melting snow from the mountains. For a moment she couldn't even breathe, it was so cold, but she managed to gasp in a breath and duck Donivan under before he could get away. There was a moment of frantic splashing and shouting, then LeAnne found herself standing with her feet on the bottom of the pool, the water up to her hips, laughing harder than she would have believed possible.

They stood together, panting and laughing and dripping, and now that she was in it, the water didn't seem so bad. It seemed a shame to waste it, in fact, considering how sweaty and sticky she'd felt only a moment before. So with a smile at Donivan she stripped out of her uniform and began to take a real bath.

She didn't expect him to hold out long, and she wasn't disappointed. His clothing joined hers on the bank, and he moved up to help her wash.

His hands were the only warmth, but they were a delicious warmth that moved in sweeping curves across her body, kneading the tension from her muscles and filling them again with shivers of excitement. She returned his massage, laughing with the play of cold and warmth as the water swirled around them.

Lovemaking in a cold running stream was definitely different from lovemaking on the grass under a blanket. They knelt on the sandy bottom, putting the water line just below her breasts, and screamed like idiots as they moved. It was over in a single wave of intense pleasure, and they struggled weak-kneed back to the bank, panting and laughing and dripping.

LeAnne sat down on the bank and squeezed the water out of her hair. An involuntary shiver shook her, but the sunlight was already at work warming her back up.

"I'd never have believed that freezing to death could be

such fun," she said with a grin as Donivan sat down beside her.

"Just goes to show that pleasure and pain are different aspects of the same thing," he replied.

"Hmm. Profound."

"Hey, I can be a real thinker when I try. How about this for a corollary: Everything can be either pleasurable or painful, depending on the circumstances."

"How so?"

"Well, take sunlight and cold water, for instance. Neither one's much fun alone, but taken together they're all right. Sunlight is great after you've been in the water, and cold water is the perfect answer to too much sun."

"Hmm. That would imply that pleasure and pain are relative concepts. That *is* profound. Come up with a unifying theory and you'll be the Einstein of the subjective universe."

"Are you being sarcastic?"

LeAnne smiled, her eyes half closed. "Just a little. People have been trying since before the holocaust to make psychology an exact science, but nobody's managed it yet."

"Probably it's from lack of experimentation. Maybe I should throw you in again, just to test my theory."

"You're welcome to try."

Neither of them moved.

"And so dies psycho-subjective relativity," Donivan said, lying back and folding his arms behind his head.

LeAnne lay back as well and watched the clouds drift past. They had been building all afternoon, small puffy things that changed shape from minute to minute. Their motion was deceptive; when they slipped behind the branches of the tree overhead she couldn't help the feeling that it was the tree that was moving instead of the cloud. But after the tree remained standing through five or six clouds she began to feel that she and the tree and the ground were all moving beneath the clouds together, that she was watching the Earth turn against the sky.

She could almost feel the motion. It was like being in the ship and listening to the drive rumbling away beneath her, feeling its acceleration in the soles of her feet and knowing that the ship was moving on and on through space. That, she realized now, was the whole point of having the drive. The Original Crew could just as easily have said that the drive was silent, but their noisemaker gave the imagination something to work with, giving the crew a subjective reason to believe as well as reinforcing the illusion of being on a ship. If they could imagine themselves being hurled through space, nothing short of stepping out of the airlock would make them think otherwise. She knew that for a fact.

But the Earth didn't need a noisemaker to stimulate the imagination. It had sheer immensity going for it. Its only sound effects were the quiet ripple of moving water and the occasional whisper of air moving through the trees, but somehow those simple sounds enhanced LeAnne's perception of motion more than any thundering roar could have. When she stood up and looked around her the Earth would again become her entire universe, but now, lying in the grass and watching the clouds, she knew that she was on a planet that was itself drifting gently through space in its orbit about the sun.

She became aware of a sound that she had been hearing for a minute or more, a sound that had grown so gradually that she hadn't consciously noticed it until it grew too loud to ignore. It was a buzzing noise, and it seemed to be coming from the sky. LeAnne sat up and looked toward the lake, and there was the source of the buzz, a black silhouette crossing in front of a cloud. It had three pairs of wings, staggered high in front to low in back just like the creature she had killed the day before.

"Donivan!"

He jerked awake. "What?"

"It's the airplane." She jumped up and grabbed their clothing, tossed him his, and ran behind a tree. "Get under cover! We don't want them seeing us, not yet."

But it was already too late. The airplane banked to the right, away from them, then to the left and around them in a circle. They kept trees between them and it, struggling into their clothing as they moved around, but the rest of their equipment lay in plain sight for the pilot to see. LeAnne made a dash for her laser on one circuit, but there was no time to take anything else.

"What now?" Donivan asked as the plane made a wide turn and settled slowly toward them.

"I don't know." LeAnne wished she could see inside. A suspicion was growing in her mind, but it was so impossible she couldn't believe it without proof.

The plane came in below tree level, then with a complicated twist it flared out all three sets of wings at once. It settled to the ground, rolled a few feet on its three wheels, and stopped just opposite the mound of raised ground. The engine noise died, and a blur at the rear became a three-bladed propeller.

"They're going to find us anyway," Donivan said. "Cover me." He stepped out away from the trees and waved toward the plane as the pilot climbed out.

He froze with his hand still upraised. They stared at one another for a long moment: Donivan the elfin human and a six-limbed creature nearly twice his height. It used two limbs for legs and the other four for arms, though from their heavier appearance it looked like the middle pair could serve either purpose. It had two eyes set wide apart in a narrow head, a ridiculously small nose above a single, fanged mouth, and no visible ears. Its skin had the same blue tinge to it that the dragon's had, a color accentuated by the stark white paint that covered its body from neck to feet. At least it looked like paint, or a thin layer of something that stuck like paint. LeAnne's skintight uniform looked baggy in comparison.

The creature broke the silence first. "You're human!" it said in a voice that sounded like an echo from a long way down an empty corridor.

"And you're not," Donivan said.

The alien lifted its middle left arm and wiggled it up and down, its four-fingered hand held flat. "That is true," it said. "I am Eyullelyan. I am not from this world."

LeAnne could hardly hold in a shout of delight. Her suspicion had been right. Aliens! The outsiders weren't people, but real live late-night-movie aliens! Her planet had aliens on it!

"That much is obvious," Donivan said. He was trying not to look at LeAnne, but his eyes kept shifting. Even from her hiding place she could see white all the way around them. At last he gave up and, staring at the alien, asked the one question foremost on LeAnne's mind:

"Are you hostile?"

"No," the alien said. "I am an archaeologist. I would not harm you in any way." It burst into an incomprehensible fit of Ys and Ls, then recovered and said, "Excuse me, please. I am excited. We had thought that there were no more humans anywhere!"

Donivan ignored the implied question, saying simply, "There almost weren't."

They stared at each other for another few heartbeats, the alien wringing its hands in a gesture that would have been human if it hadn't had too many hands to wring. At last it said, "I don't know what to say! A real human! I had never dreamed that this could happen to me. I don't know what to do."

"If it makes you feel any better, neither do I."

The alien dropped two arms to the ground and took a complicated step forward, its white bodypaint flashing in the sunlight. "May I—?"

Donivan took a wild step back. "No!" he said, and when the alien stopped, he added, "Please. Not yet. This is a little hard to take all at once."

"I understand. You are alone?"

LeAnne chose that moment to step out from behind her tree. "No," she said, making a point of tucking her laser into her waistband so the alien could see it.

If the weapon impressed it at all, it didn't show. It let out a whistle full of vowels, and when it recovered, it said, "A breeding pair! Oh, this is beyond my wildest dreams!"

LeAnne felt herself blush, then blushed even harder when Donivan began to laugh.

The alien stammered, "Forgive me! I didn't mean to—I

forgot that —I—we have only one sex. I have attempted to understand human sexuality, but I had forgotten that among you it is often a forbidden subject. Forgive me! I will not talk about sex anymore."

"Forget it," LeAnne said. She was laughing too. An embarrassed alien. An embarrassed, apologetic alien who spoke English. It was entirely too good to believe.

"Do you have a name?" she asked. "Mine's LeAnne. LeAnne Evans, and this is Donivan Hayes."

"I am Yllyia."

LeAnne tried the name, trying to slur the Ls properly. "Yllyia. Where are you from, Yllyia?"

"California," the alien said. "Most of us live in Ventura. It's the best piece of coastline left after the bombs. Or do you mean before that? We haven't found a name for our sun in your star charts—only a number—but we call it Yea. It is nearly fifty light-years from here. Do you know what a light-year is?"

"Yes," both LeAnne and Donivan replied. LeAnne said, "Fifty light-years is a long way to go for a colony. There must have been a lot of habitable planets closer than Earth. Or are they colonized already?"

She could almost see the alien—Eyullelyan, it had called itself—amend its first impression. Evidently it hadn't expected them to understand. Not surprising; two people out in the middle of nowhere, wearing dripping wet, torn clothing wouldn't immediately suggest a high degree of civilization.

It said, "We have other colonies, but not between Yea and here. Yea is at the edge of our—what is the word—our sphere of expansion. Eyullelya is much further away. But we didn't come here to colonize. At least that wasn't our primary intention. We came here to help you recover from your nuclear war, but when we found that we were too late we stayed. At least, we thought we were too late. It certainly looked that way until now."

LeAnne nodded. "I don't blame you. I saw the tapes of the war and what it looked like afterward, and *I* wouldn't have been surprised to find nobody left either. But how did you know we were in trouble in the first place? We didn't even know you existed."

"We were listening for evidence of extraYean intelligence. We learned of you almost as soon as you started using radio, but before our signal could reach you we heard the beginning of your war. There were no more radio signals after that. We held a vote to decide what to do and the group in favor of coming here won, but only by making concessions to the group who were readying for another colonization expedition closer to home. So we multiplied and we rebuilt our spaceship for the voyage to Earth, first to offer what help we could, but also to start a colony if you had destroyed yourselves. We truly thought you had."

"'The safest place for a colony is a planet that has already proven its ability to support life,'" LeAnne quoted.

"Ah, then you understand. But tell me, where have *you* been all this time? We have searched for survivors since we first arrived, yet we found no trace of anyone. And now you show up in our midst, obviously from a civilized society. Yet there is no sign of civilization anywhere around here."

LeAnne had been wondering when that question would come up. She had decided to stick to the truth in her answer. At least part of it. "We were in a starship," she said.

Donivan winked at her when she said that, but she ignored him.

The alien practically fell over in its excitement. "A starship! We hadn't thought it possible. No wonder we didn't find you. You evacuated the planet when it became uninhabitable."

"Something like that."

"Where did you go?"

"Uhh . . . that would be kind of difficult to explain right now," LeAnne said.

Donivan snorted. For a moment she thought that he might defy the computer's orders and reveal the *Starchild*'s location, but instead he cleared his throat and said, "Why don't we go sit down in the shade? There's no point in standing out here in the sun any more than we have to." He gestured beneath the trees.

"Good idea," Yllyia said. "My *lyshl* is starting to evaporate."

"Your what?" LeAnne asked.

"My . . . ah . . . garment. Clothing. Your sun is brighter than we Eyullelyans are used to, so we wear *lyshl* to protect us from it."

LeAnne took a closer look at the alien's body paint. It was actually a layer of some kind of foam, by the looks of it, hardened in place but still elastic enough to permit movement. "It looks like insulation," she said. "I'd think you'd cook in there."

"Oh no, not at all," Yllyia said. "The outside layer reflects sunlight, and the layer next to the skin evaporates and pulls heat from the body when it gets too warm. It works very well, and when it gets too thin you just spray on another layer."

"I wish I'd had some of that stuff a couple hours ago," Donivan said, leading the way back to the shade. "I just about cooked out there."

As Yllyia passed by her, LeAnne could see that the Eyullelyan had a third eye in back of its head. It swiveled to stare at LeAnne for an unnerving moment, then shifted to provide stereoscopic vision on the right as the alien passed the spacesuit jackets and the helmet. Yllyia studied them with interest, then picked a grassy spot in the shade, turned around, and sat.

Watching Yllyia sit down was—interesting. LeAnne stared unashamedly as the Eyullelyan bent backward at the knees and forward at the hips and touched its lower set of hands to the ground behind it, bending the other way a couple feet higher to keep its upper body vertical. It looked a little like a person sitting down with knees bent, but there was an extra bend and an extra pair of arms at the waist. And now that she was closer, LeAnne could see that above each eye was a tightly stretched patch of skin that had to be an ear. She wondered what it would be like to see and hear on three sides instead of two.

Even sitting down, Yllyia was tall. If the Eyullelyan was

typical of its race, then humanity was going to have to spend much of its time looking upward, LeAnne thought. She'd have preferred smaller aliens, if she'd had the choice, but she supposed these would do. They were certainly better than finding humans.

"You have trouble with the sun too?" Yllyia asked Donivan. "I would have thought that you would be—what is the word—evolved for it."

Donivan sat down with his back to the tree and pushed aside the tied-up space blanket to make room for LeAnne. He said, "LeAnne is, maybe, but not me. I evolved on board the ship."

"You did? I wouldn't have thought there was enough time for that, even if all your ancestors were crew members."

Donivan shrugged. "Evidently there was. We're all this way now, except for LeAnne."

The alien tilted its head toward LeAnne. With its three eyes, that was the only way to tell which way it was looking. It said, "You are different. Even I can see it. Are you the ship's captain?"

"What?" LeAnne said. The question had caught her by surprise. "Captain? Not me."

"I see. Then you must be a newly awakened passenger."

"Awakened? What do you mean?"

"Revived from sleep. Not sleep, but . . . ahh . . . suspended animation, that's the word. Weren't you in suspended animation?"

"No."

"No? You are a crew member too?"

LeAnne shook her head. "We're all crew. Or we're all passengers; whichever way you want to look at it. I'm different because of a genetic accident, not because I'm older than everybody else."

"You don't carry passengers in suspended animation?"

"No. I take it you did?"

"Gods yes! Otherwise you would die of old age before you got anywhere. Unless your . . . motors are far more efficient than ours."

LeAnne laughed. "No. Far from it."

"Then I don't understand. You all stayed awake through the entire journey?"

"Right."

"And your ancestors grew old and died in the ship? Generations of them?"

"Right."

"Why?" The Eyullelyan sounded like it was pleading for an answer.

"Why? I—that's just the way we—" LeAnne stopped. She was talking to an alien. Different ways of doing things, different ways of *thinking*, maybe. Different in how many unguessable ways? But there was an answer to its question. It wouldn't compromise the ship to tell Yllyia that, and it might even make a good impression.

"No," LeAnne said. "There was a reason for it. You know what we did to Earth. After the holocaust it was obvious that we had to change our whole way of thinking, and since we couldn't live on the planet until it recovered, the survivors decided that a few generations on a starship might get rid of our suicidal tendencies. That's why we did it that way."

The Eyullelyan was silent for a time while it thought that through. At last it said, "Did it work?"

Both LeAnne and Donivan laughed. The skin beneath Yllyia's eyes wrinkled and the alien made a fluid whistling sound that might have been a laugh of its own.

"We don't know," LeAnne said. "The ship's computer thinks so. That's why we're here—to find out if Earth is ready for us now that we're ready for it."

"So you have come back to live here?" Yllyia asked.

"We have. We, uh, didn't expect to find *you* here, of course, but I don't see that as a problem. Not unless you do, that is."

"Not at all, not at all! Oh, it will be perfect: an Earth full of humans again. You know, our whole race despaired when we thought you were extinct. You are the only other sentient race we have discovered in all this time, and to have lost you without exchanging a single greeting was more than some of us could bear. There were many suicides in the years after your war."

Donivan shook his head sadly. "So it was even worse than we thought. Our stupidity managed to kill people fifty light-years away."

Yllyia waved an upper arm. "Do not grieve for them. You paid the price, surely. We should be rejoicing that you are not gone after all. In fact, I should tell someone about you. No, better yet; I should bring you with me back to the university. Will you come to California as my guests?"

LeAnne and Donivan exchanged glances. LeAnne said, "Uh, I don't know. We were supposed to stay out of sight."

"Surely not. You will be a sensation. You will make my reputation, and yours too! We will all be remembered forever, the first to make contact between our races. Certainly you can't pass up that honor?"

The moment Yllyia said it, LeAnne knew that she couldn't. No self-respecting explorer could. And the computer *had* said to contact them if they thought it would be safe. Well, what could be safer than aliens who had come to help?

"I think you were right," she said to Donivan. "The computer and I were being too paranoid." To Yllyia she said, "Of course we'll go with you. We only ask that you bring us back here alone in a few days. We have to, uh, keep a rendezvous with the ship."

"Ah," Yllyia said, as if confirming a suspicion of its own. "I had wondered where your landing craft was. So, you were dropped here! No matter; I can have you back any time you want." The Eyullelyan gestured toward the airplane with an upper arm. "But if we want to make it to California before nightfall, we had best be going."

The airplane held two seats, both too large for human occupants. Yllyia took the one on the left, leaving LeAnne and Donivan the other. They threw their gear into the space behind the seats and climbed in, LeAnne taking the side next to Yllyia.

Yllyia showed them how to strap themselves to the seat,

then pushed a lever on the panel in front of them. The engine coughed to life, the noise of it quieter from inside than LeAnne had expected, and the propeller disappeared into a blur again. The plane began to roll forward, faster and faster, bumping up and down as the wheels hit irregularities in the ground. Yllyia let them pick up speed for a few seconds, then pulled back on two more levers and they lifted up into the air. The plane tilted back, lurched suddenly to one side, then picked up speed and steadied out.

The Eyullelyan had each of its four arms on separate controls, pulling and pushing and shifting from side to side as the plane climbed. It kept its forward eyes straight ahead and its rear one aimed out the back window, but that didn't keep it from talking. "These little planes are a real trick in warm air," it said. "They're all wing, and the turbulence really throws them around." As if in response to the alien's statement, the plane dropped like an elevator going down, then surged upward again a moment later. Yllyia continued on as if nothing had happened. "But they've got a lot of lift, which is good when you're digging up artifacts. You never know what you might be carrying home. Ha *ha!* It'll settle down once we get up a ways, and once we pick up some speed I'll swing the middle set of wings back and then we can do some real flying. It doesn't look it, but this thing will do two hundred miles an hour in a pinch." The Eyullelyan glanced over to its passengers. "But that's nothing compared to my other airpla—is something wrong?"

LeAnne swallowed, not trusting herself to speak. She kept her eyes on the instrument panel in front of her, but she could still sense the distance between herself and the ground, and it felt as if her stomach was still down there.

Donivan was doing no better. He was pushing himself back against her, gripping the edge of the seat in panic, his eyes wider than they had been when he first saw the alien.

Yllyia leveled the airplane out and said, "My apologies! I didn't realize that you weren't used to flying. I can land again, if you would like."

"No," LeAnne said. She looked over at Donivan, and he nodded. "We'll be all right. Just give us a minute."

"Certainly."

It took them longer than that, but they eventually forced themselves to look out the window at the ground below.

Donivan, next to the window, watched it slide along beneath them for a while, then said with a sigh, "I keep having to change my perspective. The universe keeps getting bigger on me."

Yllyia said cautiously, "Do you really live on a spaceship?"

Donivan smiled when he answered. "We really do. But it doesn't have any windows."

The Eyullelyan looked back out in front of the plane. "Strange design," it said. "No suspended animation, yet no windows either."

"Even stranger than you think," Donivan said. "Maybe we'll get to show it to you some time."

"I hope so. As an archaeologist, I would be very interested in seeing how humanity builds their spaceships. We found only satellites left in orbit, and nothing on the ground."

"What's it like?" LeAnne asked. "We haven't seen much of Earth since we got—ah, got back."

"You haven't? No, of course not, not if you were dropped off to explore on foot. Well, you won't find much. Your war was most thorough. We've had the best luck searching through the remains of small towns, where most of the damage was due to time instead of bombs. That's what I was doing when I saw you, looking for the town called Story that was supposed to be toward the mountains from Lake DeSmet."

"You still use all of our old place names?"

"Most of them. We kind of like the way your words sound."

"You do?"

"Yes. We didn't discover consonants until we heard your language. It took us years just to figure out what they were, and longer to learn to use them. We were practicing all the way out from Yea, or my ancestors were. I was born here. It really broke their hearts when they got here and there was nobody to speak to, so a lot of them just kept on using it among themselves. A lot of us still do; it's kind of an academic language."

Suddenly the Eyullelyan burst into whistling laughter. "Gods, no one will believe it when I show up with you. I'm not sure I believe it yet myself." It swiveled its hind eye to face them. "Are you really here?"

"We really are." LeAnne looked over at Donivan, caught his eye, and winked. *Yes, we are*, she thought. *At last.*

They flew above the clouds. As they flew westward, the fluffy white puff balls they had watched drift by from below had given way to an undulating layer that covered the ground completely in its own landscape of white. LeAnne leaned her head back against the seat and watched it roll past out the side window.

The alien was an excellent pilot. Once it realized that its passengers were not used to flying it had kept the airplane riding smooth and level, while at the same time inundating them with questions about every aspect of their lives.

It seemed obsessed with sex. It had read every book it could find on the subject with an eagerness unsurpassed by any shipboard teenager, but even though it understood the biology involved it couldn't understand the elaborate rituals humans had evolved to deal with it. Donivan had asked why not, and for answer Yllyia had told them how Eyullelyans reproduced.

It was no wonder that the aliens didn't understand human sexuality. The concept of combining genes to produce offspring was nothing new to them—they required four different types of genetic material to accomplish what humans did with two—but the idea of an individual carrying only one type was beyond anything in Eyullelyan experience. The Eyullelyans were hermaphroditic; any of them could supply any of the four gametes, and as LeAnne understood it, they could even supply more than one.

"Is that right?" she asked. "Could one Eyullelyan reproduce all by itself?"

Muscle cables flexed and unflexed in the alien's arms. It

breathed out with a soft whistle, then said, "It is possible, yes. It is an unnatural process, and forbidden much as your social codes forbid incest, but certain families practice it nonetheless." The plane hit an air pocket and bounced for a minute, then settled down again. "Ruling families use it to keep their blood lines pure, just as human royal families practiced incest for the same reason."

The Eyullelyan paused, as if organizing its thoughts, then said, "There is something I should tell you about this. *Ylsarli*—self-reproduction—effectively stops the evolutionary process. Some families have practiced it long enough that their members are physically different from the rest of the race."

"Different how?"

Yllyia hesitated again before saying, "Among other things, their front eyes tend to be farther apart and their teeth protrude more."

LeAnne looked at Yllyia more closely. "If your front eyes were any farther apart, they'd be crowding the hind one," she said.

"That is true."

"So you're from a royal family?"

"Formerly so, yes. My ancestors once ruled a large empire on our home planet. That was generations ago, but even though we are no longer in power the tradition has not died. Mine is one of the oldest genotypes in the species, older even than the Queen's."

"Queen?" LeAnne asked.

"Our government is a constitutional monarchy," Yllyia explained. "Most Eyullelyan governments are. It's a very stable political system. Some royal lines have been in power for millennia."

"So that's why you thought I was the captain of the ship," LeAnne said. "Your rulers are all genetic throwbacks."

"Yes."

Donivan laughed. "I bet your Queen is jealous, then, isn't she? She's not as royal-looking as you."

"You're very perceptive. The Queen *is* jealous. She sees

me as a threat, and perhaps rightfully so. My family has tried many times to regain its former power. I have not inherited that desire, but my presence is enough to make her nervous. That, besides my love for humanity, is why I became an archaeologist. I spend much of my time in remote places, which makes it easier for both of us. When I am out hunting artifacts she need not fear me, and I need not fear her."

"I was wondering about the pronoun," LeAnne said. "You use 'she' for everybody?"

"Yes," Yllyia said. "Your definition of female fits us better than male, though neither one is very accurate. We call ourselves female because we can all bear children."

"Oh. Makes sense, I guess. Do you have any of your own?" LeAnne asked.

"Not yet. Children come late in life, and I am still young."

LeAnne thought about that for a minute. "Do you mean you can't have them until you get old, or you just don't?"

"I choose not to. Most of us do, even those without my, ah, political problem. Of all the archaeologists at the university, only Ililiel, the head of the department, has a daughter, and Ililiel is nearly a hundred and thirty years old. Children take a great deal of time to raise properly, and we don't have the—what is the word—the compulsion that you humans evidently have to reproduce often."

"You don't?"

"No. We must truly want to reproduce before it is even possible. The whole concept of birth control is foreign to us."

LeAnne looked to Donivan, and saw him blushing. Was she blushing too? She couldn't tell. She said, "How could your race survive without a compulsion to reproduce?"

Yllyia laughed her whistling laugh. "We have wondered how yours survived as long as it did *with* one. Your entire history seems to be a continuing battle with population pressure."

True enough, LeAnne thought. Which was the reason for the rituals that the Eyullelyans didn't understand. No wonder they didn't, if they didn't have the problem. It took years of living with the rules every day for children on the ship to understand what they were for, and sometimes it didn't work even then. And if they traveled in suspended animation, the Eyullelyans would never understand why those rules needed to be so much stronger in a world as small as a starship.

But the colonists could relax those rules now that they had a planet to fill again, couldn't they? Or could they? LeAnne knew that population pressure was just as much responsible for the holocaust as was politics. They would have to be *really* careful if they planned to mess with the rules governing that. She would have to take it up with the computer. It could run simulations to see what would happen, whether or not the population would get out of hand after a few generations, but LeAnne could just about guess what it would say. Learning to control the population was no doubt another one of the *Starchild*'s many lessons to be remembered.

Yllyia went on. "We do have a compulsion, if you want to call it that. We call it *shalerya*. It's actually a vestigal migrating instinct, according to one theory, held over from our remote past as flying creatures on Eyullelya. After we've been on a planet for a while we find ourselves wanting to move on, to see what we will find on the next one, and the next. It's not the same migrating instinct that your Earth birds have, because we don't have the compulsion to return to the place of our birth, but we do still get the urge to leave."

Donivan said, "You mean your whole population just picks up and moves on?"

"Not all of it. We reproduce more heavily before a flight, and the children remain behind with the adults who don't feel the desire as strongly, but a large portion of us move on. More than half."

"Then you'll be leaving again soon?"

"Oh no. The instinct builds slowly over generations. It rises swiftly to a peak every thirty-second generation or so."

"And how long——?"

"Have we been here? Two generations. A little less than three hundred of your years."

"Oh," Donivan said.

LeAnne hoped the Eyullelyan couldn't sense his disappointment. It sounded like he wanted them to leave, which was true enough, but Yllyia wouldn't understand why. LeAnne did, though. He wanted to go with them.

LeAnne was only dimly aware of the conversation going on around her. Yllyia and Donivan were discussing airplanes and flying, and Yllyia was showing him how it was done, but LeAnne was busy watching the Earth slide by below. They had run out of clouds nearly an hour ago, over southern Utah, and she had taken out the world atlas and tried to follow their path on the maps. She had found Lake DeSmet on the Wyoming map, which put the *Starchild* on the front range of the Bighorn mountains, but the clouds had shrouded any other landmarks close to home. Still, she felt reasonably confident that she could find her way back if she had to. She didn't expect the need to arise, but it felt good to know that she could.

They had just passed to the south of the Sierra Nevada mountains and were coming up on what the atlas simply labeled "Coastal Ranges" when Yllyia said, "We're not far now. There's Ventura."

LeAnne looked where Yllyia was pointing, but all she could see was a smudge of gray against the horizon. "I don't see it," she said.

"Well, all you can see right now is the smoke, but it's under there. Looks like there's an inversion today."

Donivan sat up for a better look. "Smoke?" he asked. "Is something burning?"

Yllyia laughed. "It's from the factories. But I guess you wouldn't know about factories, would you?"

"I've read about them," LeAnne said. "We used to have them too. Why don't you put them in orbit?"

"We might, eventually. Right now it's easier to have them here, because we're still mining raw materials from the cities. It's much simpler."

"And dirtier," Donivan put in.

"You sound like an environmentalist," Yllyia said.

"What's an environmentalist?"

"Someone who worries about pollution."

Donivan thought a moment, then said, "You have to worry about pollution if you live on a spaceship."

"Hmm. Maybe so. Most of our environmentalists are descended from our ship's crew. They're trying to change all this, but they're up against a lot of resistance."

"Why?" LeAnne asked.

"Because they want to change our whole way of life. They claim that moving from planet to planet the way we do is the problem, that we don't care because we don't have to live with our mistakes. I wish them luck because they're right— we *are* wasteful and we *do* pollute more than we have to— but we've been doing things this way for millennia and we aren't likely to stop overnight."

"Inertia," LeAnne said.

"Exactly. Excuse me—I think we're probably in range now. I should call ahead and let my colleagues at the university know we're coming." Yllyia picked up a microphone and spoke into it in Eyullelyan. A voice responded and they talked for a moment, then Yllyia lowered the microphone and said, "They're making the call for me from the airport."

They heard voices talking back and forth for a moment, then one said, "Yllyia?"

"Right here," Yllyia said. "I'm coming in with a surprise. Gather everyone up and meet me at the airport."

"What kind of surprise?"

"Humans. Live ones."

There was a moment of silence, then, "Yllyia, are you all right?"

"Yes, I'm all right. Just meet me there. Yllyia out." She hung the microphone back on its hook and said, "They think I'm crazy. Don't disappear on me now, or my reputation is shot."

LeAnne laughed. "We won't."

"Thanks."

Yllyia began their descent, slowing the plane and gradually swinging out the middle wings until they were doing barely a third of their cruising speed. The coastal mountains slid by beneath them, and they got their first view of the ocean. Beyond the smoke layer it was a sparkling blue sheet running all the way to the horizon, a horizon that seemed at least twice as distant as it had from the mountaintop.

"The university has its own field," Yllyia said as she banked the plane to the left. "It's a good thing. If we used the regular airport I doubt if we'd make it beyond the terminal before we were surrounded by news reporters."

"Oh," LeAnne said. She looked down at the approaching city, imagining for the first time the commotion their arrival would cause there. There would be more questions than even Yllyia had asked, most of them difficult to answer if she wanted to keep the *Starchild*'s location secret. Maybe this hadn't been such a good idea after all.

But the Eyullelyans *wanted* human neighbors. And there was so *much* open land to colonize. What was she worrying about? Everything was going to work out beautifully.

While Yllyia busied herself with the landing, LeAnne and Donivan got their first close look at Ventura. It was a collection of squat cubic buildings, roads, and tall cylinders spewing smoke into the sky. The smoke was thick enough to make the ground hazy below them, and as they dropped into it they began to smell it. It was nothing like campfire smoke; it was more like the smoke that you smelled on board the ship when an ancient electronic part finally gave up.

LeAnne coughed until she realized that clearing her lungs would do no good without fresh air to breathe. Her body still tried, but she supressed it and tried to breathe shallowly.

When she saw the ground coming up at them she didn't think of breathing anyway. Donivan's arm tightened around her, and they braced themselves against the certain crash, but at the last moment Yllyia pulled the nose up and they glided onto the runway with only the gentlest of bumps. Yllyia steered toward one of the smaller buildings, where a group of Eyullelyans waited. The airplane rolled to a stop and Yllyia said, "Here we are. Welcome to Ventura, or more properly to the University of California. And there are my skeptical colleagues! Look human, now."

Half a dozen aliens converged on the airplane, babbling excitedly and pointing. They practically yanked the door out of Yllyia's hands, and they never even gave LeAnne a chance. Yllyia shouted, "Back, back, you savages! Give them room! And speak English!"

The others backed away in a hemisphere around the plane, still talking excitedly among themselves, and now that LeAnne had a group for comparison she could see other differences between Yllyia and them that Yllyia hadn't mentioned. The Eyullelyans all wore the spray-on *lyshl*—some in metallic colors and others with just bands of color on their external muscles—but where their skin did show it was noticeably lighter than Yllyia's. Yllyia's bone structure seemed thinner than theirs, and she was shorter too; some of the others were easily nine feet tall. LeAnne looked to Donivan for reassurance, then stepped down to the ground. He stepped down beside her and put his arm around her, and they stood there feeling like fish in an aquarium.

Yllyia came around the front of the plane, waving her four arms for silence. "Quiet!" she shouted. "Show some respect." When they had quieted somewhat she said, "LeAnne Evans and Donivan Hayes, humans, I present to you Eurilla, Losrell, Ililiel, Eslia, Llewella, and Napoleon."

"Who?" LeAnne and Donivan asked simultaneously.

"Napoleon," the leftmost alien said with a sigh. "Everyone asks. My mother spent most of her time studying European political systems, and she liked the name."

"Oh," LeAnne said, as if that had explained it. European?

Yllyia said, "Come on, let's get in out of this smog. To the archaeology building!" She reached into the airplane and started handing out equipment: her own pack, LeAnne and Donivan's rolled-up blanket, spacesuit jackets and helmet.

"Where did you get this?" the alien named Ililiel asked when she saw the helmet.

"We brought it with us from the *Starchild*," Donivan said.

"A spaceship?"

"Yes."

The Eyullelyans shouted in delight, all except Ililiel, who only said, "Oh," and turned away. Donivan looked at LeAnne and shrugged as if to say, *Well you can't expect to impress them all.*

Yllyia closed the airplane door and moved off toward a group of ground vehicles parked beside the building, her arms spread wide to shoo the others ahead of her. LeAnne and Donivan followed.

The ride across campus in Yllyia's car was even more terrifying than flying. The sense of motion on the ground was much stronger than it was in the air, and approaching cars seemed to barely miss them, but they managed to control their fear for the five-minute trip. Ililiel, as head of the archaeology department, had claimed the right to ride with them while the others followed in a second car, and she kept them busy with questions while Yllyia pointed out the various campus landmarks as they drove past.

"There's the astronomy department," Yllyia said with her whistling Eyullelyan laugh. "Those idiots didn't even know you were in the solar system. Still don't, I bet. Hey 'Liel, maybe we should have these two bang on old Ellela's office door and see how she reacts."

"I think not," Ililiel said quietly. "I think we should keep this discovery to ourselves at least for today. There will be ample time to announce it after we have satisfied our own curiosity."

Yllyia said, "I suppose you're right. Sure. Here we are." She turned into a wide lot beside the archaeology building and stopped the car. The other car pulled in beside them and the other five Eyullelyans piled out excitedly.

"Restrain yourselves," Ililiel said. She led them inside to a conference room and closed the door behind them. "Be seated," she said, indicating a couch across the room, and as LeAnne and Donivan sat down, the others all pulled up chairs around them.

Ililiel said, "So, Yllyia, where did you find them?"

LeAnne sighed. She'd known that question was coming,

but she could think of no way to keep it secret. She didn't suppose it needed to be secret anymore, now that the outsiders had shown themselves to be peaceful, but she was still reluctant to give up the *Starchild*'s location. She couldn't help it; she was still paranoid.

But Yllyia only said, "Out in Wyoming," which was better than it could have been. Evidently she didn't want her exact whereabouts known either.

"That is a remote place to land, isn't it?" Ililiel asked, directing her question to LeAnne.

"Well," LeAnne began, trying to think far enough ahead to keep from tripping over her own story, "we were looking for a good colony site. We were walking south along the mountains when we ran into Yllyia."

"They were just as surprised as I was," Yllyia said.

"You did not, ah, know that we were here?" one of the other Eyullelyans asked. LeAnne had already forgotten their names.

"No," LeAnne said. "We—well, we weren't really looking. We certainly didn't expect to find anyone here."

"I bet not! But it is strange that we did not see your starship arrive."

"Hyperdrive!" the one called Napoleon said suddenly. "You discovered how to travel faster than light!"

LeAnne smiled as she said, "No. Sorry."

"What kind of drive *do* you use?" Ililiel asked.

LeAnne felt on more familiar ground with that question. "It's a ramjet," she said. "It scoops up the gas and dust ahead of it for fuel and sends it out the back as energy."

Ililiel turned her head to look at LeAnne with one side eye and the hind one. Whatever the gesture meant, it was lost on LeAnne, but not the other Eyullelyans. There was a sudden shocked silence, which one of them broke by saying, "Have you much—" *whistle*. She thought for a minute, then spoke to Yllyia.

Yllyia said, "Losrell asks if you have left many colonies in other star systems."

"No," LeAnne said. "We, uh, stayed on the *Starchild*."

"They *live* on their ship," Yllyia said. "All of them."

Ililiel cut off the surprised whistles with a two-armed gesture. "Where is your ship now?" she asked.

LeAnne hesitated, then said, "I'm sorry, but I'm afraid we can't tell you that. It's a silly precaution, but we'd get in serious trouble if we did."

"Why?"

Ililiel seemed to be taking no pains to be cordial. LeAnne considered telling her to piss off, but she didn't suppose that was proper when meeting aliens for the first time, so she said instead, "It's just an order. We don't have the authority to change it. When we go back and make our report I imagine our captain or somebody will be able to tell you everything you want to know, but for now it's just Donivan and me, and we can't reveal where the ship is. Anything else, but not that."

"Of course, I understand." Ililiel stood. "If you will excuse me for a moment?" Without waiting for an answer, she turned and headed for the door.

When she had closed it behind her Yllyia asked, "What's the matter with her?"

"I don't know," Napoleon said.

One of the Eyullelyans who had until now remained silent whistled and said, "She is to be angry that *she* did not find them."

"What does this mean?" Donivan asked, turning his head sideways as Ililiel had done earlier.

Everyone laughed, a sound like the flute section of an orchestra tuning up. "Um, well," Yllyia began, "It's a gesture that evolved after we discovered that you humans only had two eyes. It means something like, 'you're not trying to sneak up on me, are you?'"

Napoleon laughed again. "It means she thinks you're lying," she said. "But don't worry about her. She doesn't even believe herself half the time. Be glad you don't have to submit your thesis to her."

"Oh," Donivan said, and LeAnne thought, *Great. All we*

need is to get caught in a lie. She was almost glad when someone turned the conversation around to sex.

A few minutes later the door opened to reveal Ililiel again. Standing in the open doorway, she said, "I just talked with Ellela over in astronomy. She confirmed it: There's no way we could have missed seeing an approaching ramscoop drive, provided you could get one to work in the first place. They're theoretically impossible." She paused to let that soak in before she said, "So maybe you should tell us what you're hiding."

That's done it, LeAnne thought. She looked around her, at the faces that had never looked away even at the interruption. She couldn't read expression there, but the fangs that she had ignored until now seemed suddenly prominent.

She looked to Donivan. He shrugged and said, "I can't see how it would matter."

LeAnne nodded. "Okay." Turning to face Ililiel, she said, "It's really quite simple. You see, our starship is underground."

Into the sudden silence, Yllyia said, "No wonder it doesn't have windows."

Ililiel ignored her. "So you live right here on Earth?" she asked. "Not in space at all?"

"That's right," LeAnne said.

"That's all I needed to know." Ililiel stepped back into the hallway and motioned with her hands, and a dozen Eyullelyans swarmed through the door. "Take them away," Ililiel said. "All of them. Maximum security. No one is to speak to them, or even see them."

LeAnne's first reaction was to reach to her waist for her stunner, but she realized too late that it was in the back of Yllyia's car, along with her laser and both of Donivan's weapons. She looked to the windows, one of them open, but she knew that she would never make it that far before one of the Eyullelyans caught her. There was no escape, no hiding in the shadows this time.

Donivan looked at her with guilty eyes. "I guess it did matter," he said.

* * *

The cell to which the Eyullelyans took LeAnne and Donivan was roughly cubical, with a door in one wall and a bed along one side. The bed was sized for Eyullelyans; it was at least ten feet long, and Donivan could have slept crossways on it without trouble. He and LeAnne sat on it with their backs to the wall while Ililiel stood opposite them and asked questions.

"How many of you are there living in this underground habitat of yours?"

"What difference does it make?" LeAnne asked.

"It makes a great deal of difference. You propose to spread out once again over the surface of this planet. We need to know what that will mean to us."

"And you need to lock us up to find that out?"

"That is regrettable, but we must be certain of your intentions before we can feel safe with you running free in our city. For instance, we must know if you still regard this as your world. Do you intend to use force to take it back from us?"

"*No*," LeAnne said, genuinely shocked. "Why would we do that? There's room enough for everyone here."

"We have read your history. Whether or not there is plenty of room does not seem to be a factor in the human decision to conquer. You do not seem to be able to coexist peacefully with other races. I point to the treatment of the Indians on this very continent as an example."

"I don't know anything about Indians," LeAnne said. "But we're different people now. A thousand years on a starship has changed us."

"And how do we know that? By visiting your 'starship' and seeing for ourselves. All you need do is tell us where it is, and if your society is as peaceful as you claim then our fears will be proven groundless."

LeAnne shook her head. "We can't. Especially not now."

Before Ililiel could say anything else, Donivan asked, "What if you don't like what you see? Then what?"

Ililiel didn't answer immediately. She folded her four arms into a braid that made LeAnne's own arms hurt, considered her response, then said, "We would have to proceed from there. If that were the case, it would change things considerably."

"How?"

"I'm not at liberty to say. We would have to negotiate directly with your leaders."

"By locking them up too?" LeAnne asked.

"I know this seems unfair to you, but look at it from our viewpoint. A dangerous species that we had thought gone for good suddenly reappears in our midst, armed and capable of doing us much harm. We must be cautious."

Donivan looked away, giving her a good view of the back of his head. He said to the wall, "Look at it from *our* viewpoint. We came here to make contact with your race, and you immediately take us prisoner. How do you expect us to feel? You're afraid of trouble, but you're doing about the surest thing you can to ensure that you get it."

Ililiel cocked her head to one side. "You have a point," she said, "but it doesn't get us anywhere." She unfolded her arms. "It is late; we can continue this discussion in the morning." She rapped on the door and waited for the guard to open it from outside. As she stepped into the hallway, she said, "Do think about what I have said. If you tell us where to find your *Starchild*, then we can clear this whole thing up quickly."

"We'll think about it," LeAnne answered.

"Good. Good night." Ililiel nodded and the guard closed the door behind her.

LeAnne looked over at Donivan and let out a long sigh. "Looks like I really got us into it this time."

"It's not your fault," he said.

"Yes it is. I shouldn't have let Yllyia talk us into coming here. I knew something like this would happen."

"It's just as much my fault. I wanted to come too." He leaned forward on the bed. "So what are we going to do?"

LeAnne stood up and paced the length of the room as she spoke. "I don't know. We really can't take them to the *Star-*

child or show them where it is, not now. But we've got to let them know we're not a threat, either."

"How do we know they're not a threat to us?"

"Say again?"

"How do we know they're not a threat to us? She says they just want to be assured that we're okay, but what if they're lying to us?"

LeAnne stopped pacing. "I don't believe my ears. I'm supposed to be the paranoid one around here."

Donivan shrugged. "Sometimes paranoia has its place." He nodded toward the door. "I don't like the way she backed off as soon as we asked her what they intended. There's something they're not telling us, too."

"Like what, do you suppose?"

"I don't know. But I don't like it, and I don't like the way she had Yllyia and everybody else arrested too. They didn't do anything."

"Hmm. True enough." LeAnne sat down on the bed beside Donivan and leaned close to whisper, "Maybe we shouldn't be talking about this. I bet they're recording us."

He nodded, and whispered back, "You're right."

LeAnne leaned back and tried to think. She bet Donivan's suspicion was right; the Eyullelyans were hiding something, too, but she couldn't imagine what it was. Yllyia had seemed completely honest, and so had the rest of the university professors. They had shown no sign of holding anything back. Only Ililiel had seemed false. LeAnne wondered if she was right to judge them by human standards, but in the end she realized that there was no alternative. She didn't know enough about the Eyullelyans to judge them by their own.

Donivan leaned over and whispered, "You know, even if Yllyia doesn't tell them exactly where she found us, it isn't going to take long for them to find the *Starchild*."

LeAnne hadn't thought of that. It wasn't a simple matter of whether or not to tell them. Now that they knew it was there, they would search until they found it. "You're right," she whispered back. "We *really* screwed up."

"Maybe not. If we can get back and warn the crew, we can come back prepared and talk it over on *our* terms."

"How are we going to get back? It's a long ways on foot."

"If we can get to Yllyia's airplane, I think I can fly it."

"You're kidding."

"No, it's not that hard. She showed me."

"Having somebody show you is a lot different than actually doing it. Besides, how are we going to get out of *here*?"

Donivan smiled. "Remember how we got into the captain's quarters?"

LeAnne looked up, and saw what Donivan was talking about. The ventilation duct was high up on the wall opposite the door, but it looked big enough to crawl through if they could reach it. It was built to be too small for a Eyullelyan, but not for a human.

Without a word, she slipped off the bed and walked softly over to stand beneath the duct. It was way above arm's reach. She didn't even think she could jump that high. She was about to try when the lights suddenly went out.

She whirled around, expecting the door to spring open and the guard to come in after her, but nothing more happened. As her eyes adjusted to the dark she saw a line of light coming in from under the door, but there were no shadows of feet just beyond, as there would have been if someone were about to open it.

"Bedtime, I guess." Donivan's voice came from the bed. She heard him get up and step carefully toward her until his hand bumped against her side, then he put his hands on her shoulder and in a barely audible whisper said, "Okay, let's try it."

Now seemed as good a time as any. She cupped her hands and held them out for his foot, then lifted him up to where his feet were even with her waist. She could feel him searching around, leaning first to one side and then the other, then he bent down again. She let him back down.

"You'll have to hold me higher," he whispered. "I can't reach it."

"Stand on my shoulders, then," she whispered back, bending down. She held onto his ankles as he climbed up, then stood again. He stretched, but finally knelt down again. LeAnne let him down.

"I can just touch the bottom of it," he whispered. "Do you think you can hold me up over your head?"

"I'll try, but how am *I* going to get up?" With the guard just outside the door, Donivan couldn't just go around and open it for her this time.

"I'll dangle my legs out once I'm in. You jump up and grab them."

"Hah. Right."

"It'll work."

She couldn't resist saying, "That's what you said last time we tried this, and look where it got us," but she got down on one knee, cupped her hands together at the wrists this time, and when he stepped in she stood up with him. That got his feet to chest level. She pushed against the wall to hold him there, dropped down to her knee again and locked her arms straight up in one quick motion, then stood again. With her arms locked, holding him was not that hard.

She felt him working at the grille for what seemed like forever, then heard a squeak of metal moving against metal. A moment later his weight lifted from her hands.

"I'm in," he whispered. She heard him shifting around, then, "Ready."

She reached upward as far as she could, but he was higher than her outstretched arms. With a deep breath and a prayer she crouched down and sprang, and she touched his feet, but she couldn't grab them in time. She let herself collapse as noiselessly as she could, then took another deep breath and jumped again. This time she caught his leg.

She heard a muffled "oof" from above, but he held tight while she pulled herself up. He bent his other leg to give her a better handhold, and she got that under one arm while she reached up to grab his waist with the other. She pulled herself the rest of the way up—and the flaw in their plan became obvious. His body was blocking the opening.

With one arm around his thigh she felt with the other until

she found the edge of the vent, grabbed that, then dropped down again until she was hanging by both hands from the opening. "Get in!" she whispered frantically.

Donivan wriggled on into the shaft, and as soon as his feet were clear LeAnne pulled herself up to follow him. It was a tight squeeze.

"You okay?" Donivan whispered.

"Yeah. Let's get out of here."

"Can you put the grille back?"

"Forget it. I can't even reach back to my nose." It was true. The shaft was just wide enough for her shoulders, but she couldn't bend her arms back more than halfway. She was glad she'd stretched them out in front of her, or she would have been pinned in.

Donivan moved off ahead of her, kicking up dust that made LeAnne want to sneeze. She fought down the urge and followed, thinking *At least it doesn't smell as bad as the stuff outside*. They must have filtered the air at the intake. They evidently cooled it too; it was a few degrees too cold in the shaft to be comfortable. LeAnne ignored it. Comfort wasn't the issue here.

She pulled herself along with a combination of toes and elbows and knees and fingers, cursing under her breath every time she hit her head on the shaft. She was just getting the hang of it when they came to a junction. Donivan bent and pulled himself around the corner without trouble, but LeAnne had to lay sideways and inch around by pulling on his feet. Her breasts got in the way, and she found herself wishing that, just this once, they were smaller. But at least she wasn't claustrophobic.

The new shaft was larger, and it ran in both directions. Light filtered in from ducts leading into other rooms, enough that she could see Donivan in silhouette in front of her, and despite his body in the way, the wind was stronger there. They had turned left at the junction, and Donivan led on, paralleling the hallway outside their cell.

They had passed two side shafts and were just coming up

on a third when they heard voices. Donivan paused at the opening, and LeAnne crawled up close behind him.

She heard one of the voices saying, "—can't get away with this. I am a member of the Yll family. I don't know who you bribed to have us arrested, but when word of this gets out you'll both be in the freezer until the end of time."

It was Yllyia.

Ililiel's voice answered her. "Word won't get out. Why do you think I had them take all of you?"

"So you could take the credit for finding the humans. Why else? But it won't work. You'll get caught, maybe not right away, but you'll eventually get caught. You can't have thought this through very far ahead."

"You'd be surprised."

"Oh?"

"What would you say if I told you that I have the Queen's backing on this?"

There was a pause before Yllyia said, "I have a hard time believing that the Queen would let you capture representatives from the civilization we came here to save. You're starting an interspecies incident that could have serious repercussions. When she hears what you've done you'll freeze for certain."

"The Queen and I are both acting on standing orders from the home world," Ililiel said.

Yllyia laughed. "The Queen and you? Standing orders? Who do you think you are?"

"I am the head of the university archaeology department. And as such I am charged with ensuring that nothing is unearthed that could harm the Eyullelyan race. In particular, humans. I had hoped that this would never happen, but I was told to be ready for it, and I am."

"You can't be—you're—why, this is preposterous! That's a standing order? We came here to help them!"

"There's where you're wrong. We never intended to help humanity, not from the start. They're too dangerous."

"Speak for yourself!" Yllyia said. "*My* ancestors came to help."

"I'm sure they did. Only a few people knew the true plan

then, just as now. But we were already trying to work out a safe method of exterminating humanity when humanity solved the problem for us. After they destroyed their own civilization we seized the chance to finish them off completely while they were weak, before they could rise up again and destroy us. That was why we came here, not to help, and not to start a colony."

LeAnne couldn't hear Yllyia's answer, if she made one at all. Ililiel went on.

"Of course we brought colonists. Earth just needed time to repair itself; why waste a perfectly good planet? But that was secondary to our main purpose, which was to eliminate the threat of humanity once and for all. Don't you see, a warlike race that breeds as fast as they do could overpower our entire empire in the time it takes to cross it. We would never be able to stop them once they got into space. We had to stop them *here*, at the source, before they could rise up again. We thought we were spared the trouble, but now you've shown us that we weren't." Ililiel paused. "I wish you hadn't; the archaeology department will be a long time recovering."

"You're going to kill us, then."

"Yes. It's nothing personal, you understand. I regret the necessity, but we have no other choice. You're all too sympathetic to the human viewpoint. None of you would be willing to go along with what we must do."

"You're not even going to make the offer?"

"No. I know you all too well."

Yllyia laughed again. "It's going to look a little suspicious, don't you think, if we all disappear at once?"

"We have a cover story already prepared," Ililiel said. "Officially you brought back an extremely contagious and deadly disease that you unearthed in your excavations. We were forced to quarantine everyone who might have been exposed to it, but unfortunately you all died despite our best efforts to save you. For safety, your bodies will all have to be cremated, and any sites that might harbor the disease organism will be incinerated with nuclear blasts."

"You're going to wipe out an entire race. Genocide."

"We're going to finish what they started themselves a long time ago. Only this way we make sure that they don't take us with them."

"Iliana would be proud of you."

The sound of a heavy slap echoed in the air shaft. "Leave my daughter out of this," Ililiel said. "Now, we're going to get it from you one way or another, so why don't you save us both the trouble and tell us where you found the humans."

LeAnne didn't know how much more of this she could take. Her universe was flip-flopping on her again. First the stardrive, then the ship itself, then her uninhabited Earth, and now the aliens. Her big, friendly, glad-to-see-you aliens. Nothing was what it seemed. She could feel a scream bubbling up inside her, a howl of grief and frustration that, once started, she would never be able to stop. Equally strong was the urge to jump out of the duct and tear Ililiel apart with her bare hands. But she was in the middle of an escape. Whichever she chose, scream or fight, it would have to wait until later. She pushed on Donivan's feet, and he began to crawl on through the ductwork.

The passage they were in terminated in a still larger junction. The wind blew even harder, and LeAnne could hear a rumbling in the distance. Donivan chose the righthand passage this time, into the wind, and though it was pitch dark again they were able to make good time on hands and knees to the end, where the fan blocked their way. They couldn't see it in the darkness, but they knew it was just ahead of them by the noise. Donivan inched forward, cautious of the whirling blades somewhere ahead, but he encountered the maintenance hatch first. It was designed to open outward; his weight pushed it open and he fell through headfirst.

The sudden light streaming in through the hatch blinded LeAnne for a second, and when she could see again Donivan was already standing up, blinking at something out of her field of view. She stuck her head down through the hatch and saw an Eyullelyan standing only a few feet away, a wrench as long as LeAnne's arm in an upper hand. When the Eyullelyan saw LeAnne she took a step back, dropped the wrench with a crash, and fled for the door, slamming it hard behind her.

LeAnne couldn't help but laugh. Pixies in the air shafts! She stuck her feet through the hole, lowered herself until she was hanging from her hands, and dropped down beside Donivan. "Are you all right?" she asked.

"Yeah," he said with a nervous laugh of his own. "I landed on its back. Come on, let's get out of here. She's going to have the whole place up in arms in a minute."

LeAnne nodded. She bent down and picked up the wrench. It was heavy enough to cave in someone's head with a single swing. She hefted it experimentally, and a crazy idea began to form. She looked toward the door again, and saw a tall tool cabinet beside it. Perfect. "Wait a minute," she said. "I have a better idea. Let's wait for them to come to us."

"Huh?"

"We're never going to get out of here with a wrench. We need a real weapon. And whoever comes through that door first is going to have one." LeAnne looked around, saw a tool rack with more wrenches hanging from it, and took down a smaller one for Donivan. She grabbed up some of the still smaller ones and gave him those too.

"Okay, here's the plan: You hide behind that big whatever-it-is there." She pointed to a hulk of dismantled machinery along one wall. "When you hear the door just *start* to open, throw a wrench right here where we're standing. I'm going to be up there above her head, and while you've got her attention with that I'll get her with this." She hefted the wrench. "When she drops her gun, you go for it."

Donivan started to protest, realized that he had no better plan, and said, "Okay." He went over to take his position, and LeAnne took a running jump, grabbed the top of the tool rack, and pulled herself up to lay across it. She took a couple practice swings with the wrench, then held it ready above the door.

Running footsteps sounded closer, stopped. LeAnne heard voices speaking in Eyullelyan, then silence.

The door burst open to a strong kick, sending a piece of the jamb flying out into the room. Donivan's thrown wrench clattered across the floor and echoed to silence. A long metal tube that was like no laser or stunner barrel LeAnne had ever seen poked in the doorway, but the Eyullelyan holding it stayed beyond her reach.

LeAnne waited, her heart pounding. It wasn't working. She had to do something, and she had to do it fast, so she did the first thing that came to mind. Shifting the wrench to her left hand, she lunged for the gun barrel with her right and yanked upward.

She heard a startled yell from beyond the doorway, and the gun came away in her hand. It was an ugly black metal thing with three handles, but LeAnne recognized the trigger at the base of the middle handle. She dropped the wrench, grabbed the gun by the middle and forward handles, pointed the barrel out the door, and pulled the trigger, hoping to scare whoever was out there away with a warning shot, but she was completely unprepared for the result. Instead of the silent beam of light she'd hoped for, a staccato roar like the previous night's thunderstorm compressed into a second's time ripped through the air, and the gun tried to twist itself out of LeAnne's grip.

She let up on the trigger, and after the echoes died down she heard shouts and footsteps receding again. Cautiously, keeping the gun ready, she slid down to the floor and peered out into the hallway, just in time to see an Eyullelyan back vanish around the corner to the right.

"Come on!" she said, waving Donivan out of his hiding place. She led the way to the left.

The gun felt awkward in LeAnne's hands. With the trigger in the middle she was forced to hold it by the two forward grips, and it didn't balance properly. It seemed awfully heavy for a hand weapon, too, but she supposed that the Eyullelyans with their larger bodies and more powerful musculature didn't mind the weight. She wished that she had some of those muscles herself just to hold onto the thing when she fired it.

She knew what it was now. Some of her favorite explorers used machine guns too.

They came to another corridor to the left. LeAnne got down on her knees and stuck her head out next to the floor for a quick look, hoping that anyone there would be looking up higher. She saw two guards standing with weapons ready, facing her way. They saw her at the same time, and she barely pulled her head back before the wall behind her burst into flying shards of stone. An instant later the sound of gunfire echoed down the corridor. She stuck the machine gun around the corner and pulled the trigger, holding the barrel tight against the wall and moving the stock back and forth to spray the entire area. When she looked out again both guards were down.

They ran down to the first guard. LeAnne wasn't prepared at all for what she saw; bullet wounds like blossoming flowers across the chest, still pouring blood. It didn't matter that the blood was a deep blue rather than red; it was blood all the same. She had just killed two thinking beings. She felt a surge of anger wash through her at the realization.

Donivan bent down and picked up the guard's gun. He held it distastefully by the barrel. LeAnne finally shook herself loose and turned away. She tried the door. Locked.

She looked back at the guard, but she didn't see a key hanging from a belt or lying nearby, and she wasn't about to go searching through her pockets for it. Motioning for Donivan to stand back, she held the gun to the lock and tapped the trigger. The lock exploded in fragments.

She kicked the door open, and was not surprised to see Yllyia and Ililiel against the side wall. She stepped through and pointed the gun straight at Ililiel. "Say your prayers," she said.

"No!" Yllyia shouted.

LeAnne looked up at her, noticing a deep blue mark on her face where Ililiel had slapped her, but she held the gun on Ililiel. "Give me one good reason why not," she said.

Yllyia said, "We'll need her for a hostage."

LeAnne considered it. She wanted *so* badly to pull the

trigger, because of what she had overheard, and because of the two guards she'd had to shoot. The guards hadn't deserved their fate, but LeAnne wouldn't mind seeing Ililiel in that condition, not at all.

But Yllyia was right.

"All right. Out the door." She stepped aside and waved the gun, and Ililiel walked out. When she saw the guard lying on the floor she said, "See, Yllyia? Wasn't I right?"

"Shut up," LeAnne growled, jabbing the gun into her back. An inch-wide circle of *lyshl* vaporized at the hot barrel's touch. "Yllyia, which way out of here?"

Yllyia hesitated. "We should free the others first. Ililiel, where are they?"

Ililiel bared her teeth in answer. LeAnne considered persuading her with a bullet through a nonvital part, but the sound of more guards approaching at a run changed her mind. Hostage or no, she didn't like the idea of being out in the open. "Let's get some cover first," she said, pushing Ililiel ahead of her down the corridor.

They barely made it to the end before the pursuit emerged around the corner behind them. Donivan, bringing up the rear, turned and fired a short burst toward them, the recoil bringing the barrel up to make the bullets stitch a line along the ceiling, but the pursuers ducked back.

But they were still in the middle of a corridor. Yllyia led off to the left, and LeAnne prodded Ililiel in the back to make her follow. They ran almost to the next junction, but they could hear footsteps approaching around that corner too. Yllyia yanked open the last door on the right, pulled Ililiel inside, and closed it softly behind LeAnne and Donivan.

LeAnne held the gun to Ililiel's side. "Not one word," she said.

The footsteps pounded up to the corner, stopped for a second, then charged on. Moments later they heard gunfire from the direction they had just come.

They're shooting at themselves, LeAnne realized, horrified, but at the same time she thought, *better them than us*.

They were in someone's office, judging by the oversize

desk next to the window. It was night outside. Yllyia looked out into the darkness, then, evidently coming to a decision, turned to search through the desk. She came up with a roll of tape, pulled some out and tugged on it, and said, "This will do. Ililiel, sit right here." She pulled out the chair.

Ililiel swiveled an eye toward Yllyia, then back to LeAnne. LeAnne caught her meaning. "Do it," she said.

Ililiel sat down, and Yllyia taped her arms together behind her back, first the top pair, then the bottom, then both pairs to each other. She wadded up a piece of paper from the desk and stuck it in Ililiel's mouth, ran a piece of tape around her head to hold it in, and with the last of the tape bound her legs to the chair.

"Okay," Yllyia said, opening the window and sticking a foot through, "we go out this way."

"What about your friends?" asked Donivan.

"We'll have to leave them. They'll be all right; Ililiel can't do anything to them while we're loose. The important thing is to make sure we get away." She swung her other leg out and dropped to the ground.

Donivan climbed out behind her, but LeAnne couldn't leave Ililiel without a parting thought. She put the gun barrel between the alien's front two eyes and said, "I heard what you told Yllyia. You're right, we're dangerous. But we came here as friends the first time. You remember that."

She wished she could read Eyullelyan facial expressions, because she wanted to know for sure that her message had sunk in, but Ililiel betrayed no emotion that LeAnne could read.

"We'll be back," she promised, and with that she followed Donivan and Yllyia out the window.

"Where are we?" Donivan asked after they had put a couple of buildings behind them. He glanced back, but the darkness held no sign of pursuit. Not yet, at least, but they knew it wouldn't be long in coming.

"We're at the military base," Yllyia said. "It's just one end of the main airport, really. We don't have much of an army.

I never understood why we had one at all, but if Ililiel was telling the truth then now I know why."

"We heard. We've got to get back and warn the *Starchild*. Can you fly us there?"

"Yes, I can do that." Yllyia laughed, a long, fluting whistle of a laugh.

"What's so funny?"

"I'll show you," she said, leading the way toward another building at the end of the street. LeAnne and Donivan had to run to keep up with her, though she was barely jogging. She led them to a side door, reached in to flip on the light, and said, "There."

LeAnne wasn't sure what to expect. What she saw was a sleek, streamlined airplane that looked as if it was in flight just sitting there. It had two main wings that attached at the midpoint and swept back at a steep angle, with an enormous engine built into each one. Smaller wings stuck out from the engine pods below and behind the main set, and two vertical fins stuck up from the rear. Above and in front of the wings sat the cockpit, a clear bubble rising smoothly above the rest of the fuselage. Along the side was painted a white star in a black circle, with bars on either side. A bright yellow arrow with the word RESCUE printed boldly across it pointed to a depression beside the star. Though it probably meant "here's how you get the pilot out in an emergency," it still seemed somehow appropriate to their situation at the moment.

As they stared, Yllyia said, "It's a little project of mine. I found it nearly intact at an airfield in South Dakota about seven years ago, and I've been restoring it with scavenged parts ever since. I just got it flying last year. Like it?"

"I like it," Donivan said.

"So do I, even if I do have to squeeze to fit in. This little bugger is *fast*. Climb aboard—no, wait. Parachutes."

"Parachutes?" LeAnne said. "What for?"

"Just a precaution," Yllyia said as she climbed up a tiny ladder on the side of the plane, reached in, and pulled out two bulky cloth bundles with straps attached. "We won't need them, but you never fly a plane like this without a parachute.

It just isn't done." She climbed back down and handed the chutes to LeAnne and Donivan. "Wish I had some human ones," she said, "but I guess we can make these work."

A car sped by outside. Yllyia froze and listened until it had turned the corner and headed off toward the building where they had been held prisoner, then she turned back and helped LeAnne and Donivan into the parachutes. She had to knot the straps so they would be short enough, and one that was designed to fit under the second pair of arms had to go simply across the chest. The leg straps had to be wrapped twice around, but they eventually got them snug enough to hold the parachute on. Yllyia got one for herself from another airplane and strapped it on with practiced ease.

"Okay, now we're ready to fly. Climb in."

There were two seats, one behind the other, both modified to fit Eyullelyans. LeAnne climbed in first and sat in the back, and Donivan sat in the same seat in front of her. Yllyia showed them how to strap in, and how to hook their parachute rings so the ejection mechanism would open their chutes for them. Hooking two people in together took more adjusting, but finally when neither of them could move more than a few inches in any direction Yllyia was satisfied. She jumped back down and punched a button beside the hangar door that started it rising, leaving LeAnne in momentary panic at the thought of being stuck in the plane if pursuit should catch up with them now.

But there was nobody beyond the door. Yllyia climbed back up and into the front seat while it slid open, pushed the ladder away to clang onto the floor, and strapped herself in. As she pulled the canopy down she shouted "Clear!" and started the engines.

"It's a tradition," she shouted over the sudden noise. "Human pilots always did that, so when I fly this plane so do I."

LeAnne felt her whole body vibrate with the engines high-pitched, shrieking howl, and thought, *Anybody searching for us will have no trouble finding us now*. Yllyia let the plane roll forward out of the hangar while she checked the controls, three hands a blur of motion while the fourth thumbed down the checklist. LeAnne watched control surfaces on the wing moving up and down in response to Yllyia's commands. Beyond the right wing she saw two Eyullelyans appear around the corner of the next building down and begin running toward them.

"Yllyia."

"I see them." Yllyia dropped the checklist, aimed the plane down the expanse of concrete in front of the hangars, and said, "Hang on, and lean back in the seat. We're going to do this a little different than usual."

LeAnne turned her head to face forward and held onto Donivan. Yllyia pushed the engines slowly up the scale, holding on the brake until the howl was almost unbearable, then she released it and jammed the throttle full forward. The plane leaped ahead, snapping them back into the seats with sudden ferocity, streaked across the ground toward the astonished Eyullelyans, then lifted straight into the sky.

There was no turbulence this time; just the steady acceleration. LeAnne felt the G-force build, becoming even worse than the initial jolt. Donivan's weight was crushing the breath out of her, his parachute pressing into her rib cage while her own greatly multiplied weight made it still worse. She gasped for air and saw swirling lights before her that she knew weren't real. The shriek of the engines grew more distant with each second, but the pressure went on and on until, just as she was sure she would pass out, Yllyia eased off the throttle and slowly brought the nose down toward level.

LeAnne drew in a shuddering breath. She felt Donivan do the same. From the front seat Yllyia shouted, "Mach one, straight up! Did I tell you this thing was fast, or what?"

PART FOUR

Facing Reality

The moment of stunned silence stretched on and on. LeAnne tried to get her mind working again, but some part of her was still trying to catch up. She concentrated on the seat in front of her, taking deep breaths and forcing her eyes to focus.

Yllyia's head popped up over the seat, her hind eye open wide. She spoke toward the front, but her voice rang loud in the cockpit. "Are you all right back there?"

Donivan managed a nod. Between breaths LeAnne said, "Barely. Whoo! Why didn't you—no, I guess you—tried to warn us. I just—didn't realize what you were talking about."

Yllyia laughed. "Best airplane ever built, on my world or yours. Check this out." She ducked back down in her seat and banked the plane to the right, nosed it gently downward, then pulled up and banked left at the same time and held it while the world spun once around over their heads.

LeAnne was glad for the darkness; without the ground rushing past she could almost convince herself that they were sitting in a dimly lit chamber and watching shadows move on the walls, save for the changes in weight. Yllyia's maneuver had kept them pressed into their seats all the way around, but at the top of the arc they had been pretty light.

"I love it!" Yllyia said, leveling out again.

Donivan found his voice. "How long will it take us to get back to the *Starchild*?"

"That depends on where it is," Yllyia replied.

LeAnne couldn't suppress her first thought, that this was all an elaborate plot to get them to reveal the ship's location, but she rejected it immediately. Yllyia couldn't possibly be in with Ililiel and the Queen. What LeAnne and Donivan had heard from the air shafts couldn't have been staged. Still, after hearing what the other Eyullelyans planned, it was hard to reveal the *Starchild*'s location even to Yllyia.

The same train of thought had evidently crossed Donivan's mind. He hesitated, but finally said, "Not far from where you found us. Just into the mountains from there."

Yllyia calculated for a moment, then said, "Then it'll be about an hour and ten minutes at this speed, if we go straight for it. But maybe it would be better if your people met us somewhere out of the way so there'd be less chance of somebody tracking us there from orbit."

LeAnne looked up into the night sky, where from this altitude the stars shone without twinkling. She hadn't thought of that. Were they being watched even now?

"Uh, there's a problem with that," Donivan said.

"What problem?"

Donivan searched for words. LeAnne had to laugh at his discomfiture. To Yllyia she said, "Nobody on the ship knows we're out here."

"Nobody?" Yllyia asked. "You mean you didn't tell anybody you were going outside?"

"It's worse than that," LeAnne said. "They still think they're in space, about a thousand light-years from anything. We tried to tell them we were on Earth and they kicked us out the airlock for it. They think we're dead."

Yllyia stuck her head up over the seat again. "You're kidding, right?"

"I wish I was."

"Oh." Yllyia sank back down, and after a moment said

quietly, "Then I don't suppose you have anyplace to land a plane, do you?"

Donivan said, "We'll have to land out where it's flat and walk up to the ship."

"Not at night we won't. And not during the day either, with Ililiel and the army after us. If we leave this plane out in the open within walking distance of your ship we might as well leave a sign pointing straight to it." Yllyia cut back on the throttle. The plane slowed, shuddered for a second, and the engine noise became suddenly louder. They had just dropped below the speed of sound, LeAnne realized. Yllyia was buying time to think.

"Now let me make sure I've got this straight," Yllyia said. "The two of you are the only humans who even know that the Earth exists, much less that we Eyullelyans are here, right?"

"Right," LeAnne and Donivan said together.

"And the others already tried to kill you once for telling them something they didn't want to hear."

"Right," LeAnne said again.

"Then what are we going to accomplish by going back there now?"

"I don't know," LeAnne said. "Maybe nothing. But we have to warn them about Ililiel."

"If they don't want to believe they're on Earth, I don't see how they'll believe something worse."

Donivan laughed. "They'll believe us when they get a good look at you."

Yllyia sighed. "I was afraid you'd say that. Ililiel, I will pull your arms off one at a time for making me do this." The agony in her voice was unmistakable.

"What's the matter. Do what?"

"Ditch the plane. Damn, damn, damn! I was so hot to escape in it that I didn't even consider what we'd do with it once we got there."

LeAnne didn't like the sound of that. "When you say ditch the plane, you mean—"

"Bail out. Jump. Parachute down and let the plane crash somewhere else. Oh, why couldn't I have taken another plane?"

"I thought you said the parachutes were just a precaution."

"Well that's why you take precautions, so they'll be there when you need them. But if you've got a better idea I'm wide open for suggestions."

LeAnne realized that she didn't. If they were going to warn the *Starchild*'s crew, then Yllyia had to come along, and if Yllyia came along, then she would have to ditch the plane. No matter how she added it up it meant jumping.

"I'm sorry," she said.

"So am I. One moment of arrogant pride, and now this." Yllyia banked the plane in a long, sweeping curve to the left, then back to the right. "I'll never do it again."

Donivan cleared his throat. "Uh, maybe I could fly the plane back to Ventura while you and LeAnne—"

"Yes! That's—no. No, it won't work. Damn. You've never landed a plane."

"No," Donivan admitted. "But I bet I can do it. It can't be that hard."

"You'd be surprised. No, I'm not going to let you kill yourself trying to save an airplane."

Donivan looked out into the darkness. "You think jumping out is safer? I think I'd rather take my chances with the landing."

"It's safe," Yllyia said. "By the time we get there the moon will be up, and we'll gain an extra hour on it as we go east. We'll have plenty of light to see, and I'll set the autopilot to fly as far away as it can before it crashes. Maybe it'll keep Ililiel busy for a few days looking in the wrong place."

There was a quiet moment before she said, "Yeah. That's probably best anyway. Besides, it's a warplane; it's fitting that it goes down to save humanity from the bug-eyed monsters."

The mountains were a wrinkled expanse of shadow below. From a few thousand feet of altitude they looked much flatter than they really were, but with moonlight illuminating them in sharp relief they looked rugged all the same. LeAnne hoped that Yllyia wouldn't miscalculate and send them down among the peaks.

The plain beyond the mountains drew closer. Yllyia had throttled down to just above stall speed, but to LeAnne it still seemed incredibly fast. And they were going to jump out at this speed! She shuddered and watched a silvery glimmer creep into view behind a mountain a little to the right of their path: Lake DeSmet.

"Get ready," Yllyia said.

LeAnne tightened her grip on the eject handle, the other arm snug around Donivan. They both faced forward, eyes closed, waiting nervously.

"Do we really want to do this?" he asked.

"No," she answered, truthfully.

"I didn't think so. Yllyia—"

"Remember, count to three, then eject!" Yllyia shouted, and at the same time she blew the canopy. Cold wind rushed in and pulled at them and the airplane lurched downward, then righted as Yllyia pulled it back into line. It was too late to change plans now. LeAnne counted slowly to three, then held tight to Donivan and pulled the eject handle.

A terrific explosion kicked her upward, and suddenly she was in free fall, wind screaming past and tearing her breath away. The seat separated from them with another kick and they began to tumble. She forgot to let go of Donivan, but it didn't matter; the wind snatched him away from her and she was tumbling alone.

The wind sucked the heat from her arms and legs almost instantly. Her hair was whipping and snapping and tangling around her face and neck, and she still couldn't breathe. She lifted a hand toward her face, thinking maybe she could scoop up some air with it, but before she could try it a still worse jolt spun her around and yanked her backward into the sky.

As suddenly as it had hit, the wind was gone. LeAnne swung gently back and forth in absolute darkness, but as the blood began to flow to her head again her night vision returned and she could see the moonlit mountains below her. She pulled the knot of hair away from her face and looked up. Her parachute was a gigantic patch of blackness blocking the stars overhead, with the moon shining brightly beneath it.

The familiar shriek of engines grew steadily fainter. In the distance LeAnne heard Yllyia cursing in Eyullelyan, her voice surprisingly clear in the night air.

"Donivan?" LeAnne shouted.

His voice sounded very close. "Here."

She twisted around, but couldn't see him.

"Where?"

"Above you. The top of your parachute is just to my left. Are you all right?"

"I think so. How about you?"

"I bit my tongue when the parachute opened, but other than that I think I'm okay. If I don't freeze to death."

"Yeah. Yllyia? Yllyia!"

"LeAnne?"

LeAnne looked toward the voice and saw a white hemisphere quite a ways off, descending faster than she was. "Now what?" she shouted.

"Nothing. Just fall. Keep your knees bent, and roll when you hit the ground. You won't hit hard; you don't weigh half as much as what the chute was designed for."

LeAnne looked down again. Yllyia's aim had been perfect. The river was a line of black dusted with silver flowing out of the mountains directly beneath her. She and Donivan would land practically at the base of the last mountain. Yllyia would be a little farther out; evidently she had ejected late.

"What if we land in the water?" Donivan shouted. His voice was getting further above now.

"If it looks like you're going to, pull on the lines in the direction you want to go. You'll slip sideways. Try not to land in the trees, either."

LeAnne reached over her head and gave an experimental tug on the lines, but she was still too high up to tell if it had any effect. Her hands were so cold she could barely hang on anyway. She tucked them in her armpits and shivered her way down.

The view was impressive, though, and despite the cold LeAnne was beginning to feel a rush of exhilaration. She'd just bailed out of an airplane and lived!

She was turning as she descended, so she got a panoramic view. The tree-covered mountains didn't reflect much; they were a jagged-topped wall of shadow to one side, but to the other side the hills stretched away like a soft blanket all the way to the horizon. She thought she might be able to see a hint of curvature out there, but it might have been her imagination. Between the horizon and her parachute the stars were cold, hard points of brilliance, except where the moon outshone even them.

She could hear the river below her. She looked down and watched it grow closer, expanding, moving off to the side. Her turning made it hard to tell whether she was going to hit to the north or south of it, but she finally decided south. Not good. The road was on the north. She was already cold enough; she didn't want to have to wade across the river as well.

It was behind her now. She waited until it was off to her left, then pulled the lines on that side until she had spun halfway around, then pulled on the right side. The water slid back until it was directly beneath her and she had to switch again. Her arms began to ache, and details on the ground came up at her, expanding, accelerating! She yowled and pulled frantically on the lines.

The water swung past. Her feet brushed a treetop, but she kicked free and pulled her feet up in time to hit the ground with her legs flexed, roll over backward, and come to a stop on her side.

She sat up, lines tangled all around her, and watched the parachute collapse.

"I made it," she whispered. She looked up and saw a patch of darkness slide across the stars. "Donivan, I made it! I'm down!"

"I wish I could say the same," he shouted. "Space, I'm headed right for a tree-eee!"

There came a swish and crash of branches breaking. A

moment of silence, then, "Wonderful. Can you help me out of here?"

Yllyia appeared like a ghost out of the night, her parachute wrapped around her for warmth as she followed the river back toward the mountains.

"There you are," she said when she spotted LeAnne and Donivan, similarly clothed, walking downstream toward her. "It looks like you're both intact."

"More or less," Donivan said. "How about you?"

"Fine. Should we find a place to sleep until morning?"

LeAnne laughed. "Not for me. After that I don't think I'll ever sleep again."

"Me either," Donivan agreed. "Besides, we should get back to the ship as soon as we can. We don't know how much time we have."

Yllyia nodded. "That is true. Very well. The moonlight is certainly bright enough to light our way. Lead on."

Nocturnal animals scurried out of their path as they strode through the grass toward the base of the mountain. Once they approached a solitary grazing deer only to have it stamp and whistle in alarm, and a herd of at least fifty more rose up out of the grass and bounded gracefully away, white tails flashing like signal flags. The grass was matted down in individual depressions where they had been sleeping, and the ground steamed from their warmth.

They found the raised line of ground that had been the road and turned to follow it, and soon they were among the trees again. The forest was all shades of silver and shadow, and as LeAnne walked through it she remembered fantasies about moonlight and enchanted forests full of elves and dwarves and stranger creatures. Suddenly, looking from Donivan to Yllyia, she burst into laughter.

"What's funny?" they both asked.

"You don't want to know." She would say no more, but for the rest of the night she kept an eye out for hobbits, and magicians in tall, pointed hats.

*   *   *

They were already a good distance up the mountain face by the time the eastern sky began to glow with the first light of day. Morning came on fast, and within an hour the sun had cleared the horizon. At one of the many stream crossings Yllyia declared a break for breakfast and began looking about for likely candidates.

"We should be able to find something around here," she said, moving toward a cluster of thorny bushes loaded with knobby red berries. "Ah, here we go. Perfect. Dig in." She began to pick with all four hands, denuding a whole bush in seconds.

Berries? LeAnne thought. She'd have sworn that with those teeth the Eyullelyans would be carnivorous. Interesting.

She picked one for herself and examined it suspiciously, remembering the warning in the survival kit's plant book about poisonous berries, but she couldn't remember which ones the book had said were safe and which weren't. This one was small, about as big as the end of a finger, and made up of dozens of easily crushed bulbs filled with a sticky red fluid. Tiny hairs covered the berry's surface, giving it a fuzzy feeling.

"Are you sure these are safe?" she asked.

"Raspberries? Sure. I eat them all the time when I'm out on a dig."

"That doesn't really mean a whole lot, though, does it? I mean, our metabolism could be completely different."

"It is," Yllyia admitted, "but humans used to eat these too. I've studied your eating habits."

"Oh. Sure, I guess you would. Well, if you say it's okay..." LeAnne shrugged, and popped the berry into her mouth. She was prepared for something sour and awful, which made the sudden flood of sweetness even more overwhelming. "Wow!" she said. "Hey Donivan, these are great!"

"I know," he said from behind her. She turned and saw him already eating from a bush of his own. "I don't argue with an empty stomach," he said with a grin.

Paranoia, LeAnne thought. *You never know when it's appropriate*.

They stretched while they ate, Donivan wincing with the cuts and bruises he had received from his meeting with a tree. "What a night," he said. "I don't think I'd mind if we never did that again."

"Nor would I," Yllyia said quietly.

"I bet. Where, uh, do you suppose the airplane, uh . . . ?"

"I don't know. I set the autopilot to fly due east at a constant eight thousand feet, but I know it didn't have enough fuel to make it to the Atlantic. Maybe the Great Lakes."

LeAnne remembered seeing the Atlantic Ocean in the atlas. "You wanted it to come down in the water?"

"It's a cleaner death," Yllyia said. "I don't think there are any mountains that high between here and there; maybe it made it."

"Maybe."

Yllyia exhaled loudly. "At any rate, it's gone, and we can't do anything more about it now. We should decide what our next move should be. What do we intend to do when we reach your *Starchild*?"

"Tell the crew where they are," LeAnne said. "And then get ready to fight Ililiel, I guess."

"If she was telling me the truth, then we'll probably be fighting a bomb delivered from orbit. I don't see how we could defend against that."

Donivan looked thoughtful. "From orbit. Your colony ship?"

"Yes. The *Lyrili-Hloo*. We use it for a space station now, but if the original colonists really did bring bombs with them then I imagine they're still on board."

"Hmm. How many people—uh, Eyullelyans—are up there?"

"Not many. Sixteen or thirty-two. The ship is mostly suspended animation chambers. Why do you ask?"

Those were strange numbers to just toss out like that, LeAnne thought. But then she realized why: Yllyia had four fingers on each hand, and sixteen and thirty-two were round numbers in hexadecimal.

Donivan looked to LeAnne, blushed, and said, "Just a

thought. I want to check it with the computer before I say anything. It'll probably have a better idea anyway."

Yllyia showed her surprise. "You have an intelligent computer?"

Donivan smiled. "Pretty close. It doesn't really think, but it can correlate information and sort through its memories for responses so fast that it sometimes seems like it."

"Is it self-aware?"

"That depends on how you mean it. It controls just about everything on the ship, so it has a kind of body awareness, but as far as abstract thought goes I don't think it could ever come up with something like 'I think, therefore I am' on its own. But we keep working on it."

"It screwed with my SHAPE test all by itself," LeAnne said.

"Shape test?" Yllyia asked.

LeAnne described the education system and how she had tried to become a drive engineer. As she talked about it she realized how far away it all seemed to her now, as if she were separated from it by more than just time. SHAPE tests and all the other shipboard problems seemed like part of a completely different life, a different dimension that she had crossed through when she stepped out the airlock. She felt a momentary pang of loss at the realization, but when she looked up at the trees around her and felt the sunlight on her skin the feeling faded. What she had gained more than outweighed the loss.

Except for her hair brush. She would give up a lot to get that back. She'd been pulling tangles out of her hair all night, and it was still a mess.

Yllyia was fascinated by the details of life on the *Starchild*. She kept up an endless string of questions while they finished their breakfast and, folding up the parachutes to carry, headed on up the mountain.

"I would have thought you'd have noticed the rotational effect from the Earth's spin," she said at one point. "Surely that should have suggested to you that you weren't in space."

LeAnne had been daydreaming as she walked, wondering

if the light-headedness she felt was from the raspberries or simply from lack of sleep and delayed reaction from yesterday's excitement, but Yllyia's question brought her to a sudden halt. "What did you say?" she asked.

"I said I would have thought the rotational effects of the Earth's spin would—"

"Of the Earth's spin?"

"Yes. You get a twisting effect when something moves from place to place across the surface of a rotating planet. It's a very small force, but it produces some large-scale effects that you should have been able to observe even inside your *Starchild*. Water swirling in a drain, for instance, or the plane of movement of a pendulum moving around in a circle. It's hard to believe you wouldn't notice it."

The look on Donivan's face was priceless, but LeAnne supposed her own expression mirrored his. "*Notice* it?" she said. "We had it pointed out to us, as proof that we *were* in space. The ship's moving in a spiral, they told us. That's why we haven't disappeared off the edge of the universe after a thousand years of acceleration. We even did school projects to determine the sweep of the spiral for ourselves. Forty-five and a half degrees."

"Our present latitude," Yllyia said.

"Our what?"

"Our latitude. Your measurements were correct, and even your conclusion, in a sense. We are forty-five and a half degrees around the curve of the planet from the North Pole, spiraling through space as it rotates."

LeAnne tried to picture it in her mind. It fit. Oh, but it had fit so well the other way too!

"What is reality?" she asked, and with a burst of laughter she resumed walking up the mountain.

Behind her Yllyia said, "But forty-five and a half degrees of spin angle still wouldn't be enough to keep you within the known universe after a thousand years of acceleration. You'd still be getting oh, say half a gravity of thrust straight ahead after you canceled out the amount lost in the spin, wouldn't you?"

"That's true," Donivan said, "but it got a lot more complex than that. The forty-five degree spin was the most prominent, but there was a long-period component of twenty-three and a half degrees that added to it—"

"Oh, of course," Yllyia said. "Earth's own axial tilt in its motion about the sun."

"Earth's . . . right. And there were theories about some *really* long-term stuff we couldn't measure, stuff due to our motion around the galaxy and precession of the spin axis and so on— but it all added up to keep us moving comfortably slower than the speed of light. Still too fast to let us go outside the ship, of course, but not fast enough to make time dilation a big consideration." Donivan chuckled. "It's easy to make the data fit the facts when you know the facts. We *knew* we were on a spaceship, and we *knew* we were accelerating at one gee and spinning at the same time. Nobody could question that. Nobody even thought to."

"No, I don't suppose they would," Yllyia admitted.

They're going to have to now, LeAnne thought. And with that thought came more than just a little apprehension at going back inside. She didn't feel ready to face the crew again.

Donivan seemed happy enough to be going back. LeAnne could see his viewpoint too. He hadn't spent most of his life dreaming about Earth, and he'd had his share of unpleasant experiences outside. His skin was starting to peel off where he had been sunburned and he was sore all over from his bruises, and even though his hand seemed to be healed after the porcupine, he no doubt remembered that too. Small wonder if he looked forward to getting back inside where it was safe.

He'd feel differently when they started their colony. They would do it right this time, make sure they had the right equipment and knew what they were doing. LeAnne decided that she could benefit from a week or two in the ship herself, doing research on house-building and farming and the myriad other things that a colony leader needed to know. She undoubtedly knew more about planetary living than anyone else on the ship, but now that she had been out once she realized that her knowledge was far from complete.

But over those plans hung the uncertainty of Ililiel. They might not have *time* to do it right. Unless they could think of a way to prevent her attack they would have to evacuate the ship completely and leave it for her to bomb. She tried to think of alternatives. The computer would probably have a better idea than anything she could come up with, but it couldn't hurt to try. She hated depending on the computer for anything.

They reached the ship in mid-afternoon. Yllyia's day-old *lyshl* had evaporated from the heat long since, but she had substituted a wet parachute for the cooling garment and was puffing along beneath that, her face almost sky-blue from the exertion. They were walking the last few hundred yards to the airlock when Donivan stopped suddenly, bent over, and plucked one of the yellow flowers that grew in abundance wherever the forest let in enough light. He held it out to LeAnne.

"What's that for?" she asked in surprise.

"To remind you of outside," he said.

LeAnne took it and twirled it in her hand, blushing. She smelled the light fragrance of the petals and felt herself falling in love all over again.

"Oh, Donivan."

"You were kind of quiet. I thought maybe that was why."

She couldn't think of anything to say to that, so she put her arms around him and kissed him.

After a long moment she became aware of Yllyia watching them intently.

"Aren't humans silly?" she said, laughing.

Yllyia laughed too. "Yes," she said simply.

LeAnne found a convenient tangle in her hair beside her ear and stuck the flower through it. "There," she said. "Okay, I'm ready now. Let's go on in."

Yllyia had to drop down onto her lower hands to fit in the airlock. LeAnne and Donivan climbed up beside her, and

Donivan was about to cycle it when LeAnne noticed something different.

"Somebody's been in here," she said. "The survival kit is gone."

Donivan turned to look in the corner where they had left it. "So it is. And so are the spacesuit legs that you cut off. Security must have been cleaning up after the execution."

"I wonder what they thought?"

Donivan laughed. "Good question. We'll ask the computer. You ready?"

"I guess."

"Yllyia?"

"Ready. And eager."

"Right. Well, welcome aboard." Donivan pushed the cycle button and the outer door swung closed, cutting off the sunlight and plunging them into darkness while their eyes adjusted to the artificial lighting. After a moment's pause, the inner door opened on more dimly lit corridor.

"Has it always been this dark in here?" Donivan asked.

LeAnne looked at the ceiling. All the lights were on. "I think so," she said.

"Wow. I guess you get used to anything after a while."

"Evidently."

They moved out into the corridor. After the heat outside, the ship's steady seventy degrees seemed cold. Yllyia dropped her parachute and stood up, her head only an inch or so from the ceiling.

"We ought to get you a helmet," LeAnne said. "You're going to be cracking your head on everything."

"I'll be careful," Yllyia said. "I'm used to exploring human dwellings."

"Oh. Right."

Donivan led the way down to the communications room, where they found the survival kit and the sliced-off spacesuit legs piled in a corner. "That's weird," he said. "Why dump it here?"

LeAnne couldn't think of a good reason. A security cleanup crew certainly wouldn't have done that. But who else would have been up on the restricted decks? It probably didn't matter, but it bothered her.

Donivan turned on the computer. He keyed in his access code, fumbled once and cursed, but got it on the second try. He shook his head. "I can't believe it; I'm out of practice already." He keyed in a request for voice, then said, "Hello computer. We're back."

"Excellent," the computer replied. "Please wait while I enter logic mode. Loading . . . okay. What did you find?"

"Aliens," Donivan said proudly. "We brought one back with us. Yllyia, say hello."

Yllyia hesitated, then said, "Hello? Um, pleased to meet you."

The computer was silent for a long moment. When it finally responded, it said, "Insufficient data. By alien do you mean of extraterrestrial origin?"

"Yes. We call ourselves Eyullelyans."

"Please wait . . ."

Donivan laughed. "This has to be a first. The computer hasn't got any experience to draw on. It's probably loading every backup memory it ever stored, trying to find anything close to instructions for something like—"

"Direct correlation failed. Probability indicates that I should bid you welcome. Please excuse me if I am incorrect."

"Welcome is correct," Donivan said with a chuckle.

"Then Yllyia, I welcome you to Earth. Donivan, I need more information. Please continue your report."

Donivan described their meeting with Yllyia, the flight to Ventura, and the subsequent trouble with Ililiel. "We're not sure what to do about that. Yllyia says they'll probably try to bomb us from orbit, which doesn't leave us with a lot of options. I had a—".

"Wait," the computer interrupted. "Wait . . . wa—"

The voice died, along with the lights.

Into the darkness, Donivan whispered, "Uh oh."

"What happened?" Yllyia asked.

"I think we overloaded its logic mode. Wow. I didn't think you could do that."

The lights flickered back on for a second, then died again.

"Evidently you can," LeAnne said. "What's happening to the lights?"

"I think it's a general system failure. That'll take out power distribution, communications, the whole works. Aaagh, vacuum. I should have realized what was happening. It must have kept loading more and more memory looking for correlations until it wrote over something vital."

"How could that happen? That doesn't sound like good programming."

"It isn't. But every program has a bug in it somewhere. Logic mode is supposed to allocate memory according to priority, but I bet nobody ever gave it an upper limit. We handed it a problem where logic mode was essential to ship's survival, so the priority was just as high as maintaining ship's functions. When it needed the memory space it wiped out its own control systems and crashed."

"That doesn't sound good."

"It isn't. It'll take hours for the techs to figure out what happened, and even longer to fix it."

The lights flickered back on and held.

Despite her feelings about depending on the computer, LeAnne felt a flood of relief. "You were saying?"

"Give it a minute. I bet they just reloaded the primary control program. When it starts loading its memories it'll kick right back into logic mode and crash again. Damn, I should be telling them what happened while I have the chance!" Donivan turned to the keyboard, but the power went out again before he could log in.

"Entropy! We'll have to go downship to the computer center and tell them."

LeAnne reached out for the wall and leaned back against it. She felt more secure touching something than standing isolated in the dark. "I think we should go downship," she said, "but not necessarily to the computer center. I think it's more important to tell the crew about Earth and the Eyullelyans."

"I don't," Donivan said. "Without the computer to back

us up we'd be going from person to person saying essentially, 'Everything you know is wrong.' Remember what happened last time we tried that?"

"We've got Yllyia this time," LeAnne pointed out.

At the mention of her name, Yllyia said, "Perhaps we can do both. Couldn't we work our way toward the computer room, spreading the news as we go?"

"I suppose we could," Donivan admitted.

"Then let's do it," LeAnne said. "Come on." She felt her way to the door and stepped into the corridor.

She heard the click as Donivan turned off the terminal, and Yllyia said, "Shouldn't there be emergency power for electrical failures?"

"There probably is," she replied. "But the batteries are a thousand years old. This deck hasn't seen maintenance since the Original Crew."

"Ah."

"Emergency Supplies still has lasers," Donivan said. "We can use those for light."

"Good idea. You lead."

Donivan moved past her and led off toward the hub, around the circular connecting corridor, and back up another radial one. He stopped at a door on the left. "I think this is it. Where's the manual open—ah, there." There was a sound of the door sliding aside.

Donivan stepped inside. "If I remember right, they're about here." He brushed against something that made a soft clunk against the wall. "Got it. Watch your eyes."

LeAnne turned away, and a bright yellow light lit up the interior of the room. Shadows wobbled as Donivan picked up two more lasers and handed them out.

"You'd better show me how this works," Yllyia said, holding hers carefully by the grip.

"Push in on the barrel and twist counterclockwise," LeAnne said, demonstrating. "When you let go it pops out and locks in place so you can't bump it to a different setting. Then just pull the trigger."

"I see." Yllyia shined her light around, trying different

grips until she found a comfortable hold with two fingers curled around either side of the handle.

"Should we take stunners too?" Donivan asked.

"Damn right," LeAnne said. No way was she going back among the crew without stunners, even with Yllyia along. They might not have any trouble, but then again they might.

Donivan produced three stunners, and LeAnne instructed Yllyia in their use as well. "There's nothing to focus; you just point and shoot. It's got a wide beam, so it's not too accurate, but you don't have to be. It just puts people to sleep for a while. If you've got to shoot somebody, use the stunner."

"This is impressive," Yllyia said. "We have nothing like it. I wonder if it will work on a Eyullelyan?"

LeAnne nodded. "I shot one of your six-winged creatures with one when it attacked Donivan, and it went down, so I imagine it'd work on you too. Be careful with it."

"I will. I hope that I will not have to use it at all."

"Me too. I guess we're ready. Shall we go?"

The computer center was on deck seventy-three. With the computer down, the elevators were not working either, which meant that they had a long descent ahead of them down the stairways. After climbing all the way up the mountain already that morning, the idea of seventy-two flights down didn't seem impossible; just painful. LeAnne was ready for that. What she hadn't counted on was the noise.

As soon as they got into the stairwell they heard a muted roaring that grew louder as they descended, until when they came to the door between restricted deck three and the first open deck they realized what it was: People. Deck after deck of people talking, cursing, and shouting as they pushed and trampled their way up and down the stairs, until their cries all blended into a single rush of sound.

Deck four landing was practically deserted compared to the noise coming from below. LeAnne looked through the narrow window in the door and saw maybe a dozen people on the other side, all talking excitedly with each other. They looked like business people. It made sense; deck four was office space.

Comparing notes, LeAnne thought. *Yes, the computer's down on our deck too*. But at least they had light. Two emergency spotlights shone down the stairwell from a battery box on the wall.

Seeing the well-dressed women made her suddenly realize how awful she must look. Tangled hair, torn uniform, dirty ... But she couldn't do anything about it so there was no point in worrying about it. "Well, here goes," she said, and pushed open the door.

She'd been wondering what she would say when the moment came, but as she stepped out onto the landing and every face turned toward her, she realized that she hadn't reached a decision among the half-dozen opening lines she'd thought of. She saw recognition in a few faces, no doubt from her notoriety as the atavistic saboteur executed just a few days ago, and decided on the simple approach.

She put on a smile and said, "Hi, I'm LeAnne Evans. I'm back from outside." Though nobody there was saying anything, she had to shout to be heard over the noise from below.

Donivan stepped through the door behind her. Still nobody moved or spoke.

LeAnne said, "This is Donivan Hayes. I'm sure you heard that we went out the airlock." No need to mention why. "Well, we want to show you what we found out there."

She turned and nodded toward the door just as Yllyia bent down to pass through.

"Hello," Yllyia said, standing straight again. "I am Yllyia. Pleased to meet you." The door swung closed behind her and latched.

Two or three people edged away, and one who had just come up from below turned and clattered back down the way he had come, but the rest stood fast. LeAnne breathed a sigh of relief. She'd half expected them all to scream and run.

As quickly as she could, she told them what had happened to her and Donivan during their days outside.

Yllyia's presence had hypnotized her audience. They stood

spellbound, entranced, but as LeAnne tried to get a response from them she thought maybe catatonic was more the word to describe them. If it took this long to get through to them on every deck, she and Donivan and Yllyia would never get to the computer center. Finally she stopped and asked, "Do you understand what I'm telling you?"

A girl, about seventeen by her looks, her eyes wide with astonishment, nodded.

LeAnne focused on her. "Good. Look, we have to go on downship. You spread the news on this deck, okay?"

The girl nodded again.

LeAnne looked to the rest of them. "You people help her. Back up her story. Tell everybody you—oh space. Catch her!"

LeAnne's shout shook the rest of them out of their trance, but too late to save the girl from hitting the floor. LeAnne bent over her and stretched her out flat while she sent someone else for a wet towel to lay across her forehead.

"Is she dead?" Yllyia asked.

"No, she just fainted," LeAnne said.

Donivan looked down the stairwell. "We don't have *time* for this," he said.

"You're right." LeAnne stood. To the others she said, "She'll be okay. Remember what I told you, and spread the word. Let's go. Yllyia?"

Yllyia was still looking down at the girl. "You're sure she will be all right?"

"I'm sure. I almost fainted when I saw you myself. Come on." LeAnne followed Donivan down the stairs. Behind her she heard Yllyia say, "I am sorry."

"Yllyia, come on!"

It got worse instead of better. The further down they went, the more crowded the stairways became, and the stronger the reaction to Yllyia. On deck five the person who had glimpsed her and run down from deck four had organized an ambush, and they had to stun their way past a mob bent on killing them with shoes, book readers, and anything else they could find to throw.

On deck six someone screamed and started a panic that spread before them all the way to deck ten, where they met with another mob, this time led by a security guard. He was a little too quick to fire, probably not suspecting that his targets also had stunners, and Donivan was able to spray his own beam before him as he fell, his legs suddenly numb from the knees down. He lay on the tenth floor landing among his inert attackers, rubbing his legs and cursing.

"This isn't working," LeAnne said as she heard someone scream "Alien invasion!" on the deck below.

"I'd have never guessed," Donivan said.

"Perhaps we should rethink our strategy," Yllyia said, twisting to dodge a paperweight thrown from above. It smashed on the wall beside Donivan and sprayed glass over the entire landing.

"We come in peace!" Yllyia shouted, and LeAnne winced. Yllyia could get a lot of volume out of that big chest of hers. But a shower of missiles proved how well her shout had been received.

"Maybe we should go back up and wait until the computer comes on line again," LeAnne said. "Then we can make a shipwide announcement."

Donivan said, "Wonderful idea, but the door's locked, and it won't take an access code unless the computer is monitoring it."

As if in response to his statement, the regular lights flickered on, and the emergency spotlights went out. Cheers rose from the decks around them, and LeAnne said, "All *right*. Yllyia, can you carry Donivan?"

"Easily."

"Good. Then let's get back where it's safe before it crashes again."

"No!" Donivan said. "The elevators will be working again— let's go on down to the computer center."

"I don't know what good we'll do there, especially if we have to stun the techs."

"We won't. They know me."

LeAnne tried to weigh the choices. The computer could crash and strand them in the elevator before they got where they were going, but she supposed that was no worse than being stranded on deck one while they waited for someone else to fix it. And they wouldn't be shot at in the elevator.

"Okay," she said. "The elevator it is." She helped Yllyia pick up Donivan and opened the door to deck ten.

The crew's reaction as they rushed past toward the elevator was much more calm than LeAnne expected. Wide-eyed astonishment, yes, but at least they weren't attacking. It wasn't until she looked back and saw Donivan slumped in Yllyia's arms, dirty and covered with cuts and bruises, eyes closed, that she understood why. Of course nobody attacked someone carrying the injured. Not even an alien.

"Emergency!" she shouted, trying to hide her grin. "Clear the corridor. Hold that elevator!"

The man who had called it obligingly held it open for her. She stood aside to let Yllyia carry Donivan in, then said, "Thanks," and stepped in herself.

"What . . . ?" he asked faintly.

"Her name's Yllyia, and she's on our side. Spread the word." LeAnne punched 73 on the keypad and the door slid closed.

She automatically tucked her feet into the grips, but Yllyia didn't realize she needed to. She whooped in surprise when the car dropped, but before LeAnne could pull her down she had already transferred Donivan to her lower pair of arms and pushed herself down with the upper ones.

"Sorry," LeAnne said. "I should have warned you."

"That's all right. One should expect free fall from time to time on a starship." Yllyia hooted in laughter.

Donivan, his eyes open now, joined in.

Deceleration pressed them to the floor for a second, then suddenly doubled, forcing LeAnne to her knees.

"What the—"

"Computer's down again," Donivan said.

The elevator came to a shuddering halt, but the light remained on. LeAnne wondered why, then realized that the elevators had to be self-contained in transit. They ran from batteries all the time, and recharged when they stopped at a deck. The computer was only responsible for controlling traffic in the tubes, but without that control they couldn't move.

"Now what?" she said.

"We wait until they get it on line again and go on down." He shifted his weight. "I'm starting to feel my legs again. Let me try putting some weight on them."

Yllyia set him down, holding her hands to either side of him until she was sure he could stand on his own. He stamped his feet and grimaced. "Wow. Worse than having an arm go to sleep at a movie." He grinned up at Yllyia. "Nothing like getting shot at by the people you came here to save, is there?"

Yllyia whistled her agreement. "It occurs to me that we would do better if the people with the guns were on our side."

"Yeah, if we could convince Security we'd have it made. But doing that's going to be hard even with the computer backing us up."

"You know," LeAnne said, "there'll probably be guards all around the computer too."

Donivan frowned. "I hadn't thought of that, but you're probably right. Entropy. They'll probably shoot as soon as they see us, too."

"Maybe not you," she said. "Yllyia and I are the ones who stand out."

Donivan looked down at himself. "And I don't?"

"Not as Donivan Hayes. You look about ten years older than you usually do, and about four shades redder. In fact you look like somebody who just lost a fight. If you went in alone you could probably get past them with a story about how you got trampled in the stairway."

"And what would you do?"

"I've got an idea that might get Security on our side. When the computer comes up again, the intercoms will work again, won't they?"

"Yeah. There'll probably be a million calls tying them up, though. What do you have in mind?"

LeAnne smiled. "A little demonstration down at the star-drive."

"What demonstration?"

"I think we've been going about this wrong. We've been trying to tell people we're on Earth, but their belief in the ship is too strong to let them believe us. What we need to do is shake their belief in the starship, and *then* tell them about Earth."

"And how does the stardri—Oh. Right. Ha *ha*. I like it. But wait; do you remember the code sequence to get in?"

"You think I'd forget something like that?"

"No, I suppose not."

Yllyia could hold her curiosity no longer. "What stardrive are you talking about? We're underground!"

"Precisely," LeAnne said, laughing.

The elevator lurched into motion again. "Okay," Donivan said, "here we go. Good luck."

"Same to you," LeAnne said to him.

They began to decelerate almost immediately, and within a few seconds the elevator connected with the deck. Donivan was out the door as soon as it opened, saying, "Emergency, take the next elevator," and LeAnne punched the door-close button before anyone could get a good look inside. She keyed in 440, the stardrive deck, and she and Yllyia were in free-fall again.

She laughed at the thought of all the times she had punched for deck 441, only to hear the computer respond with "Restricted access to that deck. Please enter your access code or re-key your destination." Restricted, ha. More like non-existent.

The drop seemed to take forever while LeAnne waited for the computer to crash and strand them again, but she knew that they couldn't fall for more than ten seconds before the deceleration coils cut in no matter how high they started. She'd timed it once, as everyone did at some time in their childhood.

Weight settled onto them gradually this time, and it took

a full thirty seconds before they connected with the deck and
the doors opened to empty corridor. The stardrive still roared
with the sound of immense power around them.

"Hold the elevator," LeAnne said to Yllyia. "I want to
make damn sure I can get the door open before I call Security
down here."

"Very well." Yllyia held a hand in the doorway.

She sprinted down to the drive room door, keyed in the
access code on the lock panel, and shouted in triumph as the
door began to slide open. The noise level rose higher.

She ran back to the elevator. "Okay!" she said. "Now we
kick this plan into action." She turned the volume up all the
way on the elevator's intercom to compensate for the noise
of the drive, and punched repeatedly at the 5. It was the first
time she had ever done that, she realized, though it had been
drilled into her from childhood. *Punch fives for Security,
because fives look like little Ss.*

She sweated out almost a full minute before they answered,
waiting for the computer to crash all the while, but eventually
a voice answered, "Security, Foster speaking."

LeAnne spoke loudly: "This is LeAnne Evans, calling from
deck four-forty. That's four four zero. I have taken control
of the stardrive, and in about ten minutes I'm going to arrange
a little demonstration. I strongly suggest that all available
Security personnel gather in front of the stardrive chamber.
Do you copy?"

"LeAnne Evans is dead. Get off the 'com, mutant."

LeAnne realized too late that she should have used a video
intercom. She thought frantically for some way she could
convince the dispatcher that she was for real, but all she could
think of was, "Ask the people on deck four, portside, if I'm
dead, and then get your people down here. You don't want
to miss what's coming." At least one person there would
attest that she was alive, but whether or not Security would
believe her was anybody's guess. She turned off the 'com
before he could reply and turned to Yllyia. "Well, whether
anybody comes or not, we promised them a show. We might
as well get set up."

* * *

Ten minutes later they were both shifting back and forth in impatience while the drive steadily battered at their senses. They waited in the doorway, Yllyia just inside and LeAnne leaning against the jamb, watching along the corridor toward the elevator and out toward the perimeter and the stairways. The computer had crashed and come back on line again while they waited, but still no one had shown up by either route. The drive had remained on despite the crash.

"Security," LeAnne said with disdain. "They never show up when you need them."

Yllyia laughed. LeAnne joined her, but stopped suddenly when the elevator door swished open and a single security guard stepped out. *Decoy*, she thought, and immediately turned to face the guards she knew would be rushing her from the outer junction, but there was nobody there.

One guard? She couldn't believe it. She told them she had taken over the stardrive and they sent one guard? But it was evidently all they were going to get, and one was better than none. She waited for him to approach, his stunner drawn and aimed. When he got close enough to hear her she shouted, "Glad you could make it. I'd almost given up."

The guard lowered his stunner. "It *is* you. You're alive!"

LeAnne recognized him. He was the same guard who had intervened at their execution when the captain had wanted to throw two corpses out the lock. She grinned. "Thanks to you."

"Is Donivan . . . did he . . . ?"

"He's still alive too," LeAnne said. "You want to know how we did it?"

"I do."

"All right." LeAnne nodded to Yllyia, out of sight beyond the door. "Prepare for free fall," she said.

Yllyia pushed the single, prominent button just inside the door, the one that LeAnne and Donivan had missed their first time in the drive chamber. The one marked OFF.

Silence descended on drive deck for the first time in a millennium.

LeAnne sighed in disappointment. Her big moment as a drive engineer, spent on an audience of one. There would be no repeat performance, for the simple reason that they could not find another switch anywhere marked ON. Once off, the drive evidently remained off.

In the corridor, the guard did the one thing that LeAnne had not anticipated: He threw back his head and laughed.

It was not the sort of laugh that invites joining in. Not quite hysterical, it was the laugh of someone who has had an incredible burden lifted without warning. He brought it under control with visible effort, but he couldn't stop smiling.

"I knew it!" he said. "You were telling the truth. I was *that* close to going out after you. I was in the airlock with my finger on the button, but I couldn't bring myself to push it. What would I have found if I had?"

LeAnne suddenly knew who had moved the survival kit from the airlock. She squinted and read the name on his badge: Deinar Jennings, the same one who had surprised her and Donivan in the control room with his prowling around on restricted decks. So that's why he'd been up there.

"You'd have found Earth," she said simply. "And something else. Can you handle another shock?"

"I think so."

"I want you to be sure."

He straightened. "I can handle it."

"All right, then. Yllyia, come on out." LeAnne stepped out into the corridor, and Yllyia moved into view in the doorway. "Meet Yllyia. She lives outside."

They stood beside the elevator, trying to decide what their next move should be. "What do you think?" LeAnne asked. "Should we call the captain down here, or do you think he would come?"

Jennings shook his head. "I don't know. The captain hasn't been entirely, uh . . . on board these last few days. I think we'd be better off dealing with the first officer, and let *him* talk to the captain."

"Okay," LeAnne said. She stepped aside so Jennings could

make the call. When he reached the first officer he said nothing about LeAnne or Yllyia, or about the drive; he simply requested his presence immediately.

While they waited for him to arrive, LeAnne told Jennings what she and Donivan had encountered outside, and about their meeting with Yllyia and the flight to California and what had happened there. As she recounted their adventures she began to yawn, and she realized that the day was beginning to catch up with her. She was going to have to find a bed sometime soon. A shower and a bed, she thought, and about ten hours in each.

With a guilty start she realized that she was wishing for exactly the same things that Donivan had talked about when he was outside. She'd been mad at him then for not sharing her excitement with Earth, but now that she was back on board she could see things in a little better perspective. The *Starchild* did have its merits.

When the first officer arrived LeAnne was almost as amazed at his reaction as she had been at Jennings's. He saw Yllyia first, then LeAnne, then looked past them down the corridor as he realized that he should have been hearing the drive, and after a second turned to Jennings and said, "I'm listening."

"Yes sir." And Jennings gave him a capsule history of events leading up to the moment, just as LeAnne had told it to him, including the threat posed by Ililiel.

The first officer pursed his lips in thought, looked again at LeAnne and at Yllyia, then nodded. "I'll want to have a look out the lock myself as soon as I get the chance, but I don't see that I have much choice but to believe you." He hesitated, then said to Yllyia, "I'm sorry your first contact with us turned out like this. I hope we can show you better hospitality from now on."

Yllyia laughed. "You have treated me much better than my people treated LeAnne and Donivan."

The first officer nodded. "I hope we can see our way through that without fighting as well. But we should warn the crew. I think the first step is to let the rest of Security in on this, and then make a shipwide announcement. Unless you already had a different plan in mind?"

"No sir," LeAnne said. "That's what we'd come up with too."

He nodded. "Good," he said, and gestured toward the elevator.

The ride upship to Security Headquarters was crowded. Four people could normally fit comfortably in an elevator, but not when one of them was an Eyullelyan. LeAnne leaned up against Yllyia, trying hard not to yawn now, but not succeeding. She was glad that the first officer had taken charge; she doubted if she could think clearly much longer.

LeAnne had never held any great respect for authority before this, but now she found that she did for the first officer. If he'd had even a moment of doubt, he hadn't let it show. This was the way a real leader acted, she realized. Not like the captain, whom the computer had chosen simply to preserve the status quo; here was someone who could instantly assess a situation and deal with it intelligently. She wondered if it was an inherent ability or a learned one.

It could be inherent. She hadn't thought about it until now, but Donivan had the same ability to a certain degree. He wasn't the leader type, but he had the same way of reacting to new information as the first officer. He'd shown it over and over again outside: While LeAnne had had to reconstruct an entire new picture of the universe to fit each new discovery, Donivan's world—and the first officer's—simply expanded to fit the new data.

Theirs was a much better system, she realized. She hoped it was something she could learn; if she was going to lead a colony project she wanted to be the best leader she could be.

Security Headquarters was a crush of activity when they arrived, but within seconds after the first officer and Jennings stepped in with LeAnne and Yllyia in tow it became as silent as drive deck. The dispatcher in his glassed-in cubicle was the last to look up, and LeAnne smiled and waved at him when he did. *Not quite dead after all*.

The first officer turned to him as well. "Get the captain

on the 'com," he said. "The rest of you mutants, listen up."
He proceeded to give an even briefer version of LeAnne and
Donivan's activities outside the ship, ending with, "And if
anybody is still in doubt, you can go on down to drive deck
and see for yourself. We left the door open."

The noise level began to rise again as people began talking
among themselves.

The dispatcher stuck his head out of his cubicle. "The
captain's on three," he said.

The first officer stepped up to an empty desk, punched line
three on the desk intercom, and said, "First Officer Koury
here." He wasted no time, but added simply, "LeAnne Evans
and Donivan Hayes have returned from outside the ship."

The captain's eyes narrowed. "They did no such thing.
They were executed four days ago."

"They were put out the airlock, sir, but they have returned
unharmed. I have LeAnne here with me." The first officer
motioned LeAnne closer to him, then reached forward and
adjusted the pickup to wide-angle.

The captain squinted into his screen. "Is this some kind of
a joke?"

"No sir. This is LeAnne Evans. She has proven to my
satisfaction that the *Starchild* is not in space."

The captain had been growing redder by the moment. He
banged his fist down out of camera range, and a pen spiraled
past his nose, but he didn't even notice. "I've had enough of
this nonsense!" he roared. "Place yourself under arrest."

"Sir, it's my duty to keep the captain informed of—"

"Your duty? You have no duty. You're relieved."

"Not until you have my report, sir."

"I don't want your entropic report, Koury! I want this
nonsense about the ship stopped." The captain noticed Jennings in his screen and said to him, "You. Place the first
officer under arrest."

Jennings looked uncomfortable. The first officer turned to
him and said, "I place myself in your custody."

"Uh, thank you sir. I think."

Turning back to the captain, the first officer said, "I am

in Officer Jennings's custody, and we are in Security head-quarters. I will continue my report. LeAnne's presence proves that the outside environment is not deadly as we had assumed. In fact, we are on Earth. She has brought back one of Earth's—"

"Silence!"

"—inhabitants. Yllyia?"

Yllyia stepped into the camera's view.

The captain jerked back as if he'd been slapped. LeAnne could see him struggling to make sense of this new development. He stared for a long moment, his eyes flicking from LeAnne to Yllyia and back, then said in a shrill voice, "Not deadly? Space, man, use your eyes. Look what it did to Donivan!"

LeAnne had to stifle a laugh. Others beyond her didn't bother. The first officer said, "No, sir. This is an inhabitant of Earth. Donivan is in the computer center, helping with repairs."

"He's *what*? You let him have free run of the ship? He was executed for sabotage!"

"I don't think you understand, sir. The *Starchild* is on Earth, just like they said it was. LeAnne and Donivan were right."

The captain spoke with exaggerated care. "LeAnne and Donivan were saboteurs, and were spaced for their crimes. If, through some means they *have* survived, then they are still sentenced to death. You will have them killed. Now. Do I make myself clear?"

"Quite." The first officer took a deep breath, and said loudly, "I can't follow your order. Before witnesses I declare you unfit for command, and request that a ship's council be assembled to determine your successor. I will send Security police to escort you to the medical—"

With a howl of rage the captain reached for the cutoff switch and his image vanished from the screen.

Seconds later, his voice roared from the dispatcher's cubicle. "You will have the first officer placed under arrest immediately!"

"I can't do that, sir."

"Get me the captain of the guard."

"I'm afraid I can't do that either, sir. He's—"

"This is mutiny! You'll all be spaced for this!" And the captain switched off again.

The first officer turned to Jennings and said, "Take a squad up to the captain's quarters and escort him to Medical. Be gentle about it, but be careful."

"Yes sir." Jennings picked out a half-dozen men and headed for the elevator.

The first officer looked up at Yllyia and said, "I'd like to have you make a statement to the crew, if you would."

"What do you wish me to say?"

He laughed. "That's a good question. Mostly I just want people to see you. Unless we drag everyone down to the stardrive one at a time, you're the best evidence we have that the ship is anything other than what the Original Crew said it was. So, I guess we'll put LeAnne on first and let her tell her story, and then you can come on and say whatever you'd like. Maybe tell us a little about your people and about Earth."

"I could do that, yes."

"Good. Excuse me a moment while I arrange it." He turned back to the 'com, readjusted the camera angle, and keyed in another number. A girl answered, and he said, "First Officer Koury here. I have a story for this evening's news."

The girl smiled. "It'll have to beat a shooting disturbance on the top stairways and a computer failure to get on tonight."

"How does an interview with LeAnne Evans, Donivan Hayes, and an alien sound?"

The girl shook her head. "That was news four days ago. Wait a minute. Alien?"

Without prompting, Yllyia moved over to stand behind the first officer. He widened the field again, and Yllyia waved, from four different directions.

"Uh . . . right," the girl said. "That certainly beats a shooting disturbance and a computer failure."

"Good. And I need a mobile camera unit in about fifteen minutes."

"You got it. Where should they meet you?"

"Drive deck. And—no, if I tell you now, he won't show up. Just drive deck."

The first officer switched off. LeAnne said to him, "Could I try calling the computer center and make sure that Donivan is okay?"

He nodded. "I was about to suggest that." He got up from the desk and let LeAnne make the call.

The person who answered didn't seem surprised to see her. He just said, "Hi. No offense, but you look almost as bad as Donivan."

"Thanks a lot. Can I talk to him?"

"Hold on." He moved out of camera range, and moments later Donivan smiled out of the screen at her.

"Lee! How'd it go?"

"Okay, I guess. We got one guard for the big shutdown, but we're up in Security now with the first officer. He had to relieve the captain from duty."

Donivan nodded. "No surprise. I think we've got the computer up again. We had to block logic mode from loading, so we're not done yet, but it won't be crashing again."

"That's good. Hold on a minute." LeAnne looked up as Jennings returned, without the other guards and without the captain.

"There's trouble," he said. "The captain took off before we got there. He convinced his orderlies and the administration guards that there was a mutiny and headed upship with them to the control room. We've sealed them in above deck three, but we can't get to them without more men."

The first officer frowned. "Your recommendations?"

Jennings said, "If we hit them from all four stairways and the elevators at once, some of us are bound to get through. There can't be more than twenty of them."

"I don't like it. Going after him like that makes it *look* like mutiny whether it is or not."

"But we can't let him have the control room," Jennings protested. "He could do anything up there."

LeAnne laughed. "Maybe he'll threaten to shut down the drive. Donivan, are you getting this?"

"Yeah. And I think I might have an idea. Anything he tries to do from the control room will have to go through the computer, so we don't have to worry about that. We can intercept his commands and send an order to surrender whenever he turns on a terminal. He'll listen to the computer, won't he?"

"He knows you're there," the first officer said. "He will know what we're doing."

Donivan thought for a moment. "Okay then, we can do even better than that. How about if we shut him down completely on all but the top deck and open both sets of doors in the airlocks? That ought to get his attention, shouldn't it?"

The first officer shook his head. "I'm afraid the captain is beyond noticing even that."

"The captain is, maybe, but I bet the rest of them won't last long. It's worth a try, isn't it, before you go after them with guns?"

"I thought you said the airlocks couldn't be opened like that," LeAnne said.

"They can if you tell the computer we're docking with another ship. Without logic mode it has to believe everything we tell it. And there's air on both sides of the lock, so it should open."

The first officer laughed. "Okay, try it," he said. "We'll give them an hour. If they don't come out by then we'll go up after them."

"Great," Donivan said. "I'll get right on it." To LeAnne he said, "I'll see you as soon as I can. Where are you going to be?"

"Taking a shower," LeAnne said. "And then on the news. You too, probably."

Donivan grinned. "Great. Well, they'll have to take me the way I am. Enjoy."

"I plan on it." She switched off and turned to Yllyia. "I'm heading for the showers. You want to come along?"

Yllyia considered for a moment, looked around her at all

the people she would be left with if she didn't, and said, "That sounds good."

"All right. I'll show you my room too." LeAnne hadn't thought of her room since she'd left the ship, but suddenly she realized how much she missed it. It was just a tiny corner of dorm deck fifty-two, but it had been her corner for five years, ever since she had moved out of the children's dorm. And it contained the only hair brush she owned.

The first officer insisted that they take a guard with them. An older woman who looked as if she had seen everything at least once during her career in Security volunteered, but on the way upship she said, "From the sound of things you need a guard the way I need more excitement in my day. It sounds like you know how to take care of yourselves pretty well."

"Thanks," LeAnne said. "We're learning."

The guard was for the crew's protection as much as for theirs, she knew. LeAnne and Yllyia alone would cause another panic just as they had on their way down the stairs, but with an official escort they were merely a sensation. LeAnne enjoyed the surprise she saw on people's faces as they walked down the corridor toward her room. Some of those people had taunted her for being different when she was younger. To the ones who were brave enough to ask, she would introduce Yllyia, but she answered the rest of their questions with "Watch the news tonight."

When they reached her room she keyed her access code into the lock panel, and just about smashed her nose into the door when it didn't open. "That's strange," she said. "I'm sure I keyed it in right." She tried it again, but again the door didn't open.

A sudden suspicion came to her then. She hoped she was wrong, but why else wouldn't it open? Hesitantly, she reached out and knocked on the door.

Too late she realized what she would look like to the person answering her knock: the ghost of the room's former occupant, come back to haunt her. She heard someone moving inside, and the door slid open to reveal a young girl, barely old enough to have a room of her own.

It was just as bad as LeAnne had expected. The girl took one look, screamed, and punched the door closed again. She went on screaming inside the closed room.

"Oh, space," LeAnne said. She bonked her head against the wall. *Stupid, stupid.* She cupped her hands against the door and shouted, "Hey, it's all right," but the screaming went on and on.

"Here," the guard said. "I'd better go in. You two stand out of the way." She traded places with LeAnne and keyed in a master code on the lock panel, and the door slid open.

The girl screamed again, louder, then burst into tears when she saw the guard standing there instead of LeAnne.

LeAnne buried her face in her hands and shook her head. She felt like crying herself. It wasn't fair. This was *her* room. To give it to somebody else so soon...

But they hadn't expected her to come back. And they would have wanted the crew to forget about her as quickly as possible, which they couldn't do as long as her room remained empty. It made sense, but understanding why was little comfort. Her room was the last link she had had with her former life, and now it was gone.

The guard's voice interrupted her thoughts. "LeAnne, come on in and show Vanesia that it's all right."

LeAnne looked across the doorway at Yllyia. Yllyia held her four hands forward in an unmistakable gesture: *I'll stay right here.*

They were sitting on the bed. The girl, slender and pale even for crew, looked even smaller tucked under the guard's arm. LeAnne stopped just inside the door and said, "I'm sorry. I didn't mean to scare you."

Vanesia sniffed. "S'all right, I guess."

"I, um, I used to live here."

"I know. I found one of your books under the mattress."

LeAnne blushed. That had to have been her copy of *The Day of the Dinosaur*. She'd duped it from the library when she was about Vanesia's age, and kept it ever since. "Did you read it?" she asked.

Vanesia shook her head. "I can't get the reader to work."

"Sometimes you have to hit it on the side," LeAnne said.

"Oh." Vanesia blinked a few times, then asked suddenly, "What's that in your hair?"

"What?" LeAnne put her hand up and felt the flower. She had forgotten all about it. "It's a flower. I brought it in from outside the ship. Would you like it?" She pulled it loose and held it out.

Vanesia took it and held it carefully in her hand. It had wilted a little, but the bright yellow petals were still soft and fragrant. She held it to her nose. "I've never seen this kind of a flower before," she said.

"They grow all over outside."

"I thought it was space outside."

"I did too, for a long time. But it's really Earth. Want me to tell you about it?"

"Okay."

LeAnne pulled out the desk chair—*her chair!*—and sat down. She took a minute to arrange her thoughts, then started describing the world outside the airlock. Vanesia's eyes grew brighter as she talked, until when LeAnne asked if she wanted to meet Yllyia she nodded eagerly.

By the time they left, she had extracted a promise that LeAnne would take her camping outside, and that Yllyia would give her an airplane ride at the very first opportunity. LeAnne left feeling somewhat mollified about losing her room, and wondering if she'd been that inquisitive when she was young.

She wound up on the news without having so much as a brush run through her hair. She consoled herself with the thought that neither Donivan nor Yllyia had had a chance to clean up either, but it was poor consolation. The interviewer claimed it was better that way—they called more attention to themselves than if they looked like just anybody off the ship. LeAnne felt like telling her that that was what Yllyia was for, but she held her opinion to herself.

The program started off with the news that the captain had resigned, and that the first officer was now acting captain of the ship until the council could recommend a permanent replacement. They made no mention of the circumstances, but Donivan whispered to LeAnne that he had lasted less than fifteen minutes after they had opened the airlocks before his orderlies had stunned him and brought him back downship.

Then they got to the real news. LeAnne and Donivan and Yllyia sat side by side, Yllyia on the floor to keep her head in the picture, while the interviewer explained who they were and asked them all the wrong questions about their experiences outside the ship. They cut back and forth between questions to scenes of the now-silent drive deck, a shaky glimpse of trees and sky outside the airlock, and finally a medium-range shot of the airlock itself with the first officer standing in it, the hull of the *Starchild* curving off into the side of the mountain to his right and covered with dirt and trees on top.

They downplayed the threat posed by Ililiel, pointing out that the ship was well-hidden and had remained undiscovered for the three hundred years that the Eyullelyans had been on Earth. Yllyia confirmed that only a small minority wanted to harm the *Starchild*'s crew, and that once the rest of them learned what had happened they would waste no time in stopping Ililiel and the Queen.

If she expected the reaction to be violent, she had not taken into account that the *Starchild*'s crew had believed themselves to be in danger of annihilation for the last thousand years. They had simply traded one danger for another.

LeAnne woke in a strange room. She was alone in the bed. She vaguely remembered going to sleep with Donivan, but he had evidently gotten up already. She smiled lazily as she realized why. He had a computer problem to work on. She'd had to practically drag him to bed or he would have stayed up all night trying to get logic mode working again.

She heard soft breathing and rose up to see Yllyia stretched out on two more beds across the room, her eyes already open.

"Good morning," Yllyia said.

"Good morning," LeAnne echoed. "Did you sleep all right?"

"Very well, thank you."

"Good. Let's pick up Donivan and go get some breakfast."

"That sounds like a good idea."

LeAnne dressed in the clothes she had recovered from Recycling: her favorite long-sleeve shirt and loose pants with pockets. Finding them still intact had made up for whatever disappointment she still felt at finding her room already occupied. She had even rescued her own hair brush. She ran it through her hair, then stuck it in her back pocket. She didn't intend to be caught without it again.

Yllyia just wore her own skin. Without sexual dimorphism the Eyullelyans had never evolved a nudity taboo, and since the *Starchild*'s temperature was just about perfect for the unclothed Eyullelyan she was happy enough to be free of the constricting elasticity of the *lyshl*.

They found Donivan in the computer center, just as they had expected. He saw them enter and waved them over to his terminal. "Morning, Lee," he said. "Morning, Yllyia. We've got logic mode up again."

"Good morning, LeAnne," the computer said. "And good morning, Yllyia. I apologize for my abrupt termination yesterday."

Yllyia laughed. "My fault. I'm glad you're not damaged."

"So am I."

"How did you do it?" LeAnne asked Donivan.

"We limited logic mode to ten gigabytes of memory, and as soon as it loaded I told it we'd already come up with a plan to take care of Ililiel, so it didn't have to search anymore."

"You lied to it?"

Donivan blushed. "Not exactly. I had an idea. You gave it to me, actually," he said to Yllyia.

"I don't remember doing so."

"It was yesterday, when you said that the bombs were on

the colony ship. I got to thinking that one defense would be to make sure nobody launches the bombs in the first place, by going up there and taking over the ship."

Yllyia's eyes drifted upward in thought, then focused on Donivan again. "You certainly don't think small, do you? It might even work, given the small crew on board, except we're in Wyoming and both the shuttles are in California." She sighed, a low, wind-through-the-trees kind of sigh. "I wish you had thought of that yesterday. We might have been able to do it. Stow away on the next flight or something." Unspoken but clear was the thought that they wouldn't have had to lose her plane, either.

"We can still get there," Donivan said. "We can use the *Starchild*'s landing craft."

Yllyia turned her head sideways. "Landing craft? In an underground habitat?"

Donivan grinned. "It's fitted out like a spaceship. And the lander is real. The computer says it came from the Manned Orbital Research Laboratory after the holocaust."

"Incredible! Will it still fly?"

"I believe so," the computer put in. "It may take minor repair, but it is an extremely durable craft. And the Original Crew prepared it for long-term storage with great care."

"You also said it would take a year to learn how to fly it, too," LeAnne put in. "By then the *Starchild* will be a radio-active crater, and the lander with it."

"That was a year for *me* to learn," Donivan said. "But we've already got a pilot right here. Yllyia can fly it."

Yllyia shook her head quickly. "I am not a shuttle pilot. Airplanes and spacecraft are very different."

"You haven't seen our lander. It looks just like a bigger version of your airplane."

"I don't know that that matters. Appearances can be deceiving."

"You should inspect it first," the computer said. "Then you can try the simulation programs that I have for it. But if you can already fly a human-built fighter plane, then you should have no problem. The lander was designed to be flown by commercial pilots."

Yllyia pulled up a chair from another terminal and sat straddling it. "You actually think this plan has a chance for success? If they see a human-built shuttle they'll know what we're trying to do."

"That is a problem, but I think we can work around it. Even if we are forced to make a direct attack, this has the best chance of completely removing the threat of any of the ideas I have come up with so far."

"You've got others?" LeAnne asked.

"Yes. We have four options so far, including Donivan's plan, none mutually exclusive."

"What are they?"

"Evacuation, decoy, diplomatic negotiations, and Donivan's pre-emptive strike. I propose to try all four, though not in that order."

LeAnne said, "What do you mean, decoy?"

"It is quite simple. Ililiel will no doubt be looking for infrared sources from orbit, reasoning that an underground habitat will generate a great deal of heat. She will not find the *Starchild* that way, since the *Starchild*'s waste heat is discharged into the Madison formation groundwater and dispersed over a large area, but she will find innumerable natural thermal vents in the Earth's crust nearby. If she were also to discover radio signals coinciding with one of these warm spots, she would very likely believe that she has found the *Starchild*. And if the radio broadcast was on a frequency that the normal Eyullelyan populace could receive, and if it announced our presence while at the same time exposing their government's duplicity, it seems likely that they would not take time to check whether—"

"I get the picture. You want somebody to find one of these hot spots and plant a radio there so they can bomb that instead of us."

"You have a gift with words. Exactly."

"I volunteer."

"I knew you would."

PART FIVE

Repeating History

It was called an All-Terrain-Vehicle, but within the first mile LeAnne decided that the name was an exaggeration. In the forest its four balloon tires bounced over every rock and fallen log with enough force to throw her from the seat, and when she landed she was invariably going in a different direction than the vehicle. She had tipped it over twice already, banging her head on the handlebars once and burning her leg on the engine the second time. Still, though it was no easier than walking, it was at least faster, especially when she found a game trail leading in the same direction she wanted to go.

She had to backtrack over and over again to get around fallen trees and drop-offs, but she made it to the base of the mountain in only three hours, and from there she was able to make even better time on the flat prairie beside the old road. She had tried the road itself for a while, but it was more eroded than the ground around it.

One day of preparation was all it had taken. The ATV had been waiting in the landing bay, sealed into a crate with a nitrogen atmosphere, along with sealed fuel cannisters and spare parts. It had taken the ship's engineers a single morning to get it running, while others repaired a radio from the top deck communication room and the computer recorded a looping message for it to transmit. The computer had also generated a map for her of known hot spots in the plain to the east and south of the ship, and LeAnne had found the design for a backpack that the specialty clothing shop had put together for her in an afternoon, and with that she was ready.

Yllyia had watched all the activity with fascination, and had finally remarked, "All this time I thought I knew what civilization was, but *this* is civilization." This while being measured for her own spacesuit, while behind them more engineers pored over the lander, inspecting and refitting it for flight.

LeAnne had never looked at it that way before, but she could see Yllyia's point. An entire society in a cubic mile of space, completely self-sufficient, with engineers ready to build anything you needed; the *Starchild* was in many ways the most advanced civilization that humanity had ever attained. A little heavy on the sciences and light on the arts, perhaps, but maybe not so stagnant as she had once believed. It would be interesting to see what they could do with an entire planet at their disposal.

The computer had drawn in the highways on the map. The one she was following turned gradually south until it met with a double line of raised ground that the computer had marked INTERSTATE, which ran south along the front range of the mountains for another ten miles or so before it joined with yet another interstate going east. The junction was at the edge of a natural bowl between high hills and mountains, and LeAnne could see the remains of a city in the bowl. The map called it *Buffalo*. Time rather than bombs had leveled this city, and the job was not yet finished; some of the buildings were still standing. LeAnne wished she could stop and look through the remains, but she reluctantly turned away and followed the highway on southward, toward the dot marked *Kaycee*. She could explore on the way back, but she had a decoy to plant first.

The interstate was much smoother driving than the little road coming out of the mountain. It had eroded far less, and in places the pavement still covered the surface. One stretch lasted almost five miles, and LeAnne slowly worked up her courage enough to shift into high gear, the knobbed tires howling on the flat surface and the wind blowing her hair out behind her. She shouted in exhiliration and triumph. LeAnne the intrepid explorer, at last!

Once a herd of grazing animals scattered before her, a sea of brown and white splitting to either side as she passed. There were too many of them to count. Over a thousand, she guessed. She supposed she would be hunting them for food in the first few years until the colony could start a domestic breeding program, but for now she was glad to be driving past on a different errand, able to watch them for their beauty alone.

The sun climbed up toward noon as she drove. She considered stopping to eat, but while the countryside was pretty to look at as she drove through it, no one place offered a good enough reason to stop. She would eat when she found one of the hot spots.

Most of them were to the south of Kaycee on the map, near towns called Midwest and Edgerton, but the computer had warned her that geothermal activity could shift over periods as long as a thousand years. She would most likely not find any of the spots in the same place, but they would probably be nearby. There were also coal deposits underground that sometimes burst into spontaneous combustion; those would do as well. Anything that vented steam to the surface would be warm enough to detect from orbit.

She had already crossed three fairly good-sized streams that hadn't been marked on her map, but when she came to a wide, sandy riverbed that was easily ten times wider than the shallow stream that meandered through it she decided that this must be the Powder River. She had evidently missed Kaycee about twenty minutes ago. The remains of a bridge lay in chunks downstream, evidence of periodic flooding, but the stream looked less than a foot deep now. LeAnne stopped the ATV and walked across the dry riverbed to it, took off her shoes and forded it barefoot, and decided that she could drive through it if she got up some speed. Leaving her pack and shoes on the far bank, she went back for the ATV and charged across, the balloon tires throwing up water and flinging mud behind her all the way.

From then on she began looking to the sides from each hilltop, stopping and shading her eyes to study the land around her. She sniffed the air, trying to catch the hydrogen sulfide smell that the computer had said would usually be associated with the hot spots. It was not a smell she would easily forget. She had smelled a sample in the ship before leaving, and the condensed odor of rotten egg had been strong enough to make her eyes water.

What she noticed first, though, was a forest of metal frameworks sticking up from the bottom of a low valley to the east. She consulted her map. It was hard to guess exactly where on it she was, but the computer had marked OILFIELD to the east of the highway fairly close to where she thought she should be, and the hot spots seemed to cluster only a mile or so to the east of that. LeAnne had no idea what an oilfield should look like, but since this was the only evidence of mankind for miles around, she supposed it was worth a look.

She drove along the ridgetops until she was about even with the frameworks, then dropped down the hillside toward them. When she got closer she could see that they were simple pivots of some sort, evidently designed to raise and lower a horizontal arm that would in turn push and pull a cable into and out of a vertical pipe stuck in the ground. It made no sense to her, but the water spilling out of the pipe did. It was unmistakably a hot spring.

Evidently the water had taken the easiest path to the surface, rising through the pipe that was already there rather than forcing its own way to the surface somewhere else. There was only a trickle running out of the one LeAnne had stopped at, but it combined with similar trickles running from similar pipes all through the valley to make a steaming pond down at the bottom. LeAnne drove the ATV to the edge of the water, shut it off for the first time since she had left the ship, took off her pack, and stretched. She was surprised; it didn't smell that bad. There was a trace of rotten egg in the air, but not anything like the concentrated sample she had smelled in the ship.

The water was too hot for skinny-dipping. Leanne felt little disappointment; she didn't feel like playing anyway. She felt uneasy being there, knowing that Ililiel was looking for just such a place from miles overhead. It made a vast magnifying glass of the sky, and LeAnne a tiny speck crawling across the ground beneath it.

She ate a quick lunch, looking while she ate for a good place to set up the transmitter. The higher the better, the engineers had said, which put it on top of the ridge she had crossed on the way in. Perfect. She could set it up on the way out, and be miles away by the time the timer turned it on.

Setting it up was easy enough; extend the antenna and prop it up with loose rocks so it wouldn't fall over, connect antenna and battery and music player to the transmitter, and turn it all on. The player was a standard personal model, the same kind that LeAnne had used all her life; she set it for a two-hour delay and continuous repeat, checked to make sure the message chip was seated tight, and headed back to the north.

She drove faster on the way back. Part of it was familiarity with the ATV, but the real reason was descending in her imagination long before the transmitter even turned on. The computer had estimated that it would take two or three more hours to pinpoint the signal after it turned on, and perhaps as many as twelve more before the Eyullelyan colony ship was in a position to launch a missile, but LeAnne considered those to be upper limits. There was always the chance that they would react within minutes; why else had the computer told her to program in a delay?

She splashed across the Powder River in second gear and was halfway up the long incline beyond when the ATV's engine sputtered to a stop. Her first thought was that water had gotten in something and shorted it out, but a few minutes with the troubleshooting chart in the manual uncovered the real problem: It had run out of fuel. She unstrapped the spare

cannister from behind the seat, broke the seal, and poured
the foul-smelling stuff into the tank. This was where pollution
came from, she thought. Burning fossil fuels for energy. She
felt a twinge of guilt as she strapped the empty cannister back
down and started the engine again, but not enough guilt to
walk home from here. Not this time.

She had made it nearly to Buffalo and was beginning to
breathe a little easier with fifty miles between her and the
transmitter when a sudden flash of light cast a long shadow
out in front of her. She felt the heat on her back, as if she
had suddenly crossed into a patch of noonday sun.

Almost instinctively she swerved to the left down the side
of the roadway, bouncing her way down the embankment
while she fought to hang on, until near the bottom she hit a
rock head on and flipped over. She landed rolling, saw the
ATV sail over her and heard it crash into another rock just
as she rebounded off one of its tires, then skidded to a stop
below it, flattened against the bank. The road aimed just a
few degrees to the east of the blast, enough to give her shadow
to hide in, but the parallel roadway just across from her
glowed brightly in the bomb's glare.

It died slowly. The ground trembled and settled down again,
but LeAnne still stayed put. In the stories she had read about
the holocaust the blast had come in separate parts, the light
and heat almost instantly, then the ground wave, then the air
wave. She didn't know how long she should wait for the air
wave to reach her, but she decided to give it a few minutes.
She was no longer in any hurry; she couldn't outrun it now.

She turned her head to look to the south and saw the edge
of the mushroom cloud. It climbed steadily into the sky, the
shock wave rising above it, a lens-shaped white cloud out-
racing even the head of the mushroom into the upper atmosphere.

The air wave arrived minutes later; a deep, resonant rumble
that went on and on, until LeAnne wanted to scream at it to
stop. It wasn't loud enough to be painful, but it was as if the
Earth were crying in agony for what she had brought down
upon it. A thousand years of peace had been broken again,

almost the moment that humanity had stepped out onto the surface. She knew that it wasn't her fault, not completely, but she had been the catalyst that brought it on. In a way the captain had been right; if they'd made sure she was dead before they threw her out the airlock, then none of this would have happened. She covered her head with her arms and wept for the planet, and for the insanity of the creatures who lived on it.

The ATV was demolished. It had come down sideways on the last rock with enough force to burst through the engine's side cover and smash parts inside. LeAnne stood beside it and watched the mushroom cloud flatten out and begin to drift eastward while she thought about her options. She couldn't fix the engine, and it was going to be getting dark in another few hours, and she didn't particularly want to spend the night out here in the middle of the nowhere, which left just one thing to do, really. With a last look at the destruction, both near and far away, she shouldered her pack and set out for the *Starchild*. She didn't look back, the whole rest of the day.

She made it to Buffalo by twilight. She walked down an overgrown road between mounds of stone that she supposed had once been houses, forded the stream that crossed her path, and climbed up to the single stone building that still stood on top of the hill beyond. One of the double doors hung partway open, the glass broken out of its center. Its hinges protested when LeAnne pulled it open the rest of the way and looked inside. It was too dark to see. She took off her pack, got out the laser, and shined it in ahead of her.

A hallway ran straight to the other end of the building, with doors opening off to either side all the way down. Stairs rose to the left and right just inside the door, and when she shined the light upward she saw that they joined together again on the second deck. It was probably some kind of public building, she supposed; a dormitory or offices or something similar.

This morning she had been eager enough to explore, but she didn't feel so fearless now, facing her first night outside alone, probably twenty miles from the ship and everything familiar. She felt sore and tired and a little bit scared, and all she really wanted now was to find a place where she could sleep without worrying about something attacking her in the night. She supposed any of the rooms would do. She walked slowly down the hallway to the first one, shined the light inside and found it empty save for desks, checked that the door would latch, and took possession.

When she woke the sun was already up and shining in through the windows. The glass was missing from most of them, making LeAnne wonder how safe she had really been from marauding animals, but she supposed the question was academic now. She uncurled and sat up, wincing with pain all along her right side. Puzzled, she took off her shirt and saw a checkerboard pattern of bruises spaced about half an inch apart: a perfect imprint of the knobs on the ATV's tire. Hitting that instead of the rock during her tumble off the road had probably saved her from broken ribs, but she was going to look pretty strange for a while.

She sat at one of the desks and looked through its contents while she ate breakfast, wondering what purpose a *Motor Vehicle Registration Form* or an *Application for Certificate of Title for a Motor Vehicle* might serve. She found a booklet entitled *Wyoming Classified Driver's License Manual* and found the answer in its brittle pages, and read on to discover that she had broken at least three state laws in driving an unregistered vehicle on the highway without properly affixed license plates and without having a valid driver's license herself.

It seemed like an awful lot of licensing went into just getting from place to place before the holocaust. She wondered if it would get that way again when she started her colony. She hoped not. *She* certainly didn't want to have to keep track of it all.

There was no trace of yesterday's explosion in the sky when she went outside to fill her water bottle in the stream. A smudge of gray near the horizon might have been the smoke of fires still burning after the blast, but the mushroom cloud had blown away in the night. LeAnne's memory of it was still vivid; she needed only to close her eyes to bring it back. She wondered if they had seen it from the *Starchild*, and decided probably not. There was a mountain in the way. Even so, they had probably felt the tremor, and maybe even heard it. Donivan would be worried about her, though she had told him not to expect her until today.

But after an hour's walking she decided that she might make it yet. Her muscles loosened up with the exercise and she was able to keep a steady pace along the top of the highway. She watched the mountain peaks in the distance slip behind the nearer ridges as she walked, and she was surprised at how quickly the miles went by. She found herself opposite Lake DeSmet by noon, and when she reached the river that fed into it she left the road and turned upstream toward the mountains.

She stopped for lunch at the same group of trees where she and Donivan had met Yllyia, but even though it was the same place, being there alone made it seem completely different. It seemed less substantial, as if having fewer people to witness it made it somehow less real. The soft rippling noise that the water made as it flowed along the banks seemed entirely subjective this time, as if she could switch it off by simply choosing not to hear it.

It was an interesting thought. Dr. McNeil had once told her his theory that the *Starchild* drove steadily onward through space without a jolt not because of an incredibly homogeneous interstellar medium but because that was what generations of crew members had imagined it doing. They couldn't imagine anything else because that was all they had ever experienced, and without people imagining it it could never happen.

It was just the sort of circular logic that McNeil loved. LeAnne had rejected it as being a hopelessly limiting theory for an entire universe to follow, but now that she was alone she realized that it did have its attractive features. Maybe the Earth had come into existence around the *Starchild* just as the airlock door began to swing open simply because LeAnne was there to imagine it. If Donivan had been alone in the airlock, who could say that it wouldn't have opened into interstellar space, or into something that only he could imagine?

Hmm. LeAnne closed her eyes. She was in a good position to experiment. Given the precarious nature of the universe, and nobody but herself for miles around to lock it into any specific form...

Change the gurgle of water to the tinkling flow of a tinier stream, up a thousand feet or so in altitude, with pine trees there and there and there... She opened her eyes. She was still in the same place. It looked like she was going to have to walk the rest of the way home.

It was well into the night by the time she reached the curving wall of the ship. She expected silence on the other side of the airlock, but when she stepped through she was greeted instead by the echo of voices and the thrum of machinery coming from somewhere inside. She pulled off her pack and carried it in her hand down the corridor to the hub, turned left toward the source of the noise, and discovered the cause of it when she reached the landing bay. An entire team of engineers was still at work on the landing craft.

Yllyia was there too, putting all four arms to use. She held open an access panel with one, held a light with another, and reached inside to work on some inner part of the lander with the other two. She hooted in surprise when she saw LeAnne in the doorway, let the access cover bang closed, and turned around to shout, "LeAnne!"

"Hi," LeAnne shouted back. "Where'd you get the uniform?"

"I had it made. You like it?" Yllyia held out all four arms and turned once around. Her clothing was unmistakably a skintight ship's uniform, built along the same lines as the dress uniform that LeAnne had been wearing when they met, only Yllyia's had slits in the arms and legs for her muscles to pass through.

"It's great," LeAnne said. "You look better than I ever did. I bet nobody even notices the extra arms."

Yllyia whistled in laughter. "You think this is good; wait until you see my spacesuit."

"You've got a spacesuit already?"

"It's not done, but it's coming along. It'll be ready in time for launch."

LeAnne whistled. "You've been busy."

"We have. We should be ready to go in ten more days."

"You're kidding. That quick?"

Yllyia waved an arm toward the lander. "Your Original Crew did an excellent job of preservation. They took out just about everything they could and sealed it in nitrogen, so our job has mostly been bolting parts back in place. They anticipated everything. They even made modifications to the design so we'll be able to take off without a runway. I've been practicing with the simulator, and it's beautiful!"

LeAnne recognized the tone in Yllyia's voice. She had heard it once before in a hangar in Ventura. She said, "I think you've got your airplane back."

"So do I. But tell me about your trip. No, wait—let's call Donivan."

A few minutes later he burst through the door, flung his arms around her with the cry, "Lee!" and hugged her hard enough to make ribs hurt even on the side that wasn't bruised.

"Careful," she said. "I'm still a little tender."

"What happened? Are you all right?"

"I'm fine." And she described her trip, and the explosion, and crashing the ATV.

"You had us worried. We took a radio outside and heard your signal start up, but when the bomb hit so soon and when you didn't make it back last night we were afraid you, well, you hadn't gotten away in time."

"It was close," LeAnne admitted. "They must have been looking for us a lot harder than we thought."

"I think we forced their hand," Yllyia said. "We've plotted their orbit with observations last night and tonight, and it looks like the ship was in a good position to launch a missile just after the transmitter turned on. They had to choose between bombing it without investigating or waiting ten to twelve hours for their orbit to carry them over the right spot again, and they couldn't afford to let the message go that long. Someone would certainly have heard it by then."

"So the hot spring wasn't even necessary?"

"We don't know. It will help now, though, because the water will fill the crater and they won't be able to tell whether or not there was anything there beforehand."

"Oh. Yeah, I guess it would. I hadn't thought of that. So do we even need to attack the *Lyrili-Hloo*?"

Donivan nodded. "They won't stop looking until they're sure they've gotten us. The computer thinks we might have a month now, but they'll eventually find us. We can't relax until we take away their bombs for good."

LeAnne sighed. "I guess not." She looked at the lander. Donivan talked as if it was simply a matter of getting there, as if capturing an alien starship was something anyone could do. She wasn't nearly as convinced. But after seeing one bomb for herself, she supposed that they had to try.

Over the next few days her confidence began to build. The attack team practiced invasion techniques with stunners modified to tingle the defenders, fighting against mock lasers and projectile weapons. They practiced maneuvering in zero gravity by riding the elevators upship from the very bottom, canceling the destination halfway, and resetting for the bottom again. Yllyia described the *Lyrili-Hloo* to the computer from memory—she had used it for a base when she had been studying human communications satellites—and the computer devised an attack plan that took advantage of the weaknesses it presented.

Their best advantage lay in the lack of rotation. Since the only Eyullelyans who actually lived on board were the crew who steered it from colony to colony and a few scientists at their destination, they had built a small rotating living section inside the hull rather than spin the whole ship for gravity, which meant that the attackers wouldn't have to dock at a central hub. They could bring the lander in anywhere, jump across to the ship, and go straight for the control room and the cargo bays.

Yllyia practiced incessantly with the simulator. At first the computer had simply created graphics on a terminal while it taught her the basics of orbital mechanics, but for learning the actual operation of the lander it used the lander controls themselves. The computer monitored the control signals and sent its video output to the heads-up display, where, with the windows blacked out, it produced an incredibly realistic sensation of actual flight.

It came up with new surprises each time, and only explained what it had done after Yllyia had either succeeded or failed to deal with them. One time LeAnne was watching her attempt a docking when the *Lyrili-Hloo* suddenly began to move off the screen under power. Yllyia whistled in alarm, yelled, "Prepare for boost!" and used the attitude thrusters to swing around.

The lander had been coming in from above, the tactic that Yllyia had hoped would offer the least chance of detection, so it was ahead of the *Lyrili-Hloo* in orbit, but LeAnne knew that with the alien ship accelerating it would not be ahead for long. Yllyia knew it too. She fired the main drive, trying to match the acceleration, but now her calculations for docking would no longer be good. She tried the docking radar— it didn't matter now if she announced her presence—but the radar gave her a string of continually varying thrust vectors that would have been impossible to follow. It was designed for docking with unpowered objects only. Yllyia turned it off with a fluid curse and began closing the distance by eye.

The *Lyrili-Hloo* had been aimed slightly outward at that point in its orbit; its thrust was bringing it up toward the lander as well as pushing it out ahead. Yllyia kept adjusting for its motion, trying to maintain a reasonable rate of closure, and she was so absorbed in doing that that she didn't see the missile launched from the starship's stern. Before LeAnne could realize that she hadn't seen it and shout a warning, it had already hit.

The display spun crazily. Alarms clamored for attention. Yllyia slapped them off and tried to stop the roll, her four hands a blur of motion on the controls, but half of her board had gone dead. The lander spiraled toward the starship, drifting off to the side now with the additional velocity from the explosion, and as Yllyia worked to steady it with only the nose thrusters the starship launched a second missile.

Yllyia cursed again, but she was already at work evading it. She ran the thrust up to three gees, watching the missile curve to follow them, and at the last moment cut the thrust to zero. The missile shot past the nose, already swinging around to return, but before it could complete its maneuver Yllyia fired the main engines again. She lined the lander up with the fleeing starship and pushed the throttle all the way up.

LeAnne, standing in the doorway to the cargo bay, felt herself grab onto the jamb for support under the imagined acceleration. The accelerometer read six gees, and the collision alarm began to howl as the starship grew larger and larger. With a sense of horror, she realized what Yllyia was going to do. She watched, unable to move or speak as Yllyia switched off the alarm and stared straight ahead, correcting with minute burns of the attitude thrusters so that the lander kept pointing directly at the center of the starship. It grew until it filled the entire screen, and kept growing.

The starship pilot attempted Yllyia's maneuver, cutting their thrust just before impact, but with a howl of triumph Yllyia cut the lander's thrust as soon as she saw it and both ships drifted together. The starship continued to grow, individual details expanding toward them, one that might have been a dish antenna coming straight toward them, until suddenly the screen went black.

LeAnne fell backward into the cargo bay with the force of her flinch. Yllyia tried to get out of her seat to help her up, but she couldn't make herself stand. LeAnne managed it alone and pulled herself forward into the copilot's chair, and the two of them sat side by side, panting for breath.

At last Yllyia said, "You had to find out if I would do it, didn't you?"

The accusation caught LeAnne completely by surprise, but the computer responded through the radio speaker before she could think of an answer of her own.

"I already knew," it said. "You were the one who needed to find out."

Yllyia growled, and LeAnne felt a shiver run up her back. She hadn't known that Yllyia could do that. Suddenly the fangs didn't seem so out of place. Yllyia said, "You knew I would. I must break this habit of sacrificing aircraft and spacecraft." She paused, then said, "And lives. Did you consider that the lander will be full of people?"

"Did you?"

Yllyia's eyes shifted over to LeAnne. "I did. I considered the lives. I had to stop and think why we were doing this in the first place, and I decided, but I used my own set of values to weigh the factors involved. Did I do the right thing by human standards? I don't know. I am not human."

"You did the right thing," the computer said.

"You are not human either," Yllyia said. "I would like to know what LeAnne would have done."

"Don't look at me," LeAnne said. "I don't know what I'd have—no, that's not true." She knew. She would have frozen. They would have died anyway, and Ililiel would have still had her bombs. So... "I guess I'd have made the same decision," she said, "but I'd probably have wasted too much time making it."

"That was the purpose of this simulation," the computer said. "You must know ahead of time what you are willing to do for the success of the mission. Now that you know, you will not waste valuable time deciding."

"What do you mean, me? I'm not the pilot."

"No," the computer replied. "The simulation was for Yllyia, but you could benefit from the same knowledge. You might face a similar decision, since you will lead the attack."

Launch day dawned cloudy and gray. The computer had predicted overcast, and it had been right, though the cover wasn't complete. LeAnne could see patches of blue off to the north and east. At her insistence, she and Donivan had spent the night outside under the stars, but they had slept very little, for various reasons. They had walked nearly a quarter of a mile up the tiny stream to ensure seclusion, but even after that no longer mattered they still couldn't sleep. Growing up on a starship notwithstanding, now that the actual moment was upon them they were both terrified of actually going into space.

As they walked back to the ship they heard the rasp of saws and the crash of trees toppling. LeAnne winced at the sound, but she knew that it was necessary. The lander didn't need a runway, but it did need room to lift off. They were clearing a big enough space for it to hover and lift without danger of catching wingtips on trees.

The landing bay door was open when they reached the ship. It had taken two days of digging to clear the dirt that had drifted in since it had last been opened, but now it was a huge rectangular hole into the side of the mountain. Deck plating had been laid out in an arc in front of the door for the lander to taxi out onto for lift-off.

The lander was difficult to see against the dark background. They had painted it black to make it harder to detect in space, but the paint worked just as well on the ground. Yllyia stood beneath it, going through her pre-flight check. She looked up when they walked toward her, hand in hand, and said, "I was wondering if I was going to have to send someone after you. We launch in an hour."

"We'll be ready," Donivan said.

A morning launch gave them the best chance of reaching orbit without being detected. Night observations from the ridgetops had traced the starship's orbit with precision, along with two other moving specks that were probably weather satellites. The computer had found a launch window that put all three below the horizon, which would give them time to get into a higher orbit, where they would be invisible to anything looking down until they were ready to make the attack.

LeAnne and Donivan walked on into the ship and took the

elevator down to their room. The ship was practically empty now; all but a minimum crew had dispersed into the mountains days ago, where they would wait until they got the all-clear signal before returning. If they didn't get the signal there would probably be nothing to return to, but at least they would be alive. LeAnne wondered how long that would be true, given her and Donivan's experiences outside, but she supposed it would be better to die in the forest than in a nuclear explosion.

They showered and dressed in their spacesuit liners; soft white skintight clothing that reminded LeAnne more of the pajamas she had worn as a child than something you would wear into space. The rest of their suits were already packed in the lander. Spacesuits weren't designed to be worn during acceleration; the attack team wouldn't put those on until after they reached orbit. They were the same suits that had been in the airlock, now refitted and resealed for vacuum. They had also been sprayed with a bright silver coating, proof against laser fire for at least a few seconds.

Nobody knew for certain what kind of weapons they would be up against. The Eyullelyans had developed laser weapons at least as efficient as the *Starchild*'s, but they also seemed fond of projectile weapons. Yllyia didn't know and the computer could not predict whether they would use them in a spaceship, but in any case there was little they could do. The suits were awkward to move in as they were; body armor strong enough to protect against bullets would have made them even worse.

The attackers would carry both stunners and lasers, and a third pistol that LeAnne hoped she would never have to try. It was essentially a hand-held welding torch fitted into a pistol grip, but it also doubled as a reaction pistol for maneuvering in free-fall. If she missed or rebounded off the *Lyrili-Hloo* she was supposed to use it to get back, but she planned on jumping accurately and sticking tight the first time.

The other members of the attack group were already in the landing bay when they returned; Jennings and a dozen other security police, two people from the computer center, and a doctor. LeAnne had organized them into six teams of three, Jennings commanding three teams and the other three following her. She supposed that as leader she should give them a pep talk before they boarded the lander, but the doctor beat her to it.

"Dramamine," he said, holding out two pills apiece. "Take them now, before you need them."

The lander had been fitted with acceleration chairs in the cargo section. They strapped themselves into those and prepared for launch, LeAnne in the front where she could be first out the hatch. Donivan sat beside Yllyia in the copilot's seat, which gave him the dubious honor of being the only other one with a clear view. He had run the simulator a few times and had once managed to get within jumping distance of the *Lyrili-Hloo* without crashing, which made him the best-qualified copilot of the crew.

LeAnne could see out well enough through the cargo bay door. The hatch had been taken out to cut down on weight, which left her with a view over Donivan's shoulder. She watched him help Yllyia with the final checklist; flipping switches and checking gauges as if he'd been doing it all his life. He saw her watching and winked.

After what seemed like nearly an hour but couldn't have been more than a few minutes, Yllyia leaned her head out the hatch and shouted "Clear!" She thumped the hatch shut and spun the lock, strapped herself back into her seat, and started the lift-off engines.

The lander was much better insulated than Yllyia's jet had been. Over the whine of the engines LeAnne could hear Donivan saying, "Wheel load ninety-eight percent, ninety, eighty-five, eighty," and when he had reached fifty percent Yllyia responding with, "Beginning forward roll."

The lander began to move, then bumped slightly as it crossed from the landing bay onto the deck plating. Yllyia turned left so that they were facing east and raised the throttle.

"Thirty percent," Donivan said. "Twenty, ten, five . . . hovering."

"Gear up."

LeAnne felt a slight sideways twist as the wheels left the ground, and a bump as the landing gear folded in. Out the window the trees seemed to sway. Yllyia increased the thrust, and they dropped away completely. From behind LeAnne came sounds of dismay.

The *Starchild*'s computer had programmed the launch time and vectors into the lander's computer, along with the midcourse corrections and the transfer orbit burn that should bring them within visual range of the *Lyrili-Hloo*, so once above ground the computer could fly them into orbit. Yllyia kept it on manual until they were out over the plain beyond the mountains and had picked up enough speed for the control surfaces to become effective, then with the warning, "Prepare for boost!" she turned over control to the computer.

The last time LeAnne had felt hard acceleration she had been wearing a parachute and Donivan had been sitting on her lap. This time, even though it was probably twice as strong, it didn't seem nearly as bad. She sank deep into her chair, the drive—a *real* one this time!—roaring just behind her, and despite her fear she felt a smile growing. Off into the unknown again!

The computer tilted them up into the sky. The direction of *down* changed slightly; now it was directly behind them, and stronger. It seemed as if the sudden increase in weight had affected the clouds as well; LeAnne watched with a sense of impending collision as the white layer dropped down toward them and suddenly flashed past, insubstantial. Her vision began to blur, but she could still see the sky growing steadily darker as they rose into it.

Within minutes the sky became completely black, but as the lander tilted back down toward horizontal the sun began shining in through the front windows. They accelerated straight toward it, gaining orbital velocity now that they were out of the atmosphere. The thrust lasted for minutes longer, then suddenly cut off. The silence was almost as much of a shock as the lack of thrust.

Strapped into her seat, it took LeAnne a moment to realize that they were in free-fall. It didn't last, though. From up front, Yllyia said, "Stand by for transfer orbit burn," and moments afterward the lander yawed sideways and the drive kicked in again. This was the burn that would shift them into the same orbital plane as the *Lyrili-Hloo*.

They endured more minutes of acceleration before the drive shut down again, this time for good. If the computer had calculated the orbits right, then in a little less than two hours they would descend on the starship without betraying their presence by using the drive. When they got into visual range Yllyia could bring them in with the attitude thrusters, but until then they would drift over the apogee of an elliptical orbit.

Yllyia and Donivan were being awfully quiet up front. LeAnne unstrapped herself and floated forward, instinctively waiting for the elevator to begin deceleration, and suddenly understood why they were silent. The entire Earth lay just below them in swirling blue and white, its thin layer of atmosphere drawing a hazy line above a horizon that curved visibly even in the narrow view from the cargo bay door. There was no sound save the quiet hum of cooling fans in the control console, no sensation of motion, not even of falling. They were too high for falling to have any meaning. They were simply suspended in space with a planet below them.

LeAnne became aware of someone watching over her shoulder. She turned her head and saw Jennings's face, upside down, and beyond him at various angles the rest of the attack team. The dramamine—or maybe the joyrides in the elevators—had evidently prevented trouble with free-fall.

Jennings voiced what they were all thinking. "I could have died in the *Starchild* without even knowing this was here."

It was a chilling thought. It had a companion: What else is there to see beyond, and how can I possibly live long enough to see it all?

Not by attacking a starship, LeAnne thought. The odds were high that they would all be dead in another two hours. But at least they had lived to see this. She turned away, pulled herself back into the cargo bay and began handing out space-suits.

* * *

Yllyia had done a good job of describing the *Lyrili-Hloo*. It was very close to the simulations that the computer had come up with, even to the tethered manufacturing modules standing out from the central cylinder. The only thing LeAnne hadn't been prepared for was its size. It was *huge*. If the *Starchild* could be put into orbit somehow, it would be no bigger.

They had been monitoring the starship's radio transmissions since coming into range, and the news was not good. Ground observers near the bomb site had seen a bright flash through the cloud cover to the north and were already headed that way to investigate. One of the weather satellites was due to cross over Wyoming on its next pass, and the *Lyrili-Hloo* had been alerted to arm its missiles for a possible strike when it came in range later in the day.

"They must have seen the drive flame's reflection on the underside of the clouds," Donivan said. They had already sealed their helmets; his voice came through the suit radio.

Yllyia responded. "At least they didn't watch us all the way into orbit."

That was true enough. The starship's crew had shown no sign of having seen them, and from the radio traffic it didn't sound like they were looking. The lander was coming in out of the sun, so unless they eclipsed it they would be almost invisible against the black sky anyway. As they drifted closer, Yllyia correcting once with a short burn from the side thrusters, LeAnne began to see airlocks in the jumble of light and shadow. They had been painted bright yellow, and a yellow beacon flashed beside each one, no doubt as a safety precaution. They were in rows of three, two smaller ones at the fore and amidships and a third larger one aft per row, with the rows spaced ninety degrees apart around the hull. They were coming in from behind so they couldn't see the forward face, and Yllyia couldn't remember for sure if there were airlocks there or not, but if there were she suspected there would only be one or two. That made twelve to fourteen locks in all, which didn't seem like many for a ship this size, until

LeAnne remembered how many the *Starchild* had. Twelve would be plenty, even for a real ship. It really didn't matter how many there were anyway; there were only eighteen attackers. Nineteen counting Yllyia, but she would stay in the lander and guard it from harm, and use the drive as a weapon if necessary.

There was no obvious indication which part of the ship held the rotating section, but according to Yllyia it was just aft of the control room. Cargo was all the way aft, and the rest of the ship in between was nothing but suspended animation chambers, sealed since the Eyullelyans had arrived on Earth.

"Okay," LeAnne said. "It looks like plan A is still good. Jennings, you lead your teams in through the forward locks we know are there and head for the control room. My team C goes with you. That gives you one team per lock. Team B and Royan from team A, you take the aft locks. Pair up and go in a hundred and eighty degrees apart. You're the bomb squad. Donivan and I will head for the control room along the outside. If we find an airlock there we'll go in first; otherwise we'll come back and join Jennings's team. Clear?"

"Clear," they replied in chorus.

"Okay. We're going to be out of contact once we're inside, so use your own judgment if something comes up. Stun anything that moves, and make sure it doesn't get up. Everybody got their cuffs?"

Each attacker carried three sets of six-ring handcuffs for immobilizing Eyullelyans. Yllyia had helped design them, and had provided the test subject for practice. With all four arms and both legs pinned behind her, she had been as good as stunned.

"Got 'em," voices replied.

"Good. Get ready to jump."

While Yllyia positioned the lander so they would be aimed straight at the ship, LeAnne pulled the handle beside the hatch and air began to hiss out into space. Her suit puffed out and stiffened, and there was a brief rush of air around her neck to compensate for the change in volume. External sounds that she had ignored until now died away, leaving only the rush of her own breathing and that of the others coming through on the radio. She waited until the pressure gauge dropped to zero, then spun the handle counter-clockwise and pulled. The door swung open and she was looking out across maybe a hundred yards of space at the side of the *Lyrili-Hloo*.

She had expected agoraphobia, and she was ready for it. Before the knot of fear in her chest could control her she grabbed the hatch with both hands, twisted her body upward until she was pointed straight out the opening, and launched herself headfirst toward the starship. She heard someone gasp, then mutter, "Watch that first step."

She hadn't made a perfect shove; she was spinning very gently sideways, just enough so that it looked like she would land on her feet. That was not the way she'd planned it. Feet couldn't grab hold of anything. Reluctantly, she took the reaction pistol from her belt and held it out at arms' length, aimed it in the direction of her rotation, and pulled the trigger.

Bright flame shot out of the nozzle and her spin suddenly stopped, but before she could let up on the trigger she began to move the other way. She switched her aim and fired again, overshooting again, and finally realized that she would get better control if she held the pistol closer to her center of mass. It would shove her away from her target point, but the ship was big enough; she wouldn't miss. Another shot from shoulder level stopped her spin completely, and she drifted in headfirst the rest of the way.

The hull was covered with handholds. They were spaced farther apart than LeAnne would have liked, but if she stretched she could always reach one from any of the others. She grabbed on with one hand and twisted around to help anybody else who might be close enough.

It took her a moment to spot them. The silver spacesuits were reflecting mostly dark sky, and the lander behind them was little more than a patch of darkness with a bright hole in it where the hatch opened to the interior. That didn't need to be there.

"Yllyia, kill the lights," she said into the radio.

"Done," Yllyia replied, and the circle of brightness disappeared.

The rest of the team drifted down in ones and twos, spread out across a wide area. LeAnne abandoned the idea of trying to help them in—she would be just as likely to miss a handhold as they would.

Jennings's voice came over the sounds of breathing: "Contact." More voices echoed his, until finally Donivan said, "Made it. That's all of us."

She allowed herself a soft sigh of relief. "Okay, spread out and do your stuff. Last one in's a mutant."

She watched silver shapes move off around the curve of the hull. They all looked the same in their suits, and she realized that they should have put some kind of identifying marks on the helmets. Too late now. One silver suit pulled itself along hand over hand toward her, feet sticking straight out all the way, until he floated beside her. Donivan. His faceplate was as reflective as the rest of his suit, but she saw his head turn sideways and knew that he was looking at Earth over her shoulder. His voice came over the radio, "It's a long way from a hole in the ground, isn't it?"

LeAnne turned to look too. Every time she saw it the planet presented a different view to her, and this time was no exception. They were coming up on the terminator, the line between day and night on the ground, and though the sun still shone brightly behind her it was dark over half the Earth. In a few more minutes they would be crossing into its shadow. She wanted to stay and watch, but she knew she couldn't. *Maybe next time,* she told herself. "Yeah," she said. "Come on, let's see what's around the corner."

They pulled themselves forward to the edge of the ship and peered over the lip. The forward end was in shadow, but they could see two more blinking yellow lights surrounding a steady white glow that came from a glassed-in bubble at the center.

"That's got to be the control room," LeAnne said. "Let's have a look inside before we try for the airlock."

"Right."

They used lasers at wide aperture to spot handholds. They were getting used to the pattern: pull and drift, reach, pull and drift, to where they made even better time than if they could have walked. They slowed when they came to the bubble and peered cautiously over the edge into a circular room that reminded them of the *Starchild*'s control room. One deck below the hemispherical dome were the same concentric banks of controls, but where the *Starchild*'s had faced inward, these faced out. There were four Eyullelyans inside, but none of them were looking up.

They were talking animatedly, with much arm waving, near a door almost directly beneath LeAnne and Donivan's hiding place. They were all oriented with their heads out—evidently they wore some kind of shoes that stuck to the floor. One carried a weapon, which it waved in front of the other three, but if they were impressed they didn't show it. They kept on arguing, then stopped suddenly when a fifth Eyullelyan burst through the door, a ragged wound leaking blue blood from its shoulder. The one with the gun listened to what the other one said, then turned and pointed its weapon at one of the other three. That one kicked backward and up, all four hands held outward in supplication, but a bright lance of red light from the gun speared it in the chest.

"What the space?" Donivan said. "They're fighting *themselves!*"

Suddenly LeAnne realized what was happening. "Mutiny!" she shouted, and she narrowed the beam on her laser and fired it through the glass at the Eyullelyan with the gun. Her shot caught it in the back. It howled and spun around, and Donivan's shot hit it in the arm that held the gun, but LeAnne had already swung her beam up to its head. It remained attached to the floor, dead.

Three astonished faces looked upward, and LeAnne and Donivan ducked back until they could just barely see in. LeAnne could almost read the thoughts below: *Who did that?*

The wounded one turned and fled back into the ship.

"You're sure we shot the right one?" Donivan asked.

"It was shooting at unarmed people," LeAnne said. "Eyullelyans. Whatever. That seems like an Ililiel sort of thing to do."

Donivan snorted. "Right. So we've got friends inside. Should we show ourselves?"

LeAnne thought it over. "Yeah. If anybody on their side has guns, we don't want them shooting at us. Tell you what; You stay out of sight, and I'll swing out. If anybody tries anything, pull me back fast."

"All right."

LeAnne reached out along a rib between windows and pulled herself out with the handhold she found there. The Eyullelyans had turned toward their injured companion, but they turned their attention upward again when LeAnne thumped on the glass with her fist. She saw them counting arms and coming to the same conclusion, then after a hurried conference one of them launched itself up toward her. It caught a handhold on the inside just opposite LeAnne, and they looked at one another for a moment before the Eyullelyan spoke.

"I can't hear a word you're saying," LeAnne said.

The Eyullelyan pantomimed pressing its head against the glass, then motioned LeAnne closer. She got the hint, and, suppressing a shudder at being only a few inches away from a face full of fangs, pulled herself down until her faceplate touched the glass. Suddenly she could hear sounds from within the ship; faintly, but she could hear.

The Eyullelyan spoke again. "Can you understand me?"

"Yes! We're on your side, I think."

"I think good. You save my life."

"Well, let's try saving some more. Can you hold the control room until we get there?"

"I am sorry. I not speak good human. Say again?"

"Can you keep everyone away until we get inside to help you?"

"I am sorry. I not understand."

"Oh, great." LeAnne held out her laser. "Get the gun. Wait here for—" but before she could finish a silver figure flashed into the control room, stunner already firing.

"Don't shoot!" LeAnne shouted, but the Eyullelyan near

the floor had already gone limp. Only its position in the dome saved the one she'd been talking to.

The figure rebounded off the far wall. "Who's that? LeAnne?" It was Jennings.

"Look up."

He did. "Entropy. You beat me to it."

She laughed. "We've got friends on board."

Jennings drifted up to a wall and caught himself on a handhold. "I was beginning to figure that out. We shot a whole bunch of them in the middle of a firefight. I left the rest of D team locking them up until we can figure out who's who."

The Eyullelyan was looking from Jennings to its now-stunned companion. LeAnne stuck her face to the glass again and said, "Don't worry. She's only asleep. Do you understand sleep?"

"Sleep?"

"Right. She'll be okay."

As she spoke, three more silver-suited figures entered the control room, stunners drawn. The lead one saw Jennings, then looked up and saw LeAnne. The doctor, Hanif, said, "C team here."

"Anyone hurt?" LeAnne asked.

"Not that I know of, but they're still fighting aft of the living section. About five or six of them got by us down a side passage."

"Damn. You did the right thing, though. The control room's most important. You four stay here and guard it. But if anybody else shows up send them downship." She rapped on the glass again to get the Eyullelyan's attention. "Where are the other Eyullelyans going?" she asked.

"Say again?"

"The ones you're fighting against. Where did they go?"

The Eyullelyan pointed with two arms. "Back. All the way. They go send *Ilarasha*—how do you say—bomb."

"Oh great. Sounds like we're not out of space yet. All right, Donivan and I will go in through one of the cargo locks and try to get in behind them. Jennings, take this one back to the ones you stunned and have her identify her friends. We can use them when they wake up."

"Got it."

"Good." To the Eyullelyan, LeAnne said, "These people are your friends. Understand?"

"Yes. Friends."

"Good. Stay with them." She lifted her head from the glass and said, "Talk to her. Make sure she believes us. Hanif, see if you can do anything for that one." LeAnne pointed at the Eyullelyan who had been shot first.

"Right," he said.

"Okay, Donivan, let's go." LeAnne pushed herself back from the window and let Donivan lead the way out to the side of the ship. As soon as they got to the edge, she said, "Yllyia, can you hear me?"

"Yes. What's the situation?"

LeAnne sighted down the length of the ship for blinking yellow lights, found them, and began to pull herself toward the farthest one. As she pulled she said, "We've captured the control room, but we didn't do all the work. The ship is in mutiny. They were fighting even before we got here."

"They were? What in the—" Suddenly, Yllyia burst into whistling laughter. "Of course. The alert. The captain had to tell the crew what they were on alert *for,* and they wouldn't go along with it."

"Somebody's evidently willing enough," Donivan said. "The one in the control room said they're still trying to launch a bomb."

Yllyia's laughter died. "Oh," she said.

"Will it do them any good?" LeAnne asked. "I mean, don't they have to wait until we're over Wyoming?"

"I don't know. The missiles could be programmable. If they are, then they can be launched anytime, and they will just wait until the right time to reenter."

"Entropy. Well, we'll just have to make sure they don't launch anything. We're headed aft."

"You'll have to use one of the midship locks," Yllyia said. "B team couldn't get the cargo locks open."

They were almost upon one as Yllyia spoke. LeAnne pulled herself to a stop beside it and said, "Okay. We're already there."

"Let me go with you," Yllyia said.

"No, you stay with the lander."

"I'm not doing any good here. I should be helping."

"You're doing plenty of good. You watch for anything that looks like they're getting ready to launch. If you see something, use the drive on it. In the meantime, just sit back and enjoy the view."

"I have been."

"Good. Keep it up. We'll check back with you as soon as we can. We're going in now."

The midship lock was a Eyullelyan-size cylinder with a hatch at either end. LeAnne twisted the single obvious handle and pushed, and the hatch swung forward. She pulled herself in headfirst, letting Donivan close the outer door, and twisted the handle on the next door. Air rushed in for a minute, then the door swung open.

They were in a small alcove set at a three-way junction between a circular corridor running around the ship's circumference and two straight ones, one running parallel to the axis and the other running radially inward overhead. LeAnne could see bright flashes down at the aft end of the axial corridor, and voices in her radio shouted, "Missed! Ha, take that, you mutant!"

It was the two computechs from B team: Walsh and Nissen. "Having fun?" LeAnne said.

"LeAnne?"

"None other. What's happening down there?"

"Video games," Walsh said. "We chased three or four of them into a cargo hold and we've got them pinned down in a crossfire with Royan and Seivers, but they're out of stunner range and they aren't sticking out enough to hit with a laser. We keep taking shots at each other, but nobody's hitting anything."

They're buying time to launch their missiles, LeAnne thought. "Hold on, we're coming down."

She kicked off and drifted down the corridor, pulling herself up to a fast speed on the passing doorways. The corridors were roomy; big enough for a Eyullelyan to stand erect in any orientation, and as she floated down toward the junction she began to get an idea.

"Have they used any projectile weapons?"

"Yeah, one," Nissen said. "They haven't fired it for a while, so maybe they're out of bullets."

"Let's hope." LeAnne slapped doorframes to slow herself down, coming to a stop just behind them. Donivan had missed the last few; he flew past into the junction, bounced off the wall, and pushed himself back, but not before laser light scintillated off his side.

"Donivan!"

"I'm all right." He grabbed LeAnne's outstretched hand to stop himself, then bent over and examined his side. The silver paint had vaporized and there was a shallow channel burned into the fabric, but it hadn't burned all the way through. "Worked just long enough," he said.

"Good," LeAnne said, but she was thinking, *long enough for what I have in mind?*

She hoped so, because she didn't see that she had a choice, not if there was even the slightest chance that they could launch a missile from in there. She stuck her head out around the corner, firing her laser to keep the Eyullelyans down, and took a quick look at the situation. The cargo bay door was halfway to the central hub, where Royan and Seivers were peering from side corridors and firing an occasional burst.

She pulled her head back in, but kept the side with the antenna just around the corner. "Royan, Seivers, can you hear me?"

"Yeah."

"All right. I want everybody to start shooting when I give the word. Keep your beams against the aft wall, and don't let them stick so much as a finger out the door. I'm going down after them."

"No!" Donivan shouted.

"Yes. It's the only way. Start shooting!" LeAnne pulled

out her stunner and pushed herself into the radial corridor before he could argue more.

Laser fire erupted from either side of her and from the central hub, centering on the cargo bay door. LeAnne swung her arms to reorient herself, kicked off the outer wall, and at the same time tucked herself into a ball, arms over her head, and spun crazily down the corridor.

She'd seen swimmers do it. Hug your knees off the diving board and you could get four or five turns before you hit the water, and if you straightened out at the last minute you could arrow in headfirst. She'd never tried it before, but the spinning part seemed to work just fine. It should keep the lasers from finding a target long enough to burn through.

But when should she straighten out? She couldn't tell where she was! If she waited too long she'd spin right past, so she supposed about *now*. She threw out her arms and legs and fired the stunner at blank wall. Space, she was facing the wrong way! She tucked again, straightened out, and fired again, this time at the door. It was easy to spot; it blazed with laser fire from either side. She saw a flash from the dark interior and felt a tug at her leg, but she kept her stunner aimed through the open door as she swept past.

"All right, stop!" she shouted. Her cover fire winked out. She kicked off the wall, lopsidedly, grabbed for support on a doorframe, then shoved off for the cargo bay door again. She played the stunner back and forth across it until she was past, caught herself again beyond it, and pulled herself back to the edge. Sticking just the barrel of the stunner over the jamb, she fired inside until she was sure nothing remained awake beyond.

Her left leg was numb. Had she stunned herself? Not unlikely, given all the gyrations she'd gone through, but just the same she didn't want to look down. She remembered seeing a flash from inside. Not the bright spear of a laser, but the muzzle flash from a projectile weapon. They hadn't been out of bullets; they'd been saving them for the attack they knew was coming.

She looked. There was a neat hole in the spacesuit just

above her knee. No hole on the other side. Now it began to hurt.

The control room was much quieter than when she had seen it last. The Eyullelyans were just now starting to wake up, and the one who had escaped stunning was off with most of the humans, trying to sort out friend from foe. Yllyia sat at one of the communication consoles, though LeAnne couldn't remember telling her it was okay to leave the lander. She hoped Donivan or somebody was keeping an eye on it. But no, Donivan was right beside her, getting in the doctor's way while he pulled off LeAnne's spacesuit.

Things were coming in flashes now. The pain was starting to take over. LeAnne couldn't remember how she'd gotten to the control room, but she did remember Donivan pleading with her to forget the bombs and let the doctor look at her leg. She'd ignored him and gone in with the rest of them to look at the racks of missiles, one drifting free where the Eyullelyans had been herding it into a launching tube. She remembered the bitter satisfaction she'd felt when she'd seen that. She hadn't gotten herself shot for nothing.

She felt Donivan's arms around her, helping pull her out of the suit. The doctor slid her legs free to reveal the white suit liner soaked in blood. LeAnne watched him cut it off. She felt light, as if she might faint, then laughed. Of course she was light.

"What's funny?" Donivan asked.

"I can't faint. There's no gravity to pull the blood away from my head."

"Or into your leg," the doctor said. "You'd have lost a lot more if you'd been standing on it."

"Does that mean I'm going to live?"

"It looks like you might." He ran something cold up the sole of her foot and nodded appreciatively when her toes curled. He looked at the bullet hole, a hemisphere of blood welling up around it now, took a cloth from his bag, and said, "This will probably hurt a little."

* * *

She came out of the pain again when she heard him say, "Stand back out of the way."

Donivan: "What for?"

"I'm going to numb her leg so I can take out the bullet."

Thank you, she thought, but she couldn't say it around the fist she was biting to keep from screaming. A moment later the pain switched off without a trace. She felt her whole body quiver as tightened muscles suddenly let go.

She took the fist out of her mouth and looked down at the doctor, who was putting away his stunner. "Why didn't I think of that?" she said.

"I'm glad you didn't. We'd have just had to wait for it to wear off again. I can't check for nerve damage in a stunned leg."

LeAnne tried to look further down at her leg, but he pushed her head back and said, "Just lie flat."

She tilted her head to the side. Donivan floated there, the concern evident on his face.

"Hey, you look worse than I do," she said. "Lighten up. We won, didn't we?"

"Why don't I feel like it?"

"Well if it's because you didn't get shot, then you've got a long session with the psychiatry department to look forward to. What's Yllyia doing?"

"She's trying to contact the Queen."

"Oh." LeAnne looked down at the doctor again. "Are you about finished there?"

"No," he said. "You just relax."

"I've got to talk to the Queen."

"You're not going to do anything but lie down when I get done here."

LeAnne started to protest, but held it back and said instead, "Fine. Since it doesn't make a whole lot of difference where I do it in free-fall, I'll lie down vertically over by the intercom. Donivan, tell Yllyia to wait until I get there."

"Right." He grinned and pushed away.

"I'm serious," the doctor said. "You should rest. You can't

feel it now that it's stunned, but your body has had a bad shock. It needs time to heal."

"I'll give it time," LeAnne said, "but I've got to do this first. This is why we *came* here."

"I thought we came here to capture their bombs."

"It doesn't do any good unless they know we've done it."

He sighed. "I could argue, but I won't." He put something bloody in a specimen bottle, then bandaged her leg. "Go ahead, but be quick about it, and when you're done I want you to go downship to the living section and lie down where you'll have some weight. I don't know what free-fall will do to your immune system, but there's no sense risking pro-longed exposure to it if you don't have to. All right?"

"All right." LeAnne waited for him to tie off the bandage, then watched him repack his bag and kick off back into the ship. She pushed herself over to the communications console, where Yllyia was still trying to get through to the Queen.

Yllyia thundered a string of Ls and Ys at the Eyullelyan on the screen, waving three arms in a complex gesture while the fourth held her from flying off into the dome. The Eyullelyan replied in softer tones, and Yllyia turned to LeAnne. "The Queen is in conference, and this *ishlyri* won't disturb her. She says if we have a message we can give it to Ililiel. Evidently she's staying in the palace now."

"Hah. Not surprising," LeAnne said. "What the space, Ililiel's good enough to start with. Put her on. I want to see her reaction when we tell her what we've done."

"Yes, that should be fun, shouldn't it?" Yllyia said. She turned to the screen and spoke again in Eyullelyan, and the picture switched to a recorded ocean scene while they were put on hold.

Moments later another Eyullelyan face peered out of the screen. LeAnne couldn't tell it from any other, but she rec-ognized the voice. "Yllyia. To what do I owe this wonderful surprise?"

"Fortunes of war," Yllyia said. She nodded to LeAnne.

Ililiel swiveled an eye. "LeAnne as well! This *is* an oc-casion."

LeAnne said, "You wanted to see our starship. Here it is."

"You are too late if you wish to surrender. We have already discovered your underground city."

"I'm not talking about the *Starchild*; I'm talking about the *Lyrili-Hloo*. Not a bad ship, actually. It's full of bombs, but we still like it."

Ililiel began to say something, stopped, and whistled softly. After a moment she asked, "What are you talking about?"

"The humans have captured the *Lyrili-Hloo*," Yllyia said.

"You have done no such thing."

"'Fraid so," LeAnne said. "We've taken your bombs away from you."

"How did—" She stopped again. "What did you do to the crew?"

LeAnne looked to Donivan and lifted an eyebrow. Ililiel concerned about the crew? Everybody was full of surprises today. "We stunned them," she said. "All but two." She looked over to where the two laser-killed Eyullelyans had been stuck by their shoes to the floor near the wall. "We had to shoot one in the act of killing the other."

Ililiel asked Yllyia, "Who are the two?"

"I don't know them," Yllyia replied. "We'll give you their names when we find out."

That news seemed to be enough for Ililiel. She said to LeAnne, "You do have a knack for complicating things, don't you?"

"I don't see that it's all that complex," LeAnne said. "We've won. You've lost. It's simple."

Ililiel said, "Are humans really as naive as that? Even if you have captured the *Lyrili-Hloo,* we can still destroy your *Starchild* from the ground. It will be more difficult, and bloodier, but you leave us with no alternative."

The words seemed to burn their way into LeAnne's brain, and she felt the by-now familiar sensation of her private universe beginning to break up. *They can't do that*. It wasn't *fair*. Couldn't anything ever turn out like she expected it to? Wasn't anything what it looked like on the surface?

Stop it. She wasn't going to think like that anymore. That wasn't the way a leader acted. So the war wasn't over. Well then, she would fight until it was. It wasn't like she didn't have weapons.

"I shouldn't have to point out the obvious, but *we've* got the ship full of bombs now. If you harm the *Starchild* or anybody on it, we'll turn Ventura into a crater."

As soon as she said it, she realized that it had been a mistake. Yllyia turned toward her in surprise, then looked back to the screen, and LeAnne was sure that some sort of nonverbal communication was going on between her and Ililiel. She didn't need to know Eyullelyan expressions to know what was being decided, either. Would Yllyia go along with a threat to Ventura? She had sacrificed herself and the *Lyrili-Hloo* in the simulator, but destroying a city full of her own people was something else. She would never agree to that, and Ililiel knew it.

LeAnne could think of only one way to salvage the situation. She had her stunner out and aimed at Yllyia's head before Yllyia could move. "I'm sorry," she said, "but we're talking about the survival of an entire race here. *My* race. We're going to reach an agreement that we can believe in or I'm going to blow every one of you right back to where you came from, friends or not." To Ililiel she said, "Now if you want to stay alive, then get your people away from the *Starchild,* now. And get your Queen on the 'com. I'm done talking to you."

Ililiel hesitated, no doubt wondering if she should accede to LeAnne's demand, but in the end she said, "I will get the Queen. It will take some time. She is in conference."

"Then get her out of it. You've got fifteen minutes. If we don't hear from you by then, we launch."

"I will do my best. Promise me that you will not harm the crew in the meantime."

"I'm not promising anything but a bomb if you screw up. Now go."

As soon as they switched off, LeAnne took the stunner away from Yllyia's head, turned it around, and held it out to her. "Here," she said. "I'm sorry, but you had to look surprised for it to work."

Yllyia held the stunner loosely in her hand. "I am surprised twice. You *were* bluffing?"

"I can't destroy a whole city. I can't imagine the type of person who could. But Ililiel can."

"So she will believe you. Yes, I think she does. *I* did, I am ashamed to admit."

"That's what I was hoping for. I figured if I could convince you, you could convince her. The question now is whether she'll convince the Queen."

"I believe she will."

"Good. Now all we've got to do is figure out what we're going to say to her."

Donivan had been silent throughout the entire exchange, but now he said, "I wish you hadn't said fifteen minutes. If we had a couple of hours we could get the computer patched in to talk to her. It's bound to be better at negotiation than we are."

"I was thinking as fast as I could. I just said the first thing I could think of to get her off the 'com before she could figure out I was bluffing."

Yllyia thought about it for a moment, then said, "I think we're still in a good position. You've bought us the time we need, whether we negotiate with the Queen now or later. We can simply restate the situation to her and tell her to wait until we do get your computer ready. She can't act against us now without fear of retaliation. And in the meantime, we can announce our presence to the people. As a member of the Yll family I can call for a public vote to remove the Queen from office, and they will listen to me."

"You can vote her out of office?" Donivan asked. "Just like that?"

"Yes."

"What's to keep her from ignoring their vote?"

Yllyia laughed. "A leader must lead in a direction that the people are willing to follow. If she doesn't, she will find herself alone. Remember what happened to your own captain.

Or for that matter, look at me. That's how my family lost its position."

"Oh."

LeAnne said, "What about Ililiel? Can you vote her out too?"

"Hmm. I hadn't thought of that. She is really nothing more than head of the archaeology department, and acting under Queen's orders, so technically she hasn't done anything wrong. Except—we might be able to argue that she should have called for a vote rather than follow her orders. I don't know. In any case, I don't think she will have any power to harm us once we remove the Queen."

"She sure seemed worried about the *Lyrili-Hloo*'s crew," Donivan said. "I wonder why?"

"I don't know. That isn't like her. She was willing enough to sacrifice the entire archaeology department, so I don't see what would—oh."

"Oh what?"

"Her daughter. Ililiel has a daughter, Iliana. Iliana is studying Earth meteorology. What do you bet she's on board?"

"You're kidding."

"Not at all. It would certainly explain her behavior."

"Can we use that?" LeAnne asked. "Hold her hostage or something?"

"Maybe. We might be able to get them to set the rest of the archaeology department free if we agree to send her down in a shuttle. But that will have to wait until we reach the final negotiations. We've still got to convince the Queen that we're serious first." Yllyia handed LeAnne's stunner back to her. "We'll need to continue the bluff, I suppose, much as I dislike the thought of a gun to my head."

"We can use handcuffs," LeAnne said. "That ought to work just as well."

Yllyia held out her arms. "That's a wonderful idea."

The Queen shared the same characteristics that made Yllyia different from the other Eyullelyans. She had the same wide-set eyes and larger fangs and narrower face, and like Yllyia her skin was darker than normal, but not to the same degree as Yllyia's. She spoke in Eyullelyan. Whether she understood English or not, she wasn't going to lower herself to use it. Yllyia, her handcuffs held prominently in front of her, translated: "With whom do I speak?"

LeAnne spoke directly to the screen, but softly, so that the Queen could hear Yllyia's translation. "I am LeAnne Evans, leader of the humans who have captured the *Lyrili-Hloo*. We have some matters to discuss."

Yllyia translated the Queen's response as she spoke. "There is nothing to discuss. You have committed an act of war against our race. You give us no choice but to retaliate."

"I think you're a little confused on what happened first. You committed the first act of war when you kidnapped Donivan and me, and you committed another when you tried to bomb us a week and a half ago. Anything we've done since then has been in response to that. But it doesn't matter who started it; we're going to finish it right here, one way or another. We'd like a peaceful solution, but we're prepared to destroy you completely if you insist. We'll use your own bombs against you. Do you understand me?"

The Queen spoke to someone off screen, and then back to LeAnne. "Perhaps we do have something to discuss after all. What do you propose?"

LeAnne let her smile show. "I propose that you keep your people away from the *Starchild*. In fact, until we can come up with a permanent agreement, I don't want any Eyullelyans within a hundred miles of it. In return we agree not to launch an attack on you."

"I agree to that."

Her suddenness took LeAnne by surprise. "All right," she said. "I, uh, it'll take us a few hours to establish a link with our leaders on the ground. When we do we'll contact you again."

"Good. However, it occurs to me that you could attempt to use that time to undermine my position by calling for a public vote. I warn you now that I will consider that as an act of aggression. If you attempt it, I will be forced to attack your city."

"You can't hope to stay in power after what you've already done."

"There is always hope. I will discuss it with your leaders when they are ready."

LeAnne looked to Donivan. He thought about it for a moment, then nodded. LeAnne supposed he was right. They couldn't afford to push too far on a bluff.

"Okay," she said. "We can wait for that."

"Good. I will await your call." And with that the Queen switched off.

LeAnne let out a long breath. "That easy? Just a few words and it's over? I expected a lot more trouble from her than that."

Yllyia held out her handcuffs for LeAnne to remove. While LeAnne unlocked them, she said, "Major governmental decisions are often made quickly. She has little choice and she knows it."

Donivan said, "What do you think she has in mind, making us agree not to call a vote right away?"

"I don't know. Perhaps she simply wants more time to think of something."

"You think I could have pushed her?" LeAnne asked.

"Possibly. I don't think it matters. We have achieved a very delicate balance; it's just as well that you didn't risk upsetting it." Yllyia rubbed her wrists where the handcuffs had been and said, "I don't like this at all, even if we have no intention of launching missiles. This is the same situation that led to your nuclear war a thousand years ago. Your United States supposedly had no intention of launching an attack either, but they were forced into it."

"Mutual Assured Destruction," LeAnne said. "I hadn't realized it, but you're right. That's just what we've done here again. Entropy, doesn't anything ever change?"

"Let us hope so. Donivan, we should contact the *Starchild* and get the computer ready. And I should go find out for certain whether or not Iliana is on board."

"What can I do?" LeAnne asked.

She hadn't noticed that the doctor had returned and was floating in the doorway. He said, "You can get downship, that's what you can do. When I tell someone to get bed rest, I mean it. Yllyia, drag her back here."

He didn't sound like he was joking. "I can go myself," LeAnne said.

"You're going to walk down on a stunned leg with a bullet hole in it? There's gravity down there."

With a grin, LeAnne said, "It's not gravity, it's acceleration."

"Whatever it is, you're not walking in it. Come on, both of you."

The crew quarters were at the bottom of the rotating section. The acceleration there was kept at a little over one Earth gravity, but LeAnne couldn't really tell the difference. The sensation of lying in a strange bed, one that was too big for her by at least three feet, was far more unsettling than a few percent difference in gravity.

Yllyia had showed her how to use the intercom by the bed, but LeAnne had left it off. Donivan could work faster without her bothering him, and there was no reason to call anyone else on the ship either. They had it all under control. LeAnne felt a little left out, but at the same time she felt relieved that she could just lie back and think. She had a lot to think about.

She'd killed someone again today. A Eyullelyan, granted, but she didn't see that the distinction mattered. It had been a thinking being, and LeAnne had ended its life. She had felt no remorse at the time, but now she was beginning to wonder. When she'd shot the guards with the machine gun in her escape from Ventura she'd felt angry at herself and at Ililiel, and later she had felt guilty, but this time she didn't know how to feel. It was a different situation. She felt guilt at taking a life, certainly, but she also felt sorry that she hadn't been fast enough to save the innocent one.

Killing one to save another. It seemed a straightforward concept, except that it hadn't worked. Both had died. But the other two Eyullelyans in the control room were still alive, and they probably wouldn't have been if she hadn't acted. Did that make it right?

If it did, then why wasn't she down in the cargo bay, getting ready to launch missiles at the Eyullelyans? If killing one to save another was right, then a first strike made all sorts of sense. Even ignoring the whole *us* and *them* bit, and who deserved to live more than the other, it worked out by sheer mathematics. If the Eyullelyans attacked first then everyone might die in the resulting war, but if the humans attacked first then at least the *Starchild* would live.

The thought made her shudder. That was the reasoning that had touched off the holocaust. Someone had seen the advantage in a first strike. Both sides had tried to make the consequences so horrible that nobody would risk starting it, but that had just led to even worse destruction when the inevitable happened. And here she had started them off on that same road again.

It was ridiculous. The Queen and Ililiel on one side, and LeAnne on the other, holding the lives of an entire world hostage while they played their little game. The average Eyullelyan didn't want war any more than the humans did, but they had all been caught up in it.

What could they do to stop it? Remove the Queen? Fine, but how could they do that without touching off the war they were trying to prevent? And besides, that was a short-term solution at best. Who was to say that the next Queen wouldn't be just as aggressive? Or the one two generations from now, or five? Or the next human leader, for that matter? With the setup the way it was, neither side could afford to give up their ability to destroy the other no matter who was in power at the moment. They needed a more permanent solution than that.

Well, what was the basic problem? The Eyullelyans were afraid of humanity, and humanity was afraid of them. They could destroy humanity, and humanity could destroy them. To solve it they would have to change that.

The solution came to her in a flash: Disarm. Let each side

give up a weapon at a time until neither one could harm the other anymore. She felt the thrill of a problem solved for at least five seconds before reality punctured her euphoria. They would have to give up everything right down to sticks and rocks to stop the possibility of war altogether. Weapons were too easy to make, and the first side that got an advantage over the other would have to use it for fear the other would do the same sometime later.

Okay, wrong solution. Back to the basic problem. Us and them. They're afraid of us; we're afraid of them. How do we change *that*?

Make it all *us*, she supposed. Mix the two groups into one. Or mix them enough to make it impossible to attack one without attacking the other. It wasn't a complete solution— it was still Mutual Assured Destruction—but at least it was a better way to go about it. It eliminated the danger of a first strike. And really, it eliminated the danger of a war at all unless everybody wanted it.

It seemed an awfully simplistic solution, but LeAnne couldn't see anything immediately wrong with it. It was really nothing more than keeping hostages. If you kept enough of them, then the distinction between sides began to blur.

She wondered if the computer would think of that. It probably would, and would probably dismiss it a moment later for some reason that LeAnne hadn't thought of, but it couldn't hurt to find out. She leaned over to the intercom and punched the sequence on the sixteen-button keypad that Yllyia had told her would reach the control room, and a moment later Donivan answered.

"Lee! How do you feel?"

"Not bad. Have you got the computer hooked up yet?"

"Not yet. We're still trying to get an uplink going from the *Starchild* to the geosynchronous satellites. Why?"

LeAnne told him what she'd come up with. "Can you think of anything wrong with it?" she asked.

"Not many people are going to want to live in Ventura unless they clean up their air," he said. "And not too many Eyullelyans are going to want to live in the *Starchild* unless we raise the ceilings. But either way it beats getting blown up. It might work. Hold on a minute, will you? There's a call coming in from the ground. It might be the *Starchild*."

LeAnne discovered with delight that the *Lyrili-Hloo*'s intercoms showed a real-time view of Earth when on hold. Donivan seemed to be taking a long time, so she pulled herself closer and tried to spot the outlines of the continents beneath the white puffs of cloud. She was still nosed into the screen when Donivan switched back on. He jerked back in surprise and so did she, but his expression kept her from laughing. "What's wrong?" she said.

"We've got trouble. That was Ililiel. The Queen is getting ready to launch a shuttle from Ventura to attack us."

"A shuttle? What does she expect—wait a minute. You mean us *here*?"

"Right. She's not even going to try to take the ship back; she's just going to try to destroy us, and then claim that we did it and use that for an excuse to wipe out the *Starchild*. She'll have all the public support she needs, then."

"Ililiel told you that?"

"That's what she said. She overheard the Queen give the order. She had Napoleon with her, and Napoleon backed up her story."

"That's crazy. Why would she do—"

"Her daughter's on board. She practically begged us to take the ship out of orbit while we can and call for a vote on the way out. She's doing the same from the ground."

"You're kidding. *Ililiel*? Does Yllyia know yet?"

"Not yet. She's still aft somewhere. I've got to find her."

LeAnne nodded. "Go ahead. I'll be up there in a minute."

Donivan looked as if he might argue, then thought better of it. "All right," he said, and switched off.

LeAnne pulled herself to a sitting position on the bed, tried to stand, and looked around for something to use as a crutch. Her eyes came to rest on the clothes closet. If she could just reach it, and if Eyullelyans hung clothing from hangers...

They did. The rod was no longer than a cane, but she

pulled it down and hobbled out of the room toward the elevator.

LeAnne heard Yllyia's voice before she even reached the control room.

"But I don't *want* to be Queen!"

"Don't give me that," Ililiel replied. "You're an Yll. Every Yll for the last thousand generations has wanted to be Queen. Besides, we need someone people will follow, and you're the obvious choice."

"Why me?"

"You're playing dumb on me. Who else do you know with fangs down to their chin?"

"That doesn't qualify me to be Queen!"

"What then? It's a hereditary job."

"But—"

"Look, if you screw it up we'll throw you out too, but right now we need someone to prop up in front of the lights and tell everyone what to do, and we need them fast because just as soon as that shuttle's ready they're going to launch it at you."

LeAnne pulled herself into the control room and floated over next to Donivan and Yllyia. "Ililiel's right," she said. "You're the best candidate for the job. You're going to need someone in power who understands humanity, because if I'm right about what's coming, we're going to find ourselves living awfully close together from now on."

"What do you mean?"

LeAnne outlined her idea for removing the threat of war by mixing the populations. When she finished Yllyia whistled softly and said, "It might work."

"There, you see?" Ililiel said. "You've got a platform and everything. Now will you get on the air and *do it*?"

The Queen lasted somewhat longer than the *Starchild*'s captain. Her army was loyal, and their fight was ideological rather than a simple denial of reality, but in the end none of it mattered. Fully half of the Eyullelyan population rose up in a single mass and surrounded her palace, while a smaller but more practical horde surrounded the airport and the shuttle, linked arms, and refused to move even if they launched on their fusion motors. A third group, by far the smallest but possibly the most important of all, commandeered airplanes and flew to the *Starchild*, where they met with the first officer and asked permission to stay.

LeAnne watched events unfold via intercom from her bed in the living section. The doctor had been furious at her for walking on her leg and threatened to strap her in if she didn't promise to stay put this time. She'd promised, but he'd assigned a guard to watch over her anyway: Iliana, Ililiel's daughter. LeAnne hadn't been sure how to take that until the two of them got to talking and Iliana admitted that she had started the mutiny on the *Lyrili-Hloo*.

She had learned to speak English from her mother, but there Ililiel's influence had stopped. Iliana was very much her own person, a scientist probing the interesting weather phenomena on a new colony world. Politics interested her even less than it did Yllyia, and she admitted that her reason for starting the mutiny was to prevent the atmospheric disturbances that the bombs would cause, not to save the "archaeological site" that her mother had said must be bombed. Only later, after the humans had boarded the ship, did she realize that she had been saving human lives as well.

"Well, about a hundred thousand of us thank you anyway," LeAnne said when Iliana told her that.

"Can there really be that many?" Iliana asked. "All living on a ship no bigger than this one?"

"There really can. It takes close attention to recycling, but we've learned how to do it."

"It's hard to imagine. We have never tried living that way in all of our history."

"No offense," LeAnne said, "but it shows. I think we can help you clean up your air a little, given what we've learned. If people start living in Ventura, then I'm sure we will."

"You are an ambitious race. Donivan is talking about rebuilding the *Lyrili-Hloo* as well."

"He is?"

"Yes. He thinks he can make it as liveable as your *Starchild*, only in his words, 'This time it will be for real.'"

LeAnne shouldn't have been surprised, not after the way he'd talked while they were camping out. So he was going to get his starship after all, with hardly more than the effort he'd need to remodel it. And that wouldn't take him long; he had a whole shipful of engineers with plenty of practice at remodeling starship interiors, all of them just itching for something to do.

It took her a moment to realize that she was jealous. It was an ungracious thing to feel—there was nothing that said Donivan shouldn't have a project of his own—but she was jealous just the same. She'd hoped to convince him that starting a colony would be fun and that they could do it together, but now that he had the *Lyrili-Hloo* she knew that he would never be content anywhere else.

She thought about it that night after Iliana had gone back to her own room. She thought about love. Weren't they in love? Didn't people in love stay together? But to do that one of them would have to give up their goal, and how could they stay in love after that? It would turn to resentment the first time one of them got bored.

It wouldn't resolve. She had stopped the war with the Eyullelyans, but she couldn't think what to do about her and Donivan.

He found her staring into the intercom. She'd put herself on hold and was watching the Earth slide by beneath the ship when he knocked softly on the door.

"Come in."

"Hi." He saw what she was doing, and said, "That's why I couldn't get you."

"I'm looking for good colony sites."

"Finding any?"

"No. The picture's too small. I'll have to use a telescope or something. But it's pretty."

He sat down beside her on the bed and they watched the

night side of the planet sweep toward them. "You're going to go ahead and start a colony anyway?" he asked. "Even with the Eyullelyans already there?"

"Of course I'm going to start a colony. That's what I've always wanted to do. Having Eyullelyans around just makes it more like an alien planet. It should be a kick."

"I, um, I've been looking around at the *Lyrili-Hloo*. I—"

"I know. Iliana told me. I've been thinking about it, and if that's what you want to do, then that's what you ought to do. Everybody should be able to do what they want." After a moment she added, "Besides, having a real starship in the sky just makes it that much more like it should be too."

He needed to justify himself anyway. He said, "We've got to do it. We're still too vulnerable. We need to spread out over more than just Earth. The Eyullelyans could have killed us all if they'd been willing to sacrifice a colony, and some of them were. We've got to make sure they don't ever have the opportunity again."

She nodded. "You're right. It doesn't make it any easier, but you're right."

He said, "But you're just as right. We can't give up our home planet."

"I'm glad you see that too." She turned to look at him and said, "So what's going to happen to us? You up here and me down there? It's not much of a love life."

"It can be. We'll find a way to make it one."

Yeah, she thought. *We probably will. We've done everything else we set out to do.*

She turned back to the intercom, and together they watched the sun rise over the new Earth.

PART SIX

Frame of Reference

LeAnne was on the com to Denver when the sonic boom rattled her office windows. She waited until it had died down enough to permit speaking again, then had to ride it out again from the Denver side as the shuttle made its southward braking turn over the mine. Vanesia came running into the office, shouting, "It's Donivan! LeAnne! Donivan's coming in!"

"I'd never have guessed," LeAnne said. "Just a minute, I'm on the com." She turned back to the mine supervisor and said, "Okay, we can hold out until Friday, but we're running out. If you don't get more nails and cement to us by next week we're going to have fifty construction crews standing around with nothing to do."

"You'll get them," the supervisor replied, "but if the *Starchild* doesn't fix our other furnace we're just going to get further and further behind. We can't run a salvage mine on one furnace."

LeAnne sighed. "All right, I'll talk to them about it. One more thing. I'm going to be gone for a week, so I'm leaving Vanesia in charge here. If you have any more trouble, talk to her about it. I'm going to be unavailable."

The supervisor glanced upward. "Enjoy yourself," she said with a toothy grin.

"I plan on it. 'Bye." LeAnne switched off and leaned back in her chair. Eyullelyans. Trust one of them to catch the significance behind a vacation with Donivan. But no, she thought, that wasn't entirely fair. Everybody had caught it, but only a Eyullelyan would say anything about it. They were always making jokes about humans and their sexual relations.

Sour grapes, she thought, and with a grin she got up to go meet him at the airport.

He was flying a different shuttle. It was smaller, barely a third the size of the *Starchild*'s original landing craft, and even sleeker than Yllyia's new F-18 replica. It came screaming in out of the south, banked into a wide turn out over the plain, and arrowed in to touch down within inches of the threshold. Speed brakes popped out of the wings and he had it slowed down quick enough to turn into the second taxiway, less than halfway down the runway. LeAnne shook her head and muttered, "Show off."

She heard laughter and turned to see the ground crew, four Eyullelyans and three humans in white coveralls, standing beside her. Even in the Eyullelyans' eyes she could see the glint of excitement behind the laughter. She looked around her at the crowd she had until now ignored, the humans all but lost among the taller Eyullelyans, and was suddenly struck by an intense feeling of déjà vu. Colonists and alien natives all gathering at the spaceport to see the shuttle land—it was a scene straight out of her earliest fantasies. The parts had been rewritten a bit, but all the players were there. She looked back to the shuttle, thinking, *They are now.*

They had to wait another ten minutes while Donivan shut everything down and the shuttle's skin cooled enough to let him climb out. He emerged carrying a duffel bag and an insulated box—experimental medicines manufactured in zerogee—which he handed over to a waiting messenger, then with a whoop of delight he dropped his bag and wrapped his arms around LeAnne and lifted her completely off the ground. That move left his face buried right between her breasts. She was acutely aware of the smiles, both human and Eyullelyan, surrounding them as he swung her once around that way and set her down again, but she didn't care. He was back. She held him to her with an intensity that surprised them both.

"I think I'll come down more often," he said when she let him up for air. He nodded toward the shuttle. "It should be easier now. Like my new toy?"

"It's beautiful. You didn't tell me you were even close to getting it ready."

"I wanted to surprise you. We just got the new fusion engine from the *Starchild* two weeks ago."

"Two weeks ago? They told me they were working on my furnace two weeks ago. And two weeks before that. Robbing parts is more like it. You've got my furnace!"

Donivan held out his hands. "Hey, I'm sorry. I didn't know. I wouldn't have leaned on them so hard to get it done if I had."

He looked so contrite that LeAnne had to laugh. "Forget it. Let Vanesia worry about it; we're going camping!"

"Thanks," Vanesia said from behind her.

LeAnne turned in surprise and said, "What are you doing here? You're supposed to be watching the office."

"I caught a ride over with Llewella." She shook her head at LeAnne's frown and said, "The world isn't going to fall apart if nobody's there to answer the com for a few minutes. I wanted to come say hi to Donivan." She grinned and said, "Hi."

"Hi yourself." He reached out and gave her a hug, then held her out at arm's length and shook his head. "You've grown a foot."

"Where? Not on my forehead, I hope."

He lowered his eyes until she blushed. "You're worse than the Eyullelyans," she said.

"I didn't think that was possible." He picked up his duffel bag, and with an arm around each of them led the way into the terminal building while the ground crew descended on the shuttle.

"I've got the backpacks already loaded and ready to go,"

LeAnne said. "All we've got to do is put in our clothing and we're ready."

"We've got them packed," Vanesia said. "She made me wear yours while she loaded the rocks in it."

"Hey, rocks even. Thanks. I was afraid I was going to have to go without."

"Nah, we thought of everything."

Donivan ruffled her hair. They passed through the terminal to where LeAnne had parked her car, and when Donivan saw it he said, "So, new transportation of your own. How's it working out?"

The car was Eyullelyan-built. The colony had been using cars almost from the beginning, but as part of her ongoing project to clean up Ventura's air LeAnne had had hers converted over to electricity to demonstrate that nonpolluting methods of transportation were feasible. "Not bad," she said. "It still throws up a lot of dust, but it doesn't smell anymore. Climb in."

She drove back toward the administration building, the only sound that of tires crunching on gravel, while Donivan looked around at the new one- and two-story buildings of wood and glass. He whistled in appreciation. "You said you'd been busy, but I didn't realize just how much you'd gotten done. It's really changed since last time I was down."

"I guess it has," LeAnne said. "You don't think much about it when you see it growing a day at a time, but we're coming along. Ventura and the *Starchild* have been a lot of help, but I think we might be self-sufficient in another year or so."

"Really?"

"Yeah. We've got all the necessities. We've been building houses faster than people can move into them, and we've been planting trees and building roads and starting farms all around here. We'll actually be exporting produce from the farms this year. Plus the university will be starting this fall, and we've even got a resident poet."

"Poet?"

"Dr. McNeil from the *Starchild*. He's been reading Thoreau

and Whitman and writing stuff about trees and rocks and clouds. Not bad, really."

"Thoreau? Whitman?"

"Old writers. Pre-holocaust. They wrote about trees and rocks and clouds too."

"Oh. I take it a colony isn't complete without a poet?"

LeAnne laughed. "I'm beginning to think so. There's so much to see out here; you need someone to distill it down for you so that you can find out what you're missing."

"Maybe I should get a chipful of his poems while I'm down here."

"I've got a copy of his book you can have," Vanesia said. "It's a real printed one, on paper. He wouldn't let us put it on a chip."

"Why not?"

"He said it wasn't appropriate to the subject matter. We had to get the *Starchild*'s recycling department to make the paper out of a pine tree and everything. It smells good."

"I bet. We've got pines growing on the *Lyrili-Hloo* too. They make the whole ship smell like forest."

"You've got pine trees up there?"

"Sure. We had all those radial corridors that were straight up and down once we started it spinning; they were perfect for trees." He laughed at Vanesia's astonished expression. "Hey, we're not all steel and silicon up there."

"What a surprise." She grinned. "So how are you coming with it?"

Donivan hesitated, glancing at LeAnne before he said, "We're making progress. We've got most of the suspended animation chambers turned into living quarters, and we've got the hydroponics section going and the computer programs transferred and—well, just about everything. You'll have to come see it."

"I'd love to. Maybe one of these days *I'll* get a vacation and I can."

LeAnne only smiled, ignoring the bait. She turned the car into the office parking lot and stopped in front of the main doors. Vanesia got out, then leaned back in through Donivan's window. "Any last-minute instructions before I screw up your filing system?" she asked.

"Nothing I haven't already told you," LeAnne said. "I've already nagged Denver about the delays, so you shouldn't have to do that again for a while. Just keep things running."

"I will. You guys have fun. If I don't hear from you in a week I'll come looking for you. 'Bye." Vanesia winked, blew a kiss at Donivan, and turned to bounce up the steps to the doors.

Donivan watched her disappear into the building. "Does she ever slow down?"

"For about ten minutes, I think, between three and three-ten in the morning."

"That's what I thought." He looked over at LeAnne. "I think some of you has rubbed off on her."

LeAnne's smile faded. "Sometimes I think all of me has."

"What do you mean?"

She pulled the car back out onto the street and headed toward her house. "Maybe it's just burnout. I don't know. Whatever it is, I've been looking forward to getting away since last winter."

Donivan nodded. "I know what you mean. Sometimes I think I could space the next person who comes to me with a problem."

"Yeah."

They rode for a block or two in silence, just enjoying being together again after three months apart. Finally Donivan said, "I don't think we need to feel guilty about getting tired. It's taken us what—six years? Six years to do what took the Originals centuries to build up to. Even the Eyullelyans took thirty years or so to rebuild Ventura. We've done okay."

"I guess so. I sometimes lose track of it in all the datawork." She shook her head. "I can't believe how much datawork there is. I swore I wasn't going to get into that, but it seems like that's all I do anymore. Budget reports, production reports, trade agreements with Ventura and the *Starchild* and you guys—it's crazy. What kind of explorer stares into a terminal all day?"

Donivan didn't have an answer for that. LeAnne turned into the driveway before her house, a brown and white split-level with a row of four-foot pine trees in front of it. She hit the button for the garage and slipped the car in under the door as it rose, climbed out and plugged it in out of habit, and led the way inside.

Donivan dropped his duffel bag by the door. They stood awkwardly in the high-ceilinged living room, looking at one another, both feeling suddenly clumsy now that they were alone. LeAnne laughed first.

"It's like this every time," she said. "We have to learn how to kiss all over again."

"Yeah, but you love it," Donivan said, and he reached up to begin.

The morning sun was barely above the horizon, casting a coppery glow over the airport and sending their shadows out a good thirty feet in front of them as they walked across the apron toward LeAnne's airplane. The shadows bulged at the shoulders; the only good way to carry a backpack is on a back.

"There's something ludicrous about flying four hundred miles just so we can walk another ten or twenty with all this weight on our backs," Donivan said, sliding his pack off and leaning it up against the right front wing.

LeAnne's plane, like her car, was a modified Eyullelyan model. She dropped her pack beside Donivan's, reached in through the passenger door to flip on the autopilot, and started her walkaround inspection. "What's ludicrous about it?" she asked.

"It's inconsistent. Why don't we just fly straight to where we're going?"

"Because that's not exploring. That's picnicking."

"Ahh," Donivan said in the voice of someone who has just learned a universal truth. "God save us from picnics." He threw his pack into the back of the plane, then hefted Le-Anne's and tossed it in on top of his. "Space, I think you put the rocks in the wrong pack. What've you got in there?"

LeAnne pulled on a middle wing, checking the joint, and said, "Oh, let's see, two space blankets, an edible plants book, some fishing line and hooks, a compass, a whole *bunch* of dehydrated food, and a medkit with a bottle of medicinal alcohol in it." She smiled over the wing. "Can you think of anything else we need?"

"Not a thing," Donivan said with a laugh.

"Good, 'cause it's a long ways back if we forgot something." LeAnne finished her inspection and climbed in beside Donivan. The autopilot had finished its system check and the instruments had come to life, and Donivan had tuned into the satellite navigation system. LeAnne verified that everything was in order, fed power to the motor, and taxied out to the runway. She used the radio to call the airport computer and get clearance for takeoff, and within another minute they were in the air and headed north.

"This is nothing like flying out of Ventura," Donivan said. "Half the time you've got to wait in line."

"Ventura's a lot bigger town," LeAnne said.

"True." Donivan looked out his window at the houses disappearing behind them. "But not for long by the looks of it."

"Tell me about it. Urban sprawl." She smiled at his blank expression and said, "I've been reading up on city management from before the holocaust. Did you know that cities gradually die from the center outward? That used to be a big problem, along with traffic jams and air pollution, and we're already getting the pollution. Not as bad as Ventura's, but we've got it. It'd be even worse if we didn't use fusion for power."

Donivan nodded. "I remember the history lessons saying that Earth might have become uninhabitable in another fifty years even without the holocaust, just because of the pollution."

"It's true. We've got a lot longer than that now, but we've still got to watch out. If we go back to the same methods the Originals used, then we're going to have the same problems. We can't burn wood and coal for heat and we can't burn oil for transportation. I'm trying to get the Eyullelyans to understand that, but it's a slow process."

"They've been colonizing planets for thousands of years," Donivan said. "You'd think they'd have figured it out by now."

"Remember what Yllyia said when we first saw Ventura. They see it, but they're just not concerned about it. Ventura's pollution problem is the worst they've ever had because the geography along the California coastline makes it perfect for inversions, but bad as it is, one city like that won't destroy a planet. They'll never pollute enough to do that, because they breed so slowly and they cut their population in half every thirty generations or so with another colony expedition."

"What I don't understand is why they're polluting in the first place. They've got fusion engines on the *Lyrili-Hloo*; why don't they use the same technology on the ground?"

"I've talked with Yllyia about that, too, and according to her it's because chemical energy is easier to use. You can heat your house with a tree and a fireplace, but a fusion power plant takes a lot higher level of technology to build and maintain. They travel in suspended animation, so when they get to a colony world they don't have a high-tech society to help them along the way we do with the *Starchild*, and that means they have to go with something they can build from scratch. The trouble with that is, once you start doing things that way it's almost impossible to get anybody to change methods."

"That fits," Donivan admitted. "I've run into places all over the *Lyrili-Hloo* where they took the low-tech way of doing things even when they could have done it better. I guess it shouldn't be any surprise that they do the same thing on the ground. But if it doesn't matter, then why worry about it?"

"I didn't say it didn't matter; all I said was that they couldn't destroy the planet that way. They can still screw it up. And besides, it's *Earth*. They should be taking better care of it. It's just one world to them, but it's the only one we've got."

"It—yeah," Donivan said. He shifted uncomfortably.

"Go ahead and say it," LeAnne said. "We can't spend a whole week together without talking about it. The *Lyrili-Hloo* is ready to go. You're leaving to find us another world and I'm staying to make sure we keep a foothold on this one and there's not a whole lot we can do about it."

Donivan looked even more uncomfortable. "You say that so casually. I don't know if I *can* leave you, Lee. Living in orbit is one thing, but—"

"Oh come on. You didn't rebuild the whole ship just to stay in orbit. You're spreading humanity to the stars, remember? Of course you're leaving."

"You sound like you want me to go."

LeAnne sighed. "No, I don't want you to go, but I don't want you putting your whole life on hold because of me, either. What we're doing is bigger than both of us and you know it. We decided that years ago."

"Did we?"

"What do you mean by that?"

"I mean when I started rebuilding the *Lyrili-Hloo* I thought I had a lifetime project on my hands. I didn't think I'd have to worry about actually taking it somewhere."

LeAnne didn't know what to say. Almost from the start she'd reconciled herself to the idea that he'd eventually be leaving, and she'd assumed he had done the same. To find out now that he hadn't was somehow like losing her own resolve.

She leveled off the plane and set their destination's latitude and longitude in the navigation computer, then turned the flying over to the autopilot. "What are you going to do, then?" she asked.

He took a deep breath and said, "We're going to take the ship out to the asteroid belt and bring back enough raw materials so that whoever wants to can build another couple of ships after we're gone. That'll take us at least another year."

A year. It was busywork—it didn't take a starship to mine asteroids—but LeAnne wasn't going to argue with him about it. He was just postponing the inevitable, and he'd be away all that time in doing it, but at least at the end of it he'd be coming back. She wouldn't let him wait forever because of her, but she would accept an extra year.

"When are you leaving to do that?" she asked.

"It looks like we'll be ready in another month or so. We've still got a lot of work left, but we can do most of it on the way." He grinned and added, "It'll give the engineers something to do."

"Right."

They both laughed, but their laughter quickly dwindled to silence again. After a minute Donivan asked, "Do you ever wish we'd just stayed on the *Starchild* and never found what was outside?"

"No," Leanne answered truthfully.

Donivan showed his surprise for a moment before he shook his head and with a smile said, "No, I suppose you wouldn't."

Yellowstone Lake slid down over the northern horizon like the shadow of a giant Eyullelyan hand reaching toward them over the rim of the world. Donivan watched it draw closer for a while, then leaned back and dug in his pack, emerging with a book reader, its side rack bristling with chips. LeAnne took a look at it and laughed. "Think you brought along enough to read?"

"Hope so," he said. "I brought tour guides and maps for the whole park."

"You brought what?"

"Tour guides and maps. I dug them out of the *Starchild*'s archives. I thought it'd be best to be prepared."

LeAnne frowned. "Donivan, we're going camping. The idea is to get out into some wild country and see what you can find, not read about it in a tour guide."

"I'd rather know not to feed the bears *before* one of them takes my arm off," he said.

"Common sense would tell you that."

"Yours might, but not mine. Remember the porcupine? This time I'm staying away from porcupines. They're all over Yellowstone, by the way. Along with grizzly bears and black bears, deer, elk, moose, buffalo, and a couple dozen other dangerous animals. You picked a hell of a spot, you know that?"

With a sigh, LeAnne said, "I picked it because it's wild and beautiful and I wanted to get away from civilization for a while. That includes your tour guide."

"It does?"

"Yes, it does."

"You had to have read a tour guide to plan the trip," Donivan pointed out.

"And I left it behind after I did, too. Once we're out here I want to make my own discoveries."

Donivan hefted the book reader in his hand, shrugged, and stuck it under his seat. "Okay," he said with a grin, "but I draw the line at bathing in ice-cold streams."

LeAnne grinned back. "Don't worry about it. Yellowstone's got hot and cold running water." She took back control from the autopilot and banked the plane to the left, aiming to the west of the lake toward Old Faithful. As she looked for the telltale wisps of steam that would mark geyser activity she wondered, not for the first time, how wise it had been to plan a camping trip with someone who felt the way Donivan did about planets. It was going to be a challenge, she could tell.

They flew back and forth over the geyser basin and spotted at least a dozen steaming hot spots within walking distance of each other, then flew on to land a few miles away in a grassy field alongside a medium-sized stream. Donivan clipped a stunner to his belt before he even stepped out of the plane, his expression daring her to say something about it, but when she did the same he relaxed and helped her unload the packs.

They tied down the wings in case of wind, stiff-armed their packs up overhead and twisted into them, and with a backward glance at their last link with civilization set off into the trees. Donivan remained quiet on the subject of ludicrousness, but after a couple of hours of sweating their way along game trails that never seemed to go in quite the direction they wanted them to go LeAnne began to think that maybe they *should* have flown straight into Old Faithful. It wasn't like she didn't know where it was.

But no, that wasn't the way she wanted to do it. *Part of exploring is the attitude you take with you,* she reminded herself, *and you can't go taking the easy way out whenever it starts to get hard.*

Eventually they came across the overgrown track of an old road slanting gently up the ridge they had been climbing. LeAnne wanted to cross over it and go on up the way they were headed, but Donivan vetoed that idea immediately, saying, "I agreed to leave the maps in the plane, but I didn't agree to ignore the roads on the ground."

LeAnne said, "We can't do much exploring if we always stick to the roads."

"What do you mean?" he replied. "We've never seen any of this. The only difference between walking along the road and climbing straight over every hill and valley is that we don't have to work as hard if we take the road."

"And we don't have to make our own decisions where to go, or keep track of where we've been, or exert ourselves to get there, either. That's not exploring; that's just being lazy."

Donivan slid his pack off with a look of exasperation. "Is it? Can you really judge the validity of the experience by the amount of sweat poured out to accomplish it? That seems like an awfully small scale to be using for the measurement."

"Well, what do you want to measure it by, then?"

"How about how much fun you have doing it?"

"I'm having loads of fun. Aren't you?"

Donivan looked at the trees around them, then back at LeAnne. "Yeah," he said, "I am. Really. I just think I'd have more of it if I didn't have to pant my way up and down all these hills."

What am I being so belligerent about? LeAnne thought. *Wasn't I thinking the same thing just a few minutes ago?*

Suddenly she felt silly standing there with her pack on while Donivan had his off. She slid out of it and said with a laugh, "Sorry. I guess I get a little too gung-ho sometimes. Forgive me?"

"I suppose," Donivan said. "Just this once." He opened one of his pack's side pockets and produced a water bottle, took a sip, and passed it to LeAnne. "Drink lots," he said just as she began to tip it back. "The more you drink the less I have to carry."

LeAnne lowered the bottle to see him looking at her, mischief in his eyes. With a mischievous grin of her own she handed it back to him without drinking and dug into her pack for her own. He'd asked for that one.

They reached Old Faithful by early afternoon. There was little doubt that they had found the place; wisps of steam drifted up from forested ridges all around a wide meadow filled with hot pools and hissing, steaming geyser cones, and the remains of half a dozen buildings clustered near the stream that ran through the middle of it all. Donivan wanted to camp inside the ruins where the corner of two still-standing walls would give them some protection from wild animals, but LeAnne persuaded him that it would be perfectly safe and more fun to camp in the trees. They set off around the edge of the meadow, and after another hour of walking they found a perfect spot just inside the forest. A small stream cascaded through its rocky bed less than fifty feet from a steaming pool, and between them a tent-size flat space offered a view of the meadow through a gap between trees. LeAnne declared it camp the moment she saw it, and Donivan agreed that it definitely beat the inside angle of two stone walls for atmosphere.

"What do we do first?" he asked, standing beside his pack with his hands on his hips, looking around them at the forest. "Build a lean-to shelter or skip that and go straight for the campfire?"

LeAnne laughed, and said, "Neither. We've got a tent and a stove. We can build a fire tonight if we want, but why don't we look around a little while we've still got time?"

"Haven't we been doing that all day?"

"Sure, but now we don't have to carry our packs. I like

the feeling of walking without the weight. It makes you feel like you're floating."

Donivan bounced experimentally from foot to foot. "You're right. Feels like about three-quarters of a gee. Say deck one-twenty or so."

LeAnne looked at him in puzzlement for a moment, then said, "Oh. Right. Well what do you say; do you want to explore for a while?"

Still bouncing, Donivan said, "Okay. Which way do you want to go first?"

"Up to the top," LeAnne answered, pointing up the slope behind their camp. "Where else?"

They pitched the tent in the last dying light of evening. Donivan had never even seen a tent before, and after a few bungled attempts at helping her LeAnne finally sent him off to gather firewood while she finished the job. When he had busted up a respectable pile of timber she showed him how to light a fire with a match instead of a laser, and they cooked dinner in the portable stove by its light.

"I learned the hard way that cooking on a wood fire is too primitive even for me," she said as she unfolded the walls and clipped the battery pack to the beamer. "When I was looking for a colony site I must have eaten burned food for two weeks before I got the *Starchild* to build this for me." She put a cup of water in each of two dehydrated dinners, put them inside, and set the timer.

Looking at it, Donivan said, "I'm not sure I understand the rules. Maps are out, but matches and microwaves are in. Is there some kind of logic that I'm missing here?"

LeAnne had to think a minute on that. "I guess I just don't want to rely on the Originals for anything," she said.

"Why not?"

"Because—well, because that's cheating."

"Cheating at what?"

"At exploring. On any other colony planet you couldn't get maps of any place you wanted to go."

Donivan mulled that over for a while before he said, "What

about satellite maps? You could get those from the colony ship."

The microwave pinged and LeAnne reached in with a spoon, stirred the dinners around, and set the timer for another few minutes. "Okay, so you could," she admitted. "But they wouldn't have the roads printed in color and they wouldn't tell you what you're going to find over the next hill."

"No, but you could program the computer to pick the best route from point to point based on the terrain, and—"

"All *right*. But I don't want to do it that way. I want to do it on my own, okay?"

Donivan held up his hands, palms out. "Okay."

LeAnne looked away, embarrassed, not knowing why. What was wrong with not wanting to use the Originals' maps? "I just don't want to do everything the same way they did it," she said. "It's our planet now, ours and the Eyullelyans', and we shouldn't limit ourselves to what's been done before. Look what happened when the Eyullelyans tried to rebuild Ventura."

It sounded pretty lame, even to her, but Donivan said, "You're right. Absolutely."

"And you're being facetious."

"I'm trying to avoid a fight."

"Oh." She looked up at him and said, "That's a good idea. I guess we've argued enough for one day, haven't we?"

They switched the subject after that, but LeAnne went to bed that night still thinking about what he'd said and wondering about her own attitude. On their first flight with Yllyia she had spent most of her time tracing their course on the survival kit's maps, and on their first explorations outside the *Starchild* she had taken old roads wherever she could, but here she was griping at Donivan for wanting to do the same thing. This was a different situation, but was it really all *that* different, or was it just hypocrisy on her part? She didn't know, but the question bothered her until she fell asleep.

She woke suddenly from a dream of exploring an ancient spaceship in vacuum, but the shrill whistle of breathing air escaping from a rip in her suit went on even after she remembered where she was. Donivan stirred beside her, sat up, and said, "What the space is that?"

The whistle rose in intensity, an eerie howl echoing all through the forest, and with it came an almost subsonic rumbling that reminded her of—"Somebody bringing a lander in on the fusion drive?" she asked.

"We'd be lit up like day," Donivan pointed out.

"Right." It was still pitch dark in the tent. "An airplane in trouble, maybe?" But as she said it she knew that wasn't it either. An airplane close enough to be that loud would have crashed already. It had to be something natural, then. Something—"Oh. Old Faithful."

"It *whistles?*"

LeAnne felt a bit of embarrassment at the admission, but she said, "Well, it didn't used to, but I've, ah, read about geysers that did. The steam escaping through the vent makes the whistle, and the water moving underground causes the rumbling."

"Oh," Donivan said. There was a flash of light from his watch, and he said, "Twelve-fourteen."

LeAnne listened a minute longer, then lay back and snuggled closer to him, feeling herself drift back to sleep, the geyser's howl turning into the hunting cry of some unseen nocturnal alien beast in her dreams.

The meadow was covered with wildlife when she got up in the morning. Through the gap in the trees she could see more elk than ground, and beyond them half a dozen great black hulks that had to be buffalo. Donivan had already gotten up and was nowhere to be seen, but she followed the sounds of singing and splashing to find him taking a bath in the stream. He had dammed the junction where runoff from the hot pool met the stream, making a perfect natural bathtub.

"Morning," he called when he saw LeAnne. "Join me?"

It was tempting. The water looked inviting, and Donivan even more so, but this morning she was more interested in exploring. "No thanks," she said. "I'm already dressed. Why don't I cook breakfast while you finish up and then we can go look at the animals."

"What animals?"

"Didn't you see them? They're all over out there."

"No," Donivan said. He turned around and looked, weaving his head back and forth to get a better view around the last trees between pool and meadow. He stopped in mid-weave, retrieved his stunner from a rock beside the pool, and climbed out, saying, "I'll, uh, come help with breakfast."

LeAnne considered telling him that neither elk nor buffalo would pose much of a threat to a person unless he bothered them, which he wasn't likely to do from within a hot pool, but she decided not to start lecturing him on wildlife first thing in the morning. Besides, the sooner they got breakfast out of the way the sooner they could go exploring.

An hour later, breakfast finished and lunch packed in a sack, they set out to see what sorts of wonders they could find. After a few cautious forays past grazing elk Donivan loosened his hold on his stunner and began to look around him for more than just the next tree to climb in case of attack, and when LeAnne suggested that they make a complete circuit of the meadow he agreed without argument.

It was a perfect day for exploring, and a perfect place. Around any curve of the forest might be a steaming fumarole or a bubbling mud volcano or simply more forest, and LeAnne found herself pushing ahead eagerly to see which it would be, then after a moment spent appreciating her discovery she would rush on to the next, and the next. Donivan had a hard time keeping up with her, but he didn't complain. He seemed to be enjoying himself at least as much as she was.

It was just after lunch when they came again to the remains of the buildings they had seen the day before. Donivan began to explore the ruins, climbing over piles of rubble and digging through them in search of interesting artifacts, but after a few minutes of watching him LeAnne began to get impatient and said, "Come on, let's go. There's nothing here."

"Sure there is," Donivan said. "I want to see how they used to live before the holocaust."

"You can read all about it when you get back. Besides, they didn't live here; this was a tourist center. Nothing but bathrooms and information booths."

"Oh." Donivan surveyed the area from atop a heap of stone, then suddenly smiled. "Hey, if I find a tour guide in here do I get to use it?"

"No."

"Why not, if I found it while I was already exploring?"

"Because I don't want to do it that way. Now come on. We came here to explore the countryside, not dig through somebody's abandoned toilets."

Donivan opened his mouth to argue, closed it again, then with a shrug said, "When you put it that way . . ." He started to climb back down, then stopped suddenly and looked back the way they had come. "Listen."

"What is it?"

"I thought I heard—yeah. It's Old Faithful again."

LeAnne strained to hear. Sure enough, it was the same whistle, somehow sounding much less eerie in the light of day. A cloud of steam rose from behind the trees about a mile back along the edge of the meadow, and LeAnne remembered finding a fumarole with a wide patch of mud around it just about there. "It can't be Old Faithful," she said. "They would have built the buildings closer to it than this."

Donivan checked his watch. "One-oh-three. You're probably right. Okay, then, it's New Faithful, named by right of first discovery. What do you think?"

"I like it."

"You *do?*"

"Sure. Come on, let's go back and see if we can see it before it quits."

Donivan jumped down and they jogged back toward it, but by the time they got there it had quit erupting and was only a steaming patch of muddy ground with a fumarole in the middle of it again. "Well," Donivan said, "if it's got a regular period, then we can see it at, let's see . . . about two o'clock in the morning. Hmm. Think I'll pass. I guess that leaves about three o'clock tomorrow afternoon."

"Oh," LeAnne said. She'd been thinking about packing up and going another couple of miles into the forest tomorrow, and the idea of waiting around a whole extra day just to see a geyser go off didn't fit with her plans. She said so.

"I thought we were going to stay here the whole week," Donivan said. "Why go dragging all that equipment around with us when we can just stay where we are and explore like we've been doing today? We haven't even begun to see everything there is to see around here."

LeAnne didn't have an answer for him. Not a good one, anyway. When she'd planned the trip she'd intended to do it just that way, but now that she was here she felt the urge to go on. She wanted to keep moving, but she couldn't say why.

"I guess it's just my reaction to being away from my desk for a change. I want to get as far from it as I can."

Donivan said, "An extra couple of miles isn't going to make any difference, except to my feet and back. I vote we stay here."

LeAnne took a long breath, let it out, and nodded. "All right."

They continued their walk around the edge of the meadow, but LeAnne's mind wasn't on exploring anymore. She was too busy wondering why she was so eager to move on. Agreeing to stay hadn't changed that; if anything it had strengthened her desire because now she couldn't do it. She felt impatient, and when they passed the ruined buildings again she felt her impatience grow, as if proximity to anything belonging to the Originals was causing it, but she knew that that wasn't the whole reason. She had explored ruins before and hadn't felt this way then.

And to make it worse, Donivan had evidently made his adjustment to the wilderness and to LeAnne's "rules" without further problem. He continued exploring with an earnestness that couldn't have been faked, and the more he discovered on his own the more LeAnne came to realize that he was enjoying the trip more than she was. She was glad to see him having fun, but at the same time she was jealous. She was supposed to be the planet person, but here he was outdoing her on her own ground.

She didn't let it ruin her day, but it still bothered her, and she was still awake when the now-familiar whistling started again in the middle of the night. Donivan fumbled groggily for his watch, announced, "Twelve-thirty. Entropy, it's not regular," and fell back asleep. But she stayed awake long after the forest became silent once again.

The next morning they tried fishing. LeAnne hadn't brought poles, but she showed Donivan how to tie the line onto a long stick and how to find worms under logs for bait, and they set off down either side of the stream that ran through the center of the meadow. Donivan caught one almost immediately, yanking it free of the water on the first bite in his excitement, then running backward and dragging it away from the stream at the end of the line until he was a good twenty feet from the water.

"Now what?" he shouted.

"Grab it and bang its head on a rock to kill it," LeAnne shouted back between peals of laughter.

"Do *what*?"

"Bang its head on a rock."

"I know we're going to eat it, but that seems kind of barbaric, don't you think? Besides, the last time I tried to grab a wild animal—"

By this time the fish had wriggled free of the hook and was flipping its way back down the bank. "It's getting away!" LeAnne shouted.

Donivan watched its energetic flapping for another few seconds, then pulled his stunner and fired it at the fish. He approached the now-inert form with caution, prodded it with his toe, then gingerly picked it up and said, "The mighty Thag returns victorious from the hunt. Do I still have to bang its head on a rock?"

"No," LeAnne said. "Just string it on your line and go find another worm." She moved off downstream to the next good hole, shaking her head, but smiling.

After another hour, though, she felt the familiar sense of restlessness coming over her. Donivan's early luck had proved to be just that—it was an hour before either of them got another bite, and LeAnne missed it. She caught one half an hour or so later, stunning it as Donivan had done instead of beating it to death, but the momentary excitement was small punctuation in the boredom. Donivan didn't seem to care if he caught any more or not, but LeAnne couldn't work up any enthusiasm for just standing on a bank with a stick in her hand. She had to keep fighting down her impatience, and she had never been very good at that.

After another hour and another fish each, she decided that they had enough for lunch. Their fishing had taken them a mile or so downstream, and as they walked back to camp, Donivan whistling softly and bouncing along as if he was still feeling only three-quarters of a gee, LeAnne abruptly said, "Why are you enjoying this trip more than I am?"

Without hesitation Donivan answered, "Because you're taking it too seriously."

LeAnne's reaction was just as quick. "I am not."

"Yes you are. You're trying to make it something it's not, and you won't let yourself relax and enjoy it for what it is."

"What are you talking about?"

"I'm talking about turning a vacation into an expedition. You're trying to make unexplored territory out of Yellowstone Park by throwing away the maps, but it isn't working. You want to discover new and wonderful things, but everything worth discovering has already been discovered once and you can't make yourself forget it."

"And I suppose you can."

"No, but I don't have to. That's the point. I'm having fun because I don't care if I find anything new. It's *all* new to me. But you want to find something that's never been found before. Explore with a capital *E*. I'm content with lower case."

When he said it that way it was hard to deny. It was true; Donivan delighted in discovering a completely different sort of thing than LeAnne did—the way a bird's nest blended into a tree's branches or the way a bit of stone glittered in a stream bed—but knowing the reason didn't cure the problem.

LeAnne had started out restless and impatient; now she felt herself growing mad. Mad at Donivan for his smug self-satisfaction, mad at herself for bringing it up in the first place, but most of all mad at the world for being what he said it was. And suddenly she seemed to step outside herself just enough to see the humor in it, and instead of the outburst she'd been working toward she laughed and said, "I feel like a spoiled kid. I didn't like my dorm deck so they gave me a whole new world to live in, and then I bitch because it's been used."

Donivan laughed with her. "It's not bad for a used world," he said. "If you're into planets, that is."

"Meaning you're not?"

"They're fun, but they're not the whole universe. If you want to explore something new, then come with me to the asteroid belt. That's where the action is now, and nobody's ever been there before, either. The Eyullelyans haven't even done any exploring out there."

LeAnne couldn't think of anything to say. It wasn't like Donivan's suggestion was new to her—she had considered and rejected the idea of going with him at least a dozen times before—but she had always thought of it in terms of following him for love. She had never considered going for the excitement.

Donivan seemed to sense where her thoughts were leading her. "You're tired of running a colony anyway," he said. "Why not try it?"

Why not indeed? Donivan had a point; this would be her first real opportunity to explore something completely new. And if she went with him they would have the whole year together instead of just four more days. She tried to imagine a year with Donivan. It seemed like forever.

But it would also be a year on a ship, doing nothing useful until they got to their destination, and probably doing nothing useful once they got there, either. What did she know about moving asteroids? What could she do besides get in the way, and get bored? If she got bored this easily out in the wilds, she could imagine what it would be like cooped up in a spaceship for a year.

"No," she said. "I've already had enough of starship life to know that I can't go back to that. I guess I'm too much into planets."

"Even used ones?"

LeAnne looked out across the meadow at the trees, and up at the puffs of cloud against the blue sky, remembering the videos of the fire storms and leaden skies of the holocaust. "You take what you can get," she said, "and like you say, this one's not bad. It could be worse."

They spent the rest of the trip soaking in Donivan's hot pool, fishing again, sitting with their backs to a tree and watching the geysers blow or the clouds drift by, huddling in the tent under the sudden rainstorms that built up the last two afternoons—and by the end of it LeAnne had reached an inner agreement of sorts. She quit looking for what wasn't there and concentrated on what was, and by the time they walked back out to the airplane she felt rested and ready to go back to being colony administrator.

The feeling of contentment lasted less than a day after her return. It might have lasted longer, but Vanesia had taken LeAnne's absence as an opportunity to prove herself capable of running the colony, and she had done such a good job of it that LeAnne found herself with a clear desk when she got back. It was the first time in months that she had seen bare wood there, and she wasn't quite sure how to take it. By the end of the day she'd grown tired of asking "Did you—?" only to have Vanesia interrupt her with, "Yes, that's done too," so she gave up looking for something to do and sat staring out the window at the mountains. And sitting there, watching the sun drop toward the snow-capped peaks less than a day after she had watched the artificial sun that was Donivan's shuttle rise up into that same sky, she felt the restlessness break through whatever barrier she had erected to contain it.

I want to do something with my life. The thought was almost tangible in its intensity, but still it made her want to laugh. What more did she want? She'd rescued the crew from a runaway starship, made contact with an alien race, set up the colony she'd always dreamed of, and still she wanted more? Most people would retire after any one of those accomplishments, content with a full life.

But she was twenty-three years old. You can't retire at twenty-three, not and stay sane past twenty-four. What was she supposed to do, go camping for the rest of her life? Climb mountains that had already been climbed? Better than growing fat behind a desk, but Donivan was right; she couldn't make unexplored territory by throwing away the maps, and though she had no doubt she could find parts of the world that had never been mapped, she knew that filling in the gaps wasn't good enough either.

Why are we here? she thought. Everyone has to find their own answer, the *Starchild*'s computer had once said, and LeAnne had thought at the time that she had, but it looked as if now she was going to have to come up with a better one.

The com buzzed for attention and LeAnne swung around in her chair, glad for the distraction. It was her private line, which meant either trouble or a friend, and at the moment she didn't really care which.

It was a friend. "Yllyia!"

"LeAnne. How was your trip?"

"Restful," LeAnne said.

"Good. You've needed to rest for a long time."

"I'm not sure about that. I think what I need is something to *do*."

"Oh?"

It was an invitation. LeAnne unloaded her thoughts, describing the trip and her abortive attempt to turn it into an "expedition," as Donivan had called it. "But I'm going to go nuts doing this for the rest of my life. There's no challenge left in it. I need excitement, adventure."

Yllyia's soft laughter made her blush.

"I know, it sounds silly just saying it like that, but it's true. At least it feels that way. Thinking about Donivan leaving has got me all messed up. Maybe after he's gone I won't feel this way, but right now I feel like I need a change. Would you stop *laughing*?"

Yllyia did, but only long enough to say, "Oh, LeAnne, you've got it *bad*. You're lucky Donivan *is* going."

"Lucky how?"

"So you can go with him, of course. I've never seen anybody with as bad a case of *shalerya* as yours."

Shalerya? The Eyullelyan wanderlust? "I don't think so," she said.

"I do. You sound exactly like one of us when hormone shift begins."

"Wonderful. I'm going through the change. But I don't want to spend the rest of my life on the *Lyrili-Hloo* either."

"Of course not. I can't understand why anyone would. That's why we invented suspended animation."

The universe seemed to accelerate to the side at Yllyia's words, leaving LeAnne about thirty feet behind. From that distance she heard herself ask, "Say that again?"

"That's why we invented suspended animation. A Eyullelyan in *shalerya* wouldn't last a year on a starship, and neither would you, but you don't have to. Have yourself frozen and—"

"Does it work on humans?"

"It should. We've frozen other terrestrial animals without any problem."

LeAnne's universe had stopped accelerating, or at least she had caught up with it again. So simple! Sleep away the journey, and go exploring a truly wild planet when they got there. "Why didn't I think of that?"

"Because you're human. Or more to the point, you grew up in a starship. It's not surprising that you—"

"I've got to call Donivan!"

"Go ahead," Yllyia said, laughing.

"All right, hold on." LeAnne put her on hold, punched up Donivan's number on another line, and when he answered she pushed both buttons simultaneously. Her screen split to show both him and Yllyia.

"Hi, Lee," Donivan said. "And hello, Yllyia. What's up?"

LeAnne said, "I changed my mind. I'm going with you."

"You're what?"

"I'm going with you. On the big trip."

"You *are?*"

"Yes."

The camera followed Donivan as he sat down. For a long moment he didn't say anything, then he shook his head and said, "What changed your mind?"

"Yllyia did."

Donivan's eyes shifted to the side. "What did you say to her?" he asked.

"I merely pointed out that she would have a much better chance of finding a new world to explore if she went with you," Yllyia said.

"Finding a new world? But—" His eyes suddenly widened. "Oh. Right." He nodded, then laughed outright. "I guess I'll have to leave a couple extra tanks installed in the hospital, then. And find someone else to be captain."

It was LeAnne's turn to be surprised. She hadn't thought of that aspect of it. "You'd go ahead and have yourself frozen too?"

"Of course," he said. "What does it matter? The ship will still be here when I wake up, and that way so will you. Even if you're down on the surface." He paused again, then asked, "Are you coming on the asteroid trip too?"

"No," LeAnne said. "I've got a million loose ends to tie up before I go. I'll need the whole year to get ready. And— space yeah. I'll need as much time as I can get just to practice exploring!"

"Practice?"

"Of course. I've still got *plenty* to learn; why not learn it on Earth where I've got a better chance of surviving my mistakes?"

"I guess that makes sense." Donivan turned to Yllyia again

and asked, "How about you? Can we convince you to come along too?"

Yllyia shook her head. "No. I haven't produced an heir yet. And even if I had, my place is on Earth. I'm an archaeologist, remember."

LeAnne nodded. From Yllyia's point of view Earth was probably the most exciting planet in the galaxy.

She felt a sudden pang of loss at the realization that she would never see Yllyia again after they launched. Or Vanesia, or McNeil, or—"Entropy. No matter which way I do it I've still got to say goodbye to somebody I love."

"True," Yllyia said. "You've come to a decision point. Life is full of them, but people have to do what's right for them and hope that the rest will understand. Your friends will realize that you can do nothing else."

"I—thanks." Yllyia was right. LeAnne knew that this was something that she had to do, knew it with a certainty that she hadn't felt since she'd decided to become a drive engineer. And if she'd learned anything in the years since then, she'd learned that she couldn't expect even the clearest of goals to be accomplished without sacrifice. But knowing that didn't make the sacrifice any easier. "I just wish for once it would be easy," she said.

"No you don't," Yllyia replied.

Donivan laughed and said, "When it gets easy is when you start looking for something else to do."

LeAnne laughed with them, for Donivan had described her motivations exactly. When life got too simple, when she'd achieved the goals she'd set for herself, she started looking around for new ones. She realized now that goals were no more permanent than the situations that created them; change the frame of reference and you changed the whole picture. Even in the excitement of going with Donivan she knew that that wouldn't necessarily be the last thing she would do with her life. After she'd had her fill of exploring she would probably find something else that needed doing.

She looked forward to it, whatever it might be.